A PLAYBOY
IN PERIL

BOOKS BY KELLY REY

A PLAYBOY
IN PERIL

a Jamie Winters mystery

Kelly Rey

Special thanks to Gemma Halliday for so many reasons, I don't know where to begin.

Thanks also to Lisa Kelly, the voice of the Jamie Winters Mysteries audiobooks, past and future. When Jamie talks to me, she does it in Lisa's voice.

Mom, I wish you were here to see this. I think you would have loved it.

Thanks to Katharine McDowell for Archibald Dougal Ritz. I hope he lived up to the name.

And to my readers, without whom Jamie and Maizy would exist only in a pile of papers in my filing cabinet. I'm so grateful for your support. Thank you.

CHAPTER ONE

———

"Nicky D's dead," Maizy Emerson whispered in my ear.

Maizy was an almost-eighteen-year-old with Smurf blue hair, a collection of body piercings, and an IQ that was off the charts. She was also my landlord Curt Emerson's niece and the *ept* half of our inept crime-solving partnership, so when Maizy whispered, I listened. Even if I had to mute Bert Convy on the Game Show Network to do it. I had a thing for Bert Convy. I think it was the dimples.

"Who's Nicky D?" I whispered back as I held my phone to my ear.

"Why are you whispering?" she asked. "Oh my God, is Uncle Curt there? He is, isn't he? Are you guys doing nicky-nack?"

Hardly. Thanks to the miracle of air conditioning, I was dressed for a sweltering Northeast summer in sweatpants, a long-sleeve tee, and thick gym socks; if any skin was left showing, it was purely by accident.

"Nicky D?" I prompted her.

"They found him dead in the dressing room," Maizy said. "An amplifier fell on his head."

"That's horrible," I said. "Who's Nicky D?"

A sigh huffed into my ear. "Virtual Waste."

I frowned at the phone. "Give me a break. I'm not that bad. I just had a long day."

I could practically hear her eyes roll. "Virtual Waste is a *band*. Nicky D's the drummer. He's kind of a stud muffin." She paused. "Well, not so much anymore, I guess, since the amplifier landed on his head. I haven't been able to get backstage, but you wouldn't think something like that would improve his looks, right?"

Eww.

"Why would you want to go backstage?" I asked.

"Are you kidding?" she asked. "I went to the trouble of renting a Cordoba from Honest Aaron and pushing it all the way to the Pinelands Bar and Auditorium so I could sneak into the Virtual Waste concert. Who wouldn't want to get backstage?"

I clamped my mouth shut. Trust me, nothing good was waiting to come out. Honest Aaron was a shyster who operated on a cash-only basis, had no regard for legalities such as a current driver's license, and carried no inventory newer than 1975.

"You're not saying anything," Maizy said. "You're wondering why a Cordoba, right?"

"I'm wondering so many things," I told her.

"Let me help," Maizy said. "It's easy to sneak in here. There's only one bouncer, and she's always too busy putting out dumpster fires to notice who might be avoiding an arbitrary Friday night cover charge."

"I think the word you want is *evading*," I said. "And what's with all the dumpster fires?"

"Beats me," Maizy said. "They just seem to happen every time I come here. And FYI, I'm going to need you to start saving kindling for me. Newspaper, shopping bags, whatever you've got."

Ashley, the cat I'd acquired through questionable means from a murder suspect who'd turned out to be nothing more than a freaky little guy with lax property management skills, strolled in from the kitchen and stood in front of the recliner, staring at me. After a few seconds I caved and moved to the sofa. That's how it was with Ashley and me. That's how it was with almost everyone and me. Assertiveness wasn't my strong point. My name's Jamie Winters, I'm in my early thirties, I work practically for loose change as a legal secretary in a personal injury mill, I've never owned a home, and I drive an ancient Escort held together only by rust. Those are the high points of my life. Those, and a smoking-hot landlord that makes the rest of it tolerable.

"I'm sorry that happened," I said, "but what do you want me to do?" Hopefully not drive down to the Pineland Bar and Auditorium, wherever that was. I wasn't sure I had enough gas even to make it to work on Monday morning. And I wasn't a big fan of the New Jersey Pine Barrens. The Pines were dark and spooky and full of the Jersey Devil.

"I want you to drive to the Pinelands Bar and Auditorium," Maizy said.

I sighed. "Why don't you just come home, Maize?"

"I can't," she said. "The Cordoba broke down, and I need a ride."

"You know your father and uncle bought you a nice reliable Civic. It's all yours as soon as you actually get a license."

"I'll get around to it," she said.

I wished she'd get around to it before I hit retirement age. I was getting tired of Honest Aaron and his unending parade of automotive misfit toys, especially since *I* got the calls to rescue her when doors fell off or rusted floors dropped out onto the highway. In fairness, she couldn't really call her dad. Cam was a cop with no knowledge of Maizy's relationship to the Monty Hall of the junkyard set.

Something gave a screeching kind of wail in the background. I hoped it was a lick on an electric guitar. The alternative gave me a full-body shudder. "But I won't get there for almost an hour and a half."

"That's okay," she said brightly. "I'll just start investigating while I wait. You know, laying the groundwork."

Oh, boy. Groundwork. "Investigating?" I repeated.

"You don't think that amplifier fell on Nicky D's head all on its own, do you?"

"Well...yeah."

"Then I wasn't clear," Maizy said. "It fell out of someone's hands. And I think I saw the someone going backstage before it happened." She paused. "And I think he saw me. I mean, I'm not positive 'cause he had the hoodie up over a baseball cap, and it was kind of dark. But I think we looked right at each other for just a second."

I went still. "Maizy, are you saying what I think you're saying?"

"You bet I am," she said. "We've got another case."

CHAPTER TWO

———

The Pine Barrens sprawled over a million acres, almost a quarter of New Jersey, encompassing portions of seven different counties. It boasted cranberry farming and white sugar sand, tea-colored cedar water lakes, and enough ghost stories to bleach your hair. At night under a sky stippled with patchy clouds and a timid moon, those stories weren't so hard to believe.

When I cruised past the sign announcing my arrival at the Wharton State Forest, I released my sweaty grip on the wheel long enough to roll up the window and lock the door. Which was the equivalent of a flickering candle in a drafty house when it came to ghosts, but you work with what you've got. The road unfurled in front of my headlights like a silky black ribbon, its edges fringed by unbroken lines of pine, oak, and cedar trees. No houses. No sidewalks. No traffic lights. Just a disorienting darkness that threw shadows beneath my wheels as I drove.

Eventually I reached a break in the trees, and there was the Pinelands Bar and Auditorium, nestled into a copse of towering pines, behind a small phalanx of EMT vehicles and police cars. The dirt parking lot was full and blocked off, so I parked on the shoulder of the road and went to find Maizy.

The "Auditorium" part was clearly wishful thinking. It was a low-slung L-shaped building with a single front window plastered with beer signs. The short arm of the L retreated into the woods in the back. I guessed that was the auditorium. It didn't strike me as the sort of place I'd want to go see a band perform, but then I wasn't seventeen and ideological. I was thirty-two and exhausted and hot. For three months of the year, New Jerseyans lived in a broiler laden with greenhead flies and mosquitoes. It was like trying to swim through hot motor oil under heavy insect bombardment.

A decrepit Cordoba sat at the edge of the lot with two people leaning against it. One of them was tall and beefy in a black T-shirt, jeans, and motorcycle boots. The other inexplicably wore a black hoodie three sizes too big yet still not up to the job of containing a mushroom cloud of blue hair. Maizy.

She hurried over. "Thanks for coming. You didn't tell Uncle Curt, did you?"

"I haven't seen him," I said. "Aren't you hot?"

"That's nice of you to say, but looks aren't important to me."

I rolled my eyes. "Ready to go?"

Maizy nodded. "We'll start investigating tomorrow."

"Investigating what?" I asked.

"Nicky D's murder," Maizy said. "I saw the killer, remember? Weren't you listening?"

"Not after the part about 'I need a ride,'" I said. "Did you tell the police what you saw?"

"Are you kidding?" she said. "I'm underage, in a bar. Even with persuasive ID, I don't want to risk getting anyone in trouble."

My eyebrow lifted. "You mean fake ID."

"An excellent fake," she said. "That's what makes it persuasive. Anyway, don't worry. We can go inside tomorrow."

Like I was worried. "I don't want to go inside," I said. "I want to go home." I tipped my head toward the Cordoba. "Who's your friend?"

"Huh? Oh, that's Bryn Harper. She offered to fix the car, but I told her it must've thrown a head gasket. She was just keeping me company while I waited."

Maizy did a come-here gesture, and Bryn detached herself from the car and joined us. Up close, she was even bigger and more intimidating. The sweeping curves of her quads and shoulders were apparent. Clearly Bryn was no stranger to the gym. I could relate. I'd been to a gym once. Of course, I'd been following a suspect at the time. Fortunately, he'd left before I'd been forced to pick up a dumbbell and expose my inner weakling.

"Bryn's the bouncer," Maizy told me. "She's also a ninth-degree black belt, third dan."

"Impressive," I said, although I had no idea what that meant.

"My Uncle Doug taught me," Bryn said in a lilting, girly voice about two octaves higher than I'd expected. Little pink combs swept back her hair. Her eye shadow was sparkly peach. "He practically raised us, and I learned a lot from him. It's not easy to be a woman in a man's world, he always said."

"Preach," Maizy said.

I rolled my eyes.

"Bryn was a Marine," Maizy told me. "She's fierce."

"Semper fi," Bryn said with a little fist pump.

"She offered to give me lessons," Maizy added. "I'm going to be a lethal weapon."

"I can teach you, too, if you want," Bryn said. "It's a dangerous world out there."

"It's a dangerous world in *there*," I said, tipping my head toward the bar. "Did she see the guy go backstage?" I asked Maizy.

Bryn snapped to attention. "What's this?"

"It was before Mike found Nicky D," Maizy said. "I don't know who it was, but he didn't belong there. I know unauthorized-access-into-a-restricted-area when I see it."

Bryn crossed her arms. "I don't like the sound of that. Any idea who it was?"

Maizy shook her head. "I didn't get a look at his face. Didn't you see him?"

"Afraid not," Bryn said. "I was taking out the garbage."

"Doesn't the janitorial staff do that?" I asked.

"She means she went nuclear on some goober," Maizy said.

Oh, *that* cleared it up.

"Can you describe this guy?" Bryn asked.

Another headshake. "But I'll find out who he is," Maizy said. "It's what I do."

"I thought you were a PhD candidate in economics," Bryn said.

Good grief.

"Come on," I said. "We should be heading home."

"I'll be back," Maizy told Bryn. "Just so you know."

"Let me know if I can help," Bryn said. "Good luck with the dissertation defense."

I gave Bryn a wave and pulled Maizy in the direction of the Escort. "Dissertation defense?" I asked in a low voice, in case Bryn had bionic hearing to go along with her Steve Austin physique.

"That reminds me." Maizy grinned. "Next time we're around Bryn, call me Doctor. I'd hate to disappoint her."

"I hate to disappoint *you*," I said, "but you're still in high school."

"Only in body," she said. "Mentally, I left years ago."

Couldn't argue with her there.

We got in the car. "Don't tell me she buys that story."

"Sure she does. Bryn trusts me." Maizy snapped her seat belt into place. "She said I remind her of her little sister Brianne. You know, a real sensitive soul. Hey, look at that ubergoober over there."

"Sensitive soul," I repeated dryly. "Is Brianne a lethal weapon like Bryn?"

"Probably not anymore," Maizy said. "She killed herself eight months ago. Something to do with a guy, I think. I know they were really close. Bryn said Brianne came to all the Virtual Waste shows and hung out, but I didn't want to ask too many questions. It made Bryn sad to talk about it."

I glanced at her, surprised. "That's pretty mature for a girl with blue hair."

She did a dismissive wave. "The hair's window dressing. Like Bryn's muscles. They help 'cause she's working in a male-dominated field. Below all that brawn she's pretty girly."

"Maybe so, but I wouldn't mess with her," I said.

"Who's messing?" Maizy asked. "We may *need* her help to find out who killed Nicky D. She's got connections."

"About that." I started the car. "Why are you so sure anyone killed him? Maybe the amplifier *did* fall on him by accident."

"I don't think so." Maizy's fingers drummed on her thigh. She sported a summer motif on her nails: green polish with a tiny white daisy on each middle finger. Sometimes Maizy's means of communication were less than socially acceptable. "Virtual Waste plays two sets on Friday nights. I was talking to Tommy between sets when I saw some guy sneaking backstage, toward the dressing room. It was only like ten minutes later that Mike started shouting for help."

I aimed the Escort back in the direction from which I'd come before realizing I had no idea where my first turn was. How was it possible that every road looked exactly alike? No landmarks or signposts. Just trees, trees, and more trees. And maybe I was wrong, but that lake should be on the other side of the car.

"Who are Tommy and Mike?" I asked. I should've invested in a GPS.

"Are you serious?" Maizy asked. "Mike Crescenzo? He's the bass player. All the girls think he's pretty hot, but he's old. He's like 27."

I shrugged. I thought her Uncle Curt had cornered the market on hotness. All that dark hair and those dark eyes and that innate sense of direction. Very sexy.

"And Tommy is the bartender," Maizy was saying. "Not that I was drinking, being underage and all. Well, I mean, he offered me a Screaming Mimi—he named that after his wife— but I said no, alcohol kills brain cells, and I have just the right amount."

Pretty sure I hadn't driven five miles on this same road before. How did anyone find their way around in this godforsaken wilderness? Every tree, every dirt road shooting off into darkness, every unmarked intersection looked exactly alike.

"You've got a signal on your cell, right?" I asked her. "You called me."

"I used the phone at the bar." She pulled her phone out of the acres of hoodie and checked the screen. "I got nothing.

Why?" Her eyes got wide. "Are you lost? You're lost, aren't you?"

"I'm not lost," I said. "I'm temporarily misplaced."

"Dude, it was like two turns," she said. "How could you get misplaced?"

"Because my initials aren't GPS," I snapped. "Do you have any idea where we are?"

Maizy looked out the window at unbroken blackness. "No clue," she said.

"Haven't you been here before?"

"I've been *there* before," she said, jerking her thumb over her shoulder toward the bar. "Not *here*. I know. Let's go to Apple Pie Hill, and then we can probably get a cell signal."

"Great." I nodded. "Where's Apple Pie Hill?"

"Beats me," Maizy said. "It's supposed to be the highest point in South Jersey. How hard can it be to find?"

We leaned forward to scope out the horizon. No hills or high points of any kind. Only trees.

"We must have passed the fork," Maizy said. "You probably didn't see it. I hear cataracts can distort night vision."

"I don't have cataracts," I snapped. "And I didn't see any fork."

"My point exactly," Maizy said. "Maybe you should let me drive."

I glanced at the gas gauge. "I'm getting really low on fuel. Think there's a gas station around here anywhere?"

"Oh, sure," Maizy said. "Right up there next to the Walmart and the Home Depot."

I gave her a look. "Not helpful, Maize. We're only in this situation because I was trying to help you out."

A set of headlights appeared in my rearview mirror.

"We're not the only survivors," I muttered. "Could do without the high beams, though."

"Maybe we could flag him down," Maizy said. "Ask him where we are."

"Are you kidding?" I said. "We're two women in the wilderness in the middle of the night. We're an episode of *CSI* waiting to happen."

"Not if we have a rocket launcher," Maizy said.

My jaw went slack. "Do you have a rocket launcher?"

"Where would I put it? I'm just saying." She glanced in the side mirror. "He's really moving, isn't he."

She was right. The car had just about closed the distance between us. The glare from the high beams lit up the Escort's interior brightly enough to read a road map. If I'd had a road map to read. The headlights sat up high, which had to mean either a pickup truck or an SUV. Either way, my car was no match for it.

I was getting a bad feeling, maybe thanks to all those old *Movies of the Week* I'd watched featuring women in jeopardy making inexplicably poor decisions, like pulling over on a desolate road in the middle of the night.

"Lock your door," I told her. I waited until I heard the click of the lock before I slid over toward the tree line, giving the truck ample space to pass. Because of the high beams, I couldn't tell what make it was or see who was driving it. But I could tell it had no intention of passing, because a second later it nudged up against my bumper and pushed. The Escort lurched sickeningly.

"Hey!" Maizy twisted to look behind us. "What's he doing?"

I had both hands on the wheel, fighting to stay on the pavement. "I think he's trying to run us off the road. Can you see who's driving?"

She tried to shield her eyes against the high beams. "It's too bright. Or too dark. Anyway, I can't tell."

Thump.

The Escort's front right tire veered into dirt shoulder and skidded along for a foot or two before I pulled it back onto the pavement.

"That cuts it," Maizy said. "First Nicky D, now this. I've had it." Clutching her cell phone, she unbuckled her seat belt, rolled down her window, and pushed herself up so she was sitting on the passenger door, half inside the car and half outside.

"What are you doing!" I yelled at her. "You're going to get killed!"

"I'm filming this moron," she yelled back. "Just keep us on the road!"

Thump. Swerve. Straighten. Maizy kicked me in the shoulder.

"Hold it steady!" she yelled. "I can't get a clean shot!"

"Get back in here, and put your seat belt on!" I yelled back. I sounded panicked even to my own ears. I *was* panicked. The Escort wasn't exactly an impenetrable fortress. It wouldn't take too many hits before it disintegrated into a pile of metal chips and tattered upholstery. At least I didn't have enough gas in the tank to explode into a fireball. So we had that going for us.

"I'm gonna put this on YouTube, you doofus!" she shouted at the maniac behind us.

"Don't—" I began, but before I could say anything else, it abruptly dropped off our bumper, veered sharply to our left, cut its headlights, and rocketed past us, its deafening horn blasting through the darkness. It was a pickup. I stared after it, trying to commit details to memory. Panic kept me from perceiving the make, but it had two or four doors and a short or maybe long bed and was some shade of blue. Maybe dark green. Or red. At that point I didn't know if it had four tires.

Seconds later, the pickup I'd committed to memory disappeared into the night.

Maizy dropped back into her seat. Her windblown cheeks were pink. Her poofy blue hair was unchanged. "That was pretty smart," she said. "I couldn't read the plates in the dark, and I didn't get a look at the driver. He was up too high. I bet the state police would like to have a word with him. It's illegal to leave the scene of an accident."

"That was no accident," I muttered.

"Agreed," Maizy said. "I just didn't want you to fry your wires. Now hit it. We need to get a partial plate, at least. I want to know who that goober is."

"I don't care who it is," I said. "Probably someone from the bar trying to get some kicks by terrorizing two helpless women."

Maizy rolled up her window. "First," she said, "Virtual Waste fans are not homicidal maniacs. Generally speaking. And second, we are not helpless women. I've got the video to prove it." She shoved her cell phone back into a pocket. "And third, where's your sense of adventure? Live a little. What's the worst that could happen?"

"We could catch him," I said. Immediately I realized what a ridiculous idea that was. I couldn't catch a tumbleweed in my glorified go-kart. I could barely top sixty without fear of shaking the engine loose.

"Yeah," Maizy said, "and what if we could? It'd be *radical*, right? I bet he dented your bumper. Even worse than normal, I mean. That thing was *huge*."

I frowned. That hadn't occurred to me.

"And if he bent the frame," Maizy said, "your car is toast. You know what that means."

"It means I want to know who totaled my car," I growled, stomping on the gas. The Escort coughed once, bucked, and died. We coasted to the side of the road and looked at each other.

The chase was over. We were out of gas.

CHAPTER THREE

———

"You might want to think about a new car," Maizy said. "This one is a speed bump away from a major repair. I can talk to Honest Aaron, if you want. He runs a special every week."

"We just ran out of gas. That's all," I said. I pulled into the driveway behind my landlord's Jeep and killed the engine.

"Yeah, but why?" Maizy asked. "Your gas gauge doesn't work anymore, right?"

Gas gauge, radio, dome light. It was still better than one of Honest Aaron's traveling crime scenes.

"What's your point?" I asked sourly.

"My point," Maizy said, "is it's a good thing that cop drove by."

I stifled a yawn. "What's good about it? We sat there for almost two hours before he showed up." Worrying that the maniac would turn around and try again. Worrying that I'd have to try to sleep in my car. Worrying that the maniac would turn around and try again and *catch* me sleeping in my car.

"At least he got us some gas," Maizy said. "And he gave us directions. It's funny how different things look in the dark."

Funny, yeah. I grabbed my bag and poured myself out onto the driveway. I'd been afraid to leave the car since I figured it was better to be lost with shelter than on foot. I'd also been afraid to roll down the window more than a few millimeters. The night had devolved from subtropical to fires of hell hot, which I hadn't expected. Summer days were supposed to be suffocating, but the nights were another story. One I usually slept through.

The house was dark, which was reasonable since it was nearly three a.m. I lived on the renovated second floor of Curt Emerson's tidy bungalow, which had tan siding, a brown roof, a drag strip of a driveway, and an immaculate lawn, regardless of the season. It sat in the middle of a block full of tidy bungalows with bright shutters and midsized sedans in the driveway.

Maizy followed me around back, and we clomped up the stairs leading to my apartment. "Have you got anything to eat? I'm hungry."

"How can you be hungry? It's almost three o'clock in the morning," I said. "Aren't you tired?"

She snorted. "Hardly. Do you know how many years of your life you waste sleeping?"

"Not enough," I said. "You can make yourself a PB&J if you do it quietly."

"I'd rather have a strawberry banana smoothie with flaxseed," she said.

I jammed the key in the lock. "Then you'd better go knock on your uncle's door. I'm fresh out of flaxseed."

"Yeah, I guess I could visit Uncle Curt." She hesitated. "He might not like it if I wake him up, though. And he might sleep in the nude. I don't want to embarrass him. Guys are funny about stuff like that."

I almost dropped my key at the thought of Curt sleeping in the nude. I couldn't imagine any scenario where he'd be embarrassed by that. Curt was built like Thor right down to the big hammer. Curt should be *proud* to sleep in the nude.

Wait.

"How do you know guys are embarrassed by stuff like that?" I asked.

"My friend Sydney told me," she said. "She read it in *Cosmo*. She learns a lot of stuff from *Cosmo*. Like what boobs would say if they could talk. You'd be surprised. Boobs are pretty opinionated. Anyway, the unexpected drop-in is one of the seven things that'll turn off a guy."

Only seven? I'd managed to find a lot more than that. I turned on a table lamp, and Ashley lifted her head on the recliner, blinking in irritation at the disruption to her twenty-two daily hours of sleep. My apartment was on the small side: a kitchen, a bathroom, and a living room that doubled as a bedroom thanks to the sofa bed. Thanks to Curt, it had neutral colors, upgraded appliances, brand new carpet, and more closet space than I needed since I had no wardrobe to speak of.

Maizy plopped down cross-legged in front of the recliner, stroking Ashley's head. "I'll bring you the article. It's very helpful, if you're into that sort of thing. Personally, I find it kind of anachronistic."

Yeah, that's just what I thought.

"By the way," she said, "do you have a hand mixer? According to *Cosmo*, you can use a hand mixer to—"

My phone rang, making me jump. I snatched it up before it could do it again.

"Just tell me one thing," Curt said in my ear. "Was it legal?"

I mouthed *Curt*, and Maizy called out, "Ask him if he has any flaxseed."

I frowned at her. "Of course it was legal," I told Curt. "She...*we* just went to a concert."

A tick of silence. "What concert? There's no one in town."

"Volatile Waste."

"*Virtual* Waste," Maizy said. "Tell him about Nicky D."

I shook my head. Telling him about Nicky D would only lead to telling him about the maniac driver, and *that* would only lead to telling him about running out of gas, which would only lead to a lecture on good automotive upkeep. Been there.

"Who's Nicky D?" Curt asked.

"He's in the band," I said.

"Drummer," Maizy said. "He's the drummer. Was. Before he died."

A longer tick of silence.

"Another dead person," Curt said.

We'd been *there* before, too, a couple of times. Curt thought I was a human divining rod for dead people. My defense was I never went looking for them. They just seemed to find me. Curt considered that defense lacking. But he hadn't shredded my lease yet, so how annoyed could he be?

Still, it couldn't hurt to distract him.

"Are you naked right now?" I asked.

Maizy gave me the thumbs-up.

"Nice try," Curt said. "Maizy told me all about that *Cosmo* article. She wanted to know if it was instructional."

I narrowed my eyes at her. She did the wide-eyed who-me? shrug and went back to petting Ashley.

I turned my back and lowered my voice. "What'd you tell her?"

"Come on downstairs," he said. "You can find out for yourself."

My stomach gave a little flutter.

"What happened to this Nicky D?" he asked.

I forced myself to focus. "An amplifier fell on his head."

"When someone dropped it there," Maizy added.

"You don't know that," I told her. "Just because you saw some guy going backstage and Nicky D was found dead not long after that doesn't prove anything."

"What about the guy who tried to run us off the road?" she asked. "Did that prove anything?"

"What'd she say?" Curt asked sharply.

"Don't worry," I said. "You know Maizy's prone to exaggeration. It was just a meaningless little road rage encounter. That's all."

"That's not a thing," Maizy said.

"I agree with her," Curt said. "Tell me this. If I go outside right now, will I find dents in your car?"

"Is that a trick question?" I asked.

"Right." He sighed. "Don't move." He hung up.

"Great." I turned to Maizy. "He's coming up."

"Is he going to be nude?" Maizy asked. "Because if he is, I'm going to wait in the bathroom."

"I'm sure he won't be nude," I said.

"You don't know," she said. "Sometimes Uncle Curt likes to flout convention. We wouldn't want to see his giblets at three a.m."

We wouldn't?

"I'm sure Curt's giblets will be safely out of sight," I told her.

"I hope so," Maizy said. "'Cause you can't unring that bell."

Footsteps thumped up the stairs, and Curt burst through the door. He wasn't nude, but it wouldn't take much to make him that way. He was already barefoot and shirtless, and that was a good start. I fought the urge to lick my lips as I took in the faded jeans slung low on his hips. He needed a shave. His hair, dark and thick, stood up in unruly little spikes from sleeping. His eyes, so dark they were nearly black, were penetrating and a little scary in a I'm-going-to-throw-you-over-my-shoulder-and-haul-you-off-to-bed kind of way. His agitated breathing made his six-pack abs flex and relax in time. Forceful Curt.

Yum.

"Talk," he said.

I peeled my eyes off his abs and my mind off his giblets. "It wasn't as bad as Maizy made it sound."

"That's true," Maizy said. "Running out of gas was much worse."

Curt stared at the ceiling for a few beats. "Someone tried to run you off the road *and* you ran out of gas?"

"Not at the same time," Maizy said. "The gas thing happened while we were chasing the dink who tried to run us off the road."

"You *chased* him?" Curt said.

Maizy nodded. "Only for two yards. Then we ran out of gas, not that it mattered. Jamie could have had a full tank and all night, and she still wouldn't have been able to catch him."

"Thank you," I said with ice.

"It's not your fault," she said. "My hair dryer has more RPMs than your car."

"Again," I said, "thank you."

Curt's voice was steel. "Why would you do that?"

"I wanted to get at least a partial license plate," Maizy said. "So I could report him to the police." Her eyes got wide and innocent. "Wasn't that the right thing to do, Uncle Curt?"

Maizy had a gift for making the insane sound logical. I could practically see Curt trying to conjure up a counterargument.

"Did you get it?" he asked finally.

Maizy shook her head. "But I got some film while he was busy rear-ending us." She pulled out her cell phone.

I pretended not to see Curt glaring at me. I knew he thought I was a bad influence on Maizy. Personally, I thought it was the other way around. If not for Maizy, I'd have been snug in bed with Ashley draped over my head, dreaming of a life that didn't involve homicidal maniacs and lawyers.

We huddled around Maizy's phone. The video was shaky and dark except for occasional flashes from the maniac's headlights when he dropped back to make another run at the Escort. Watching it gave me the willies all over again.

"How did you shoot this?" Curt asked her. "It looks like you were on the roof of the car." He looked at her. "You weren't on the roof of the car, were you?"

"Of course not," Maizy said. "I was sitting on the door. And yes, the door was closed at the time."

"That makes me feel much better," Curt said.

We watched the video all the way through until the pickup's headlights went black and it tore past us and vanished. I could feel Curt's tension radiating off him in waves. I could see it in the little muscle working in his jaw as he watched the screen. And in the way his dark hair curled adorably onto the back of his neck.

Okay, maybe that was a different type of tension.

"Did you hear that?" Maizy asked. "That's not factory equipment. He's got an air horn."

"I heard it the first time," I said. I didn't know an air horn from a fog horn, but I knew *loud* when I heard it.

"That'll make him easier to find," Maizy said.

"Why would we want to find him?" I asked.

Curt crossed his arms and looked at her.

Maizy was unfazed. "Because I want to prosecute the doofus who tried to paste us to a tree." She held up her phone. "I've got proof, remember?" She restarted the video. "You can't see anything," she said, disappointed. "I thought maybe we would at least be able to see a face."

She was right. The cab of the pickup was only partially visible to begin with, given how high it sat. Something sat crumpled on the dash; I could make out the number 20 on it in white print. Maybe a discarded bandana? A silver circle with what looked like a silver crucifix inside glinted as it swung from the rearview mirror. Beyond that, the cab was swathed in shadows that shifted with each movement. Nothing was distinguishable except that the driver had a head. And—

"Is that a baseball cap?" I asked.

Maizy squinted at the screen. "I think so. It's hard to tell."

"Didn't you say the guy going backstage wore a baseball cap?"

She nodded. "But a lot of guys at the b—the concert wore one."

"Where *was* this concert?" Curt asked.

"It wasn't a bad place," I said. "It's called the Pinelands Auditorium."

"It's in a lovely bucolic setting," Maizy added.

We turned to stare at her.

"Well, there are trees," she said.

"This wouldn't happen to be the Pinelands *Bar* and Auditorium, would it?" Curt asked.

Maizy did her wide-eyed thing again. "You know, come to think of it, there *may* be a bar in the front."

I rolled my eyes.

Curt glowered at her. "Hand it over, Maize."

"I don't know what you're talking about," she told him. "I only did what millions of other teenagers do on a Friday night."

"Use fake ID to get into a bar," he snapped.

"It's not *fake* ID," Maizy said. "The ID is legit. It's the application that's open to interpretation."

"Don't tell me," Curt said. "It says you're a forty-year-old Russian."

"Nyet," Maizy said. "But that's not a bad idea. Can I use that?"

Curt sighed.

"I don't know why you're getting so agitated about this," Maizy said. "It's not like I drank anything. Alcohol kills brain cells."

"And she has just the right amount," I added helpfully.

"More than she needs." Curt shook his head. "Hand it over," he repeated.

Muttering to herself, Maizy pulled a laminated ID card from her pocket and slapped it into his hand. "Way to abrogate my rights as a citizen, Uncle Curt."

He shoved it into his jeans pocket. "You don't have any rights yet."

"We'll see what the ACLU has to say about that," she muttered.

Curt ignored her. "What brought you into this?" he asked me.

I glanced at Maizy. She frowned and did a tiny head shake. "Her friend bailed on her," I said. "She called me for a ride home."

"You could have called me," he told Maizy.

"Jamie wanted to meet the band," Maizy said.

His eyebrows lifted. "You're a Virtual Waste fan?"

Did he always have to be so skeptical?

"I'm not a fan, exactly," I admitted.

"She's a little old to be a fan," Maizy said. "The median age of the audience was 21. She's way over that."

I crossed my arms. "I wouldn't say *way* over."

"What time did you go to bed last night?" she asked me.

"I don't know. After the news."

"Six o'clock?" She shook her head. "See? Old."

"The *eleven* o'clock news, Maizy," I said tightly.

I saw a flash of Curt's dimples. Was he laughing at me? He had a lot of nerve since he was a year older than me. Of course, it was different for men. Especially men like him. Curt was going to draw admiring stares when he was seventy. Judging from my premature gray hairs, poor eyesight, and complete lack of curves, I was going to draw flies.

"Did the cops question this mystery man you saw going backstage?" Curt asked.

Maizy shook her head. "I don't think so. He must have gone out the side door. I didn't see him again once Mike found Nicky D."

"Who's Mike?" he asked.

"He plays bass," she told him. "There's Bones, TJ, Plop, Nicky D, and Mike."

"Plop?" Curt repeated.

"His real name's Marion," Maizy said. "They call him Plop because—"

Curt held up his hand. "Don't want to know." He moved over to the recliner, scooped Ashley up, sat down, and repositioned her in his lap. She licked his hand, squinted up at him adoringly, wrapped her tail around herself, and went back to sleep in a fog of contentment. "Let me ask you this," he said. "Do the cops even know about the mystery man?"

"It would be grossly unfair to make assumptions about what the cops know," Maizy said.

"So you didn't tell them," Curt said.

Maizy stuck her hands in her pockets. "I couldn't do that, Uncle Curt. I wasn't supposed to be there in the first place."

Uh-oh.

"I could use some hot chocolate," I said brightly. "Anyone interested?"

"You weren't supposed to be in the *bar*," he said. "It's legal for you to watch a concert in the auditorium." He hesitated. "You *were* in the auditorium, right?"

"Maybe some tea?" I asked. "I can probably find some old tea bags in the back of the cabinet. They might be dusty, but that can only enhance the flavor, right?"

Maizy frowned a little. "Well, this happened in between sets, Uncle Curt."

He stiffened. "Were you at the bar, Maizy?"

"No, of course not." She shook her head. "I was bar adjacent."

"Bar adjacent," he repeated.

"Not drinking," she added helpfully.

Curt was quiet for a very long time, during which I think I saw a few of his hairs turn gray.

Finally, he said, "So when are we going to talk to the band?"

Maizy and I exchanged a glance.

"You mean you aren't going to ask me any more about the bar?" Maizy said.

He looked pained. "Would there be any point in it?"

"Doubtful," she said. "But I'd hate to deprive you of the practice."

"I'll bear up," he said. "I'm guessing you know how to find them."

"They play the Pinelands every weekend," she said. "But they had another gig midweek, so they were going back to pack up their stuff. Bones said they'd be there around noon."

"Then we'll head out around eleven," he said.

We stared at him.

"If you think," he said, "that I'm going to let you two run back and forth to the Pine Barrens in *that* car—"

"Hey," I protested. "It only ran out of gas."

"—so that you can play detectives again—"

"Hey," Maizy protested. "We don't *play*."

"—you're dead wrong," he finished. "It's going to be 'we' or letting your father ground you until you turn 21. Your choice."

Didn't seem like much of a choice to me. I'd go with "we" every time. Curt provided the muscle and the restraint to counterbalance my inherent cowardice and Maizy's impetuousness. Plus he had a reliable vehicle. And bonus, he was eye candy.

"I'm fine with it," I said.

Curt's gaze shifted to Maizy.

Her fingers drilled a frustrated beat on her crossed arms. "Don't misconstrue my agreement as sanctioning that clumsy attempt at blackmail."

"Duly noted," Curt said soberly. "And there was nothing clumsy about it. Now I'm going back downstairs to bed. We're going to function on the honor system here. That means the second I leave, you two aren't going to do something stupid like drive back to the bar. Right?"

I yawned hugely. "Bed sounds good to me."

"Bed? At three a.m.?" Maizy looked disgusted. "Old people are so boring. *God*."

CHAPTER FOUR

———

I'd made the mistake before of letting Maizy stay the night, but I was forever trying to turn over a new leaf and find optimism underneath, so I climbed into bed hoping this time would be different.

It wasn't.

For the next four hours, Maizy kicked me, kneed me in the kidneys, slapped me in the face, and stole my blankets. I wasn't an early riser, but I could only take so much abuse. By the time seven thirty came, I was showered, dressed, and waiting on the toaster to produce something to carry me through until lunchtime while I sipped orange juice.

Maizy came into the kitchen rubbing her eyes. "Have you got any oatmeal?"

I shook my head. "Cap'n Crunch."

She opened my cupboard and stared at the solitary box of Cap'n Crunch. "Almond milk?" she asked hopefully.

I shook my head. "Whole."

She closed the cupboard with a shudder. "Maybe I'll have some toast."

As if on cue, my slice popped up, beautifully golden brown and deliciously fragrant. Maizy snatched it from the toaster and snarfed a third of it before I could get out of my chair. She sniffed her sleeve while she ate. "Think I need to go home—"

"Yes," I said.

"—and change?" she asked.

Oh. "Depends," I said. "How long have you been wearing that shirt?"

She gave me a strange look. "About fourteen hours."

"You're fine," I told her. "I'd be more worried about the underwear."

"What underwear?"

I had no intention of going *there.*

She brought the box of Cap'n Crunch to the table and started eating it by dry fistfuls. "I should probably call Honest Aaron. He's got a customer waiting on that Cordoba today."

"You're kidding." I held out my hand. She poured some cereal into it. "Who'd want to rent that hunk of junk?"

Yeah, I know, pot and kettle.

"I don't ask," Maizy said. "It's better that way. All I know, whoever it is prepaid the disposal fee."

The disposal fee honed Honest Aaron's competitive edge. If you needed the car for the sort of unsavory criminal purposes that were apt to leave behind ample bodily fluids, you could pay an extra $15 and just drive the car into a quarry. For $20, Honest Aaron would do it for you, no questions asked.

"Oh, well." Maizy got up to pour herself some orange juice. "He can take the LTD. No one's wanted to rent that since the Campbell divorce got a little messy in '14."

I wasn't sure what that meant, but *eww.*

Someone knocked on the door. I got up to find Curt on the landing with a Dunkin' Donuts bag and a cardboard tray holding three lidded cups. "Chocolate frosted, right?"

"You shouldn't eat that," Maizy said over my shoulder. "Too much sugar isn't good for you."

"You've got Cap'n Crunch all over your lips," I told her. I took the bag.

Ten minutes later, it was empty along with half the box of Cap'n Crunch.

"I did a little reading up on Virtual Waste this morning." Curt settled in with his coffee. "Doesn't sound like Nicky D made himself a lot of friends."

Maizy emptied the doughnut bag crumbs into her palm. "He was full of himself. Like a lot of good-looking guys."

I appraised Curt. Curt wasn't full of himself at all, even though he had every reason to be. But I could see Maizy's point. Take Wally Randall, the Boy Lawyer at Parker Dennis, the law firm where I worked. Some women would consider Wally good-looking in a guy-lining, self-tanning, tooth-whitening kind of way. Problem was, Wally owned a mirrored compact and wasn't afraid to use it.

"What'd he look like?" I asked. "Just for background purposes."

Curt snorted into his coffee. "A fan, huh?"

"Don't blame her," Maizy said. "We had the cheap seats. She could barely see the stage."

"I can *see*," I insisted. "What'd he look like?"

Maizy pulled out her cell phone, worked the screen for a few seconds, and stuck the phone under my nose.

I sucked in a sharp breath. Nicky D was more than good-looking. He had the kind of face that made you forget your name. Caribbean blue eyes, perfect Roman nose, lips bordering on girlishly full. High cheekbones. Carefully disheveled hair in three shades of gold.

Yowza.

"Like what you see?" Curt asked.

Oh, no. I wasn't stepping into *that* trap. "He's alright, I guess." I handed Maizy her phone. My hand shook a little.

"I know what you mean," Maizy said. "Bones is a lot better looking. He plays lead guitar." She tapped away the photo of Nicky D and another very different photo appeared. "See?"

Bones, in action onstage. Shoulder-length black hair tied back in a loose ponytail, showing silver hoops, barbells, and studs lining the curves of both ears. Multiple chains around his neck. Leather straps around his wrists. The whole rock jewelry suite, right down to the dark sunglasses that made it impossible to see his eyes. I didn't need to see his eyes. I'd seen enough. And so had Curt, if his horrified expression was any indication.

"You find this guy good-looking?" Curt asked in a pained voice.

"This guy," Maizy said, "isn't conforming to Madison Avenue's perception of attractiveness. He's honoring his own individual truth. *That's* good-looking."

"Point taken," Curt said. "I'm proud of you, Maize."

"Plus he's got a cute butt," Maizy said.

Curt just looked at her.

"For some reason, the two Susans always chased Nicky D around instead." She shrugged. "Go figure."

Curt cleared his throat. "The two Susans?"

Maizy nodded. "Susan One and Susan Two. They claim to be Virtual Waste groupies, but they're really Nicky D groupies. They went to every show in the area and never once paid attention to Bones."

Suspicion shaded Curt's expression. "What happened to Brody Amherst? He really likes you, doesn't he?"

Another shrug from Maizy. "I guess so. Brody's gone all corporate ever since he started delivering pizzas for Domino's. Now he's part of the problem."

Curt glanced at her cell phone. "There might be more than one problem."

"I'll say," Maizy agreed. "Virtual Waste needs to find another drummer. That's a *big* problem. Which reminds me." She glanced up at the wall clock. "We should leave around ten. I want to talk to Archie before he leaves for New York. He's trying to line up a gig for the band at the garden."

"Madison Square Garden?" Curt sounded impressed.

"Nah," Maizy said. "The beer garden at the county fair."

I drained my hot chocolate and got up to toss the cup. "Who's Archie?"

"Virtual Waste's agent," Maizy said. "Archibald Dougal Ritz. You haven't heard of him?"

"I never even heard of Virtual Waste before last night." I noticed Curt's eyebrows lifting. Oops. "I mean, of course I've heard of Archie Ritz. Who hasn't?"

"I hadn't," Maizy said. "Not until two months ago, after they fired their last agent, Gilbert Gleason."

"Why'd they fire Gleason?" Curt asked.

Maizy shrugged. "Not sure. Nicky D probably did nicky-nack with his wife. He was like that."

"Then they should have fired Nicky D," I said indignantly.

"You'd think so," Maizy agreed. "But you don't kill the golden goose. Gilbert tried, but he just put a hole through the snare drum. Mike was pretty upset about that since a new one wasn't in the budget."

I stared at her. "Are you saying Gilbert tried to *shoot* Nicky D?"

"Does that surprise you?" she asked.

"Yes, Maizy," I said. "That surprises me. Did he try to shoot Nicky D because he got fired?"

She shrugged. "Chicken and egg. I'm working on that."

"Seems like Gilbert Gleason is someone we might want to talk to," Curt said.

"I know what you're thinking," Maizy said. "But Gilbert couldn't have done it. Word is his wife dumped him and he disappeared after the snare drum incident."

"Why'd she dump him?" I asked.

"I'm working on that, too," Maizy said. "Anyway, no one's seen him. And Mike looked."

"So what?" I said. "He could have been lying low while he figured out a plan to get back at Nicky D."

Maizy thought about it. "Yeah, I guess so. From what I hear, he didn't seem like the planning type, or the laying low type, but you never know, right? Except..." She shook her head. "There's a picture of him with the band at Pinelands, and I don't think that's who I saw going backstage. The sneaker was *soft*. Like middle-aged spread soft." She looked at Curt. "You know what I mean."

"No," Curt said. "I don't."

I noticed his abs flexing.

"Don't hurt yourself," Maizy said. "That wasn't an insult."

I tossed Curt's empty cup in the trash. "Maybe we should get going."

Curt stood and shoved in his chair with a little too much force. "Aren't you going to ask me if you can drive, Maizy?"

"Not today," she said. "You could use the exercise. I hear it's hard to fight belly fat after thirty." She headed back to the living room.

Curt stared after her, grinding his teeth.

"Don't take it personally," I said. "She'll get older, too."

"Maybe she will"—Curt's eyes narrowed into slits—"and maybe she won't."

CHAPTER FIVE

———

An hour later we pulled into the dirt lot at the Pinelands Bar and Auditorium and parked next to an old blue VW van, with a chromed-out Harley on our right. The Cordoba was gone, retrieved by Honest Aaron. A couple nondescript later-model cars sat scattered about the lot. The general ambiance was a whole lot less *Psycho* in the daylight.

"Bryn's here." Maizy pointed at the Harley.

Curt lifted a questioning eyebrow at me.

"The bouncer," I told him. "And trust me, the bike fits."

Maizy pointed to the other side, at the VW van. "That's the band's tour bus. Mike drives it."

Curt blinked. "*That's* the tour bus? Things not going too well?"

Maizy hopped out of the Jeep and leaned in the open door. "Are you kidding? Do you have any idea what VW vans sell for at classic-car auctions?"

"Twenty bucks?" he asked.

Maizy snorted and slammed the door. We got out and headed for the bar after her. Overhead, puffy white clouds wafted across an azure sky. Pine scent saturated heavy air. Every winged insect known to modern entomology capered around us, pinging against our arms and legs in search of a landing spot.

Inside, it was about what I expected. Two red-felted pool tables. Pockmarked wooden tables anchored by a U-shaped mahogany bar with overhead racks for glasses along both arms of the *U*. No music. No booths. No dance floor. On the back wall hung a cardboard fist with one pointing finger, reminding me of the Ghost of Christmas Future. Beneath the fist, someone had tacked a handwritten sign: *AUDITORIUM.*

A beefy sixtyish man in jeans and a gray T-shirt under a denim vest off-loaded chairs from the tabletops. He paused when he noticed us. "We're not open yet, folks."

Maizy took a step closer to him. "It's me, Tommy."

"Alana?" A smile creased his weather-worn face. "What brings you around? Did you leave something here?"

Curt looked at me and mouthed *Alana?*

I shrugged. I'd seen plenty of renditions of Alana before.

"I need to talk to Archie," Maizy said. "Is he here?"

Tommy shook his head. "Haven't seen him since last night. The band's in the back, though. Hey, I almost forgot. I got something here for you." He went behind the bar for a moment before holding up a folded piece of paper. "Here it is. You must have an admirer."

I caught sight of *Blue-haired Girl* scribbled on the front before Maizy turned away to read it.

Tommy went back to off-loading and wiping down chairs. Curt stood beside me, taking in the ambiance while waiting to leave it.

Maizy spun around. "Who gave you this?"

Tommy paused in mid wipe. "No one. It was left on the bar."

"By who?" she demanded. "Did you see who left it?"

I glanced at Curt. If I didn't know better, I'd say Maizy sounded a little freaked out.

He shook his head. "It was pretty busy last night. I found it under a glass when I was cleaning up."

"How do you know it was meant for her?" I asked him.

"Ain't too many blue-haired girls around," he said. "She kinda stands out."

In more ways than one. Right now she was standing out because tension was vibrating off her in waves.

Curt was watching her. "What's it say, Alana?"

Maizy refolded it and stuffed it into her pocket. "Nothing. Someone likes the way I dance is all."

I narrowed my eyes at her. I'd never seen Maizy dance, even when she'd crashed a wedding reception. Something didn't add up. That note.

"Hey, buddy, quick hand here?" Tommy called out.

Curt went off to help move a few tables. I turned to Maizy.

"Is that from *him*?" I whispered.

She did a quick nod. "Don't tell Uncle Curt."

"Did he threaten you?"

"Not really." She stuck out her chin. "It was a pathetic attempt at psychological warfare."

I stuck my hands on my hips. "Maizy, did he *threaten* you?"

"He saw me." She looked away. "That's all."

"That's *all*?" I yelled.

Curt glanced over at us with a frown. I forced a smile and a no-worries wave.

"What do you mean, that's all?" I whispered savagely. "That's enough. He *saw* you?"

"He saw *this*." Maizy gestured to her blue hair. "Not this." And to the rest of the picture, which was typical teenager, except for the body piercings and lower-back tattoo. "In a weird way," she added, "my hair is like a shield. It's all people notice."

"You have to change it," I told her. "Immediately. Tonight."

"That's like asking Samson to get a little trim," she said.

I shook my head. "I don't care. You're going to lose the blue, or I'm going to tell Curt about that note." Either way, I planned to tell him. He needed to know his niece could be in the cross hairs of a killer.

"Okay, *fine*. I'll be a conformist until we solve the case. *God*." She crossed her arms. "It just better be fast. My hair is my mojo."

Curt and Tommy were back.

"Anything else I can help you with?" Tommy asked.

"Depends," Maizy said. "Did you see someone here last night taller than me but shorter than him—" pointing at Curt "—wearing a dark baggy hoodie and work boots?"

"Maybe a baseball cap?" I added.

Tommy unloaded another chair and gave it a perfunctory wipe. "You're kidding, right? You just described eighty percent of the customers. Men *and* women."

"How about anyone who was acting suspicious?" Curt asked.

"What do you mean?" Tommy asked. "Like drinking some fruity drink with an umbrella in it?"

"Like gonging people in the head with an amplifier," Maizy said.

"Or making plans to run innocent women off the road," I added.

It was possible I'd come with my own agenda.

"I didn't see no one I didn't expect to see," Tommy said.

"Who'd you expect to see?" Curt asked.

"The regulars. The band and the lawyer that works for them. Alana." Tommy swiped at a tabletop. "And a whole bunch of strangers. That's about it, until that kid turned up dead and the cops got here. What's this all about, anyway?" He gave the table a couple more swipes and straightened. "Wait a second. You telling me someone killed him?"

"You didn't hear it from me," Maizy said.

"I *didn't* hear it from you," Tommy said. "You heard it from *me*. But the cops said it was an accident."

"Yeah," Maizy said. "They do that."

Tommy seemed perplexed. "Wouldn't they know about that hoodie person?"

"You'd think so," Maizy said. "What were *you* doing while Nicky D was getting himself killed?"

He moved on to the next table and started off-loading chairs. "I was behind the stick all night, except for a quick run to the back for a case of JD."

"Did you see *anything* unusual?" I asked him.

He slung the rag over his shoulder. "Not that I can think of. Look, I appreciate the interrogation, but I got work to do here. Whyn't you go on back. Bryn's there helping the boys pack up. Until they get another drummer, they're pretty much done." He glanced at Curt and me. "These your folks?"

I stuck my fists on my hips. "Do I look like I could be her mother?"

"Well…" He cocked his head sideways, assessing. "Yeah."

Curt choked back laughter.

"She's my partner," Maizy said. "We solve crimes together."

"You do, huh?" He seemed bemused. "What kind of crimes?"

"Murders, mostly," Maizy told him. "Missing persons. Pretty much anything except shoplifting. Anyone can catch shoplifters. *You* could probably catch shoplifters."

Tommy frowned at Curt. "This kid for real?"

"Alana's as real as it gets," Curt said. He grinned at me. I gave him nothing. I didn't like to encourage him.

"Here's a case for you," Tommy said. "My libido seems to be missing. I think my wife stole it." He let out a cackle.

"TMI, dude," Maizy told him. "Also, don't believe inherently flawed gender-based memes about sexual performance. Maybe the problem is *you.*"

Tommy's mouth fell open.

"We'll be backstage when Archie gets here," Maizy said. "Let me know if there's anything you want to tell me about last night."

CHAPTER SIX

————

With Maizy in the lead, we wound around the tables and into the rear wing of the bar that served as the auditorium. There were rows of chairs packed tightly together facing a no-frills stage. No curtain, no windows, one door in the back corner that provided access to the backstage area for the acts. I figured it was probably how the killer had escaped without notice. It was the kind of door that locked automatically when it closed so that you could get out but not in. Which meant the killer hadn't sneaked in from the parking lot but had been in the audience or at the bar before Nicky D's death.

Curt glanced around. "You know you've made it when you play here."

"Don't judge," Maizy said. "Virtual Waste started out playing proms."

"And then things went downhill," he said.

I was kind of proud of myself for noticing the door. It wasn't often that I scooped Maizy. I nudged her. "That door can't be opened from the outside."

She barely glanced at it. "It might've been propped open, for all we know. Or someone could have let the killer in."

I blinked. "You mean an accomplice?"

"Not necessarily," she said. "He might have knocked, and someone just opened it. You know, like at the movie theater."

"That's how you get into the theater?" Curt asked. "You do realize that's a *business*."

Maizy shrugged. "I buy popcorn. Hey, look. There's Bryn!"

Bryn had emerged from backstage busily looping a long electrical cable.

"Wow," Curt said.

Yeah. That's what I'd been thinking. She wore skinny jeans that were a misnomer in the case of legs like hers, along with a bright pink midriff top that showed off the bottom of her six-pack abs.

We followed Maizy up to the stage and waited while Bryn stowed the cable in a travel case.

"I didn't expect to see you so soon," she told Maizy. "But I'm glad you're back. And you brought friends." She beamed at us like a grandmother offering freshly baked cookies to hungry kindergarteners.

"They're not friends," Maizy said. "They're my partners. Hortense and Bruce."

That cut it. I was buying Maizy a book of twenty-first-century baby names.

Bryn turned her megawatt smile on me.

"We met," I said. "Last night. Outside."

She nodded, the way you do when you're just being polite. I wasn't offended. Being memorable wasn't in my skill set.

She pivoted to Curt. "Hello, Bruce."

Well, I didn't like the sound of *that.*

"Nice bike you've got out there," Curt said. "'53 Panhead, right?"

Bryn's smile brightened even more. "That's right. My Uncle Doug gave it to me as a graduation gift. I got my love of bikes and cars from him. Want to take it for a spin?"

He shook his head. "Thanks, but I'm happy on four wheels."

"I've got those, too," Bryn said. "I also restore muscle cars." She batted her eyelashes at him. "I'm always happy to show them off."

Gee, I hoped we didn't accidentally back over her Harley when we left.

She turned back to Maizy. "You said you were going to find out who killed Nicky D, but I know you're busy preparing to defend your thesis, so I thought I could help. I did some asking around."

Curt mouthed *thesis?* at me. I don't know why he bothered. Not like he should have been surprised.

"Do go on," Maizy said.

I rolled my eyes. She might be taking that Dr. Alana thing a bit too far.

"I might have a lead for you," Bryn said. "That's what it's called, right? A lead?"

Maizy shrugged. "Lead, suspect, killer. Tomato, to-mah-to."

"Well," Bryn said, "someone told me he saw Mike and Nicky D arguing right after the first set. He said it got pretty heated."

"What were they arguing about?" Curt asked.

Bryn shook her head. "He didn't know. He was watching them from across the room. But the argument's not the most important thing." She glanced over her shoulder and lowered her voice. "He said that right after that, Mike propped open the back door and made this strange arm motion. Like he was signaling to someone outside."

"Like this?" Maizy did a come-here gesture by crooking just her forefinger.

Bryn shook her head.

"Like this?" Maizy did a whole-arm get-over-here wave.

Bryn shook her head.

"Why don't you demonstrate," Curt suggested.

Bryn took a step back, lifted her right arm, and batted it around hard enough to wrench her shoulder out of its socket.

"That's weird, alright," Maizy said. "Did he see anyone sneak in after that?"

"He wasn't paying attention," Bryn said. "I think he said he left not long after that. He hadn't planned on sticking around for the second set anyway."

"What was this guy's name?" Maizy asked. "We'll need to talk to him."

"Don something." She frowned. "Maybe Dan. Or Derek. I'm not sure. He's only been here a couple of times."

"Try to find out if you see him again," Curt said.

Bryn's expression softened into a smile. "I can call you if I do."

I *really* didn't like the sound of *that.* I was just about to unleash the full force of my wrath, which surely would have frightened her into incoherence, when lucky for her, I got distracted by something banging backstage, followed by someone cursing loudly and colorfully.

Bryn gave a start. "I should get back to work," she said. "They offered me a hundred bucks to help them pack up their gear today." She leaned in. "It gives me the chance to keep an eye on Mike, right?"

"You want to be careful with that," Maizy said. "Investigating isn't a hobby."

It wasn't a job, either. At least not the way *we* did it.

CHAPTER SEVEN

———

Someone wandered out from backstage, noticed us standing there, and flashed us a peace sign.

"Hey." I nudged Maizy. "Who's that?"

She glanced over. "Oh, that's Plop. He's the keyboardist. Come on. I'll introduce you."

Plop was a slob in a Grateful Dead tie-dyed T-shirt, sagging jeans that settled at mid butt, and untied Nikes. His face was round and pink and unshaven. He wore round glasses with a pale blue tint. A miasma of cigarette smoke surrounded him.

"This guy should come with a Surgeon General's warning," I whispered to Curt.

He smirked. "Try not to take deep breaths."

Plop gave his jeans a hike with both hands. "Hey, Alana." The cigarette in the corner of his mouth bobbled when he spoke. "Didn't expect to see you today."

"How you doing, Plop?" Maizy gestured to us. "These are my friends. They're cool."

"Good enough for me," Plop said. He stuck out his hand to Curt. "Nice to meet you, man."

"You know that'll kill you," Curt said flatly.

Plop drew back in horror. "Shaking hands? Since when?"

"He means smoking," Maizy said. She turned to Curt. "Don't worry. If I was interested, I could've gotten cigarettes from Herbie Hairston at school. He keeps a dozen cases in the trunk of his car. He steals them from the 7-Eleven."

"Can you hook me up?" Plop said.

"That was *Hairston*, right?" Curt asked.

I'd heard all about Herbie Hairston. Herbie was the poster child for juvenile delinquents everywhere.

"Let me ask you something," Maizy said. "Did you see Mike and Nicky D arguing last night?"

"You mean about all the lawsuits?" Plop asked.

"What lawsuits?" I cut in. This was familiar territory. Lawsuits paid my rent. Okay, *some* of my rent. On the months when I didn't have a hefty car repair. Or a need to eat.

Maizy elbowed me, not too gently. "Yes," she said. "About all the lawsuits. Is that what they were arguing about?"

"Beats me," Plop said. "I didn't know they were arguing."

"What about the lawsuits?" I asked.

"Beats me," he repeated. "I didn't know there were lawsuits."

"But you said 'all the lawsuits,'" Maizy reminded him.

"Did I?" He frowned. "I don't remember."

Oh yeah, this was going to be easy.

"Is Archie here?" Maizy asked.

He labored to consider the question. "Haven't seen him since last night, chilling with Bryn. Why?"

"We want to talk to him about Nicky D," she said.

I could have been wrong, but I thought a shadow darkened Plop's face. Or maybe it was a stray wisp of smoke because he was pulling on his cigarette so hard his cheeks were caving in.

He didn't say anything for a few seconds while he blew out smoke in a stream. "What for?"

Without a word Curt reached out, took the cigarette from him, dropped it, and ground it under his heel.

"Dude." Plop stared at the remains. "That was so not cool."

"Maybe you can help us," Maizy said. "What can you tell us about Nicky D?"

"Let's see." Plop rolled his eyes upward, thinking. "He's dead."

Curt muttered something under his breath.

"Can you be more specific?" I asked him.

More exertional thinking. "He's *really* dead."

"Do you know anyone who might have wanted him that way?" Maizy asked.

"Everyone wanted him dead," Plop said.

"What do you mean?" Curt asked. "Why?"

"Yo, Plop, you want to pick it up out here? We haven't got all— Hey, Alana!" The anti-Plop swooped down to kiss Maizy's cheek. Clean shaven, military haircut, stain-free clothes. Nice cologne. This guy would look right at home in *GQ*, modeling $2,000 suits.

He straightened up and offered Curt his hand. "Mike Crescenzo. I'm with the band."

This was Mike? He didn't look like a cold, calculating, door-propping accessory to murder. He looked like someone you'd see modeling underwear on a billboard along the New Jersey Turnpike.

"Are you Alana's father?" Mike asked.

I snickered because Curt *so* had that coming.

"Is the rest of the band more like you," Curt said, "or more like…" He cocked his head toward Plop, who was humming to himself while scrounging in his pockets for another smoke.

Mike's smile showed even white teeth. "Don't let Plop fool you. He may seem bizarre, but he's a genius on the keyboard." He turned to Maizy. "What brings you back here? I thought you had to teach a relativistic quantum field theory class today."

Curt stared at Maizy. I was unfazed. I was pretty sure she could do it.

"I was twenty minutes late to class," she said without hesitation. "So, you know." She shrugged. "Fifteen-minute rule. Listen, what were you doing last night when Nicky D died?"

He drew back, startled. "Excuse me?"

"What she means—" Curt said.

"—is what were you doing last night when Nicky D died?" Maizy said.

"We were between sets," Mike said. "You must remember that."

"Sure, sure," Maizy said impatiently. "But *where* were you between sets?"

He seemed to hesitate. "I was at the bar talking to Archie."

"What if someone said you were fighting with Nicky D?" Maizy asked.

Mike's fingers were getting twitchy at his sides. In my experience that was never a good sign. "Who said that?"

"I never reveal my sources," Maizy said.

I did a surreptitious scan of the vicinity. Bryn had disappeared.

"What's this mean?" Maizy flapped her arm around, mimicking Bryn mimicking Mike.

"I give up," Mike said. "What is this, anyway?" His tone was terse. Terse tones *and* twitchy fingers meant trouble. "He died by accident. You think I dropped that amplifier on Nick's head?"

"Of course not," I said.

"You might have pushed it," Maizy agreed.

Twitch, twitch. "Let me save you some time," Mike said. "I didn't. You can check my alibi with Archie if you want to."

"I don't think we need to call it an *alibi*," I said. Interesting that *he* would call it that when Nicky D's death had been deemed accidental.

"She's right," Maizy said. "We could call it an excuse instead. But that wouldn't be very nice, would it."

"Like I said," Mike repeated, "feel free to talk to Archie."

"We'll talk to everyone," Maizy said. "That's how it's done."

Mike frowned. "How *what's* done?"

Curt stepped forward, angling himself partially between them. "Looks like you've got a lot to do. We don't want to hold you up."

Mike gave Maizy a lingering glance before turning to Curt, tension visibly draining from his face. "Listen, if you happen to hear of a drummer looking for work, would you send him our way? We have a gig on Thursday after next, and I don't want to cancel it."

Talk about compassion. Nicky D hadn't been dead twenty-four hours yet.

"We could use a couple of backup singers, too," Mike added. He cocked his head at Maizy and me. "You two do any singing?"

"Yes," Maizy said.

"No," I said.

"Don't pay attention to her," Maizy said. "She just gets stage fright. Sometimes it's hard for her to sing, what with all the vomiting. We just put a bucket near her, and it's on with the show."

Oh, *gross*.

"What a trouper," Mike said. "I like it."

Maizy looked at me. "Good thing that didn't get in your way on the Geezer Tour."

Oh, no.

"Geezer Tour," Mike repeated. "Never heard of that one. Where was it?"

"Nursing homes, mostly," Maizy said. "Assisted-living facilities. Retirement communities. The shows were short, on account of the audiences were in bed by nine, but we packed a lot into that twenty minutes."

Mike stared at her.

"What's it pay?" she asked.

"A bill a gig," Mike said. "Give it some thought."

"We'll do it," Maizy said.

I elbowed her. "He said give it some *thought*."

She elbowed me back. "I *heard* him."

"Great." Mike gave us his billboard smile. "Now all we need's a drummer."

"I might know somebody," Curt said. He gestured toward the stage. "Do you mind?"

Mike's face lit up. "You've got to be kidding me."

My jaw went slack. "You've got to be kidding me."

Curt settled himself behind the drum kit, picked up the sticks, and launched into a complicated riff for a minute or two before settling into an easy groove. He showed me double-barrel dimples, and I fought the urge to hurl my panties onstage.

Plop stopped scrounging to listen.

I turned to Maizy, hands on hips. "Did you know he could do this?"

She shook her head, unconcerned. "I thought he only played the guitar."

A smallish guy wandered over to stand next to Mike. "Who's that?"

"Name's Bruce." Mike nodded toward us. "He came with Alana."

"Hey, TJ." Maizy pulled me forward. "This is Hortense. TJ's the lead singer," she told me. "He's a songwriter, too."

I shook his hand. "Have I heard anything of yours?"

"Sure," TJ said. "On Nick's solo CD."

Was that a motive I heard?

"That's theft of intellectual property," Maizy piped up. "You could sue. Just so happens my partner here knows a few good lawyers."

"No, I don't," I said immediately. I wasn't lying. I worked for Sleepy, Grumpy & Dopey, LLC.

"Doesn't matter," he said. "I can write more songs. Not like it's going to be a problem anymore."

I took a harder look at him, wondering if he was strong enough to wield an amplifier. He was on the thin side, but it was the wiry kind of thin that could be deceptively strong.

TJ turned his attention back to the stage. "Dude sounds good. We gonna hire him?"

Mike glanced at Maizy. "Is he looking for work?"

Curt in a band? I hadn't even known Curt could play an instrument. And here he was onstage, going all Dave Grohl on me. But he couldn't be seriously auditioning. Curt already had a job, eschewing his business degree and the nine-to-five existence that came with it in favor of the cubical-free life of package delivery.

Oh, who was I kidding?

Then it occurred to me: this was Curt's midlife crisis. Joining a band instead of covering up gray hair or getting in shape or buying a Corvette. He had no gray, he already had a killer body, and the Jeep was more his style. More horrifying, if he joined a band, would that make me a groupie? I didn't want to be a groupie. I couldn't afford it. I didn't have the body for it. And I liked to be asleep by eleven.

Maizy nudged me. "Don't overthink this."

Hard to do that when my whole world had just been drummed off its axis.

"It's not that bad," Maizy said.

How could it not be bad? The Curt I knew was up onstage morphing into a sexy rock guy right in front of me. It wouldn't be long before he stopped shaving and grew his hair long and got naked-lady tattoos.

"It could be worse," Maizy said. "He could get a ruler tattooed on his—"

"Will you stop that?" I snapped.

She shrugged. "It's not my fault you think out loud."

Pretty sure I didn't. Just in case, I took a step farther from TJ, which is when I noticed Mike had gone onstage to talk to Curt.

"That guy your father or what?" TJ asked Maizy.

"He's one of my partners," Maizy told him.

TJ frowned a little, clearly unsure of the context. "I just hope he knows how to show up on time and be professional."

Note to self: steal Curt's watch and take the batteries out of his wall clocks.

"Why?" Maizy asked. "Wasn't Nicky D professional?"

Onstage, Curt was shaking his head and Mike had a pained expression. The new job was falling through. Hope surged through me.

TJ snorted. "Oh, sure. A professional wannabe."

Ouch. Also, *hm.* TJ seemed to be throwing plenty of shade at Nicky D.

"We're trying to do this for a living," he added. "The guys all bought into the concept of group. Nicky D bought into the concept of Nicky D."

Serious shade.

"What do you mean?" I asked. "Like stealing your songs?" Now that I had new hope, I was back in the game.

Plop had moseyed offstage and disappeared. Darn. I was hoping to ask him where *he'd* been between sets.

"Nick thought he could get away with anything," TJ said. "He treated people like dirt. Don't get me wrong… A good-looking guy never hurts a band's appeal. I mean, look at Jim Morrison, right?"

"*He's* a good-looking guy," I said, gesturing toward Curt, who was in deep discussion with Mike.

"But he's a noob," TJ said. "He's got no say. Nick was with us from the beginning. He thought *he* invented Virtual Waste."

"So you're not sorry that he's gone," Maizy said.

"Not especially." TJ hesitated, coloring slightly. "Not that I'd want to see him dead or anything."

Of course not. His abiding affection for Nicky D came through loud and clear.

"So where were *you* between sets last night?" Maizy asked him.

TJ didn't hesitate. "I went outside for a smoke."

She nodded. "Anyone with you?"

"The Marlboro Man," TJ said. "What are you, a cop?"

"A concerned citizen," Maizy said. "Did you see anything out of place last night? Someone where they shouldn't have been, that kind of thing?"

"It was a full house," TJ said. "I didn't notice anyone in particular."

"Think about it," she said. "Anyone with a navy hoodie, work boots, maybe a baseball cap?"

"Yeah," he said. "Bones. He likes to hide in plain sight."

I could relate. I practically made a religion out of going unnoticed. That might have had something to do with the fact that only water retention made me top a hundred pounds and my cat had more curves than I did. See? Not groupie material. Not backup singer material, either, but I was pretty sure Maizy hadn't been serious about that.

Maizy seemed crestfallen. "Did Bones have a problem with Nicky D?"

"Everyone had a problem with Nicky D," he said.

"Is Bones here?" I asked.

"He didn't show up this morning, and he's not answering his phone." TJ smirked. "Probably had another accident. That dude drives worse than my grandmother."

Bad enough to rear-end a moving car while escaping the scene of a homicide? Maybe it was me, but that had *flee the country* written all over it.

Curt and Mike rejoined us. Hard to read anything from their expressions. Curt seemed amused, maybe because I was shooting death rays out of my eyes. That sort of thing tended to amuse him. Which tells you how threatening I can be.

"Did I miss anything?" he asked me.

"No," I snapped, "but I think *I* did. Do I have to go buy some high heels and low-cut tops now?"

He kissed the top of my head. "No, but I really wish you would."

"That's not funny." I stuck my fists on my hips. "Did you take the job?"

"I have a job," he said mildly. He leaned in close and lowered his voice until I felt it more than heard it. "But wouldn't it be nice to have someone on the inside, Hortense?"

I drew back to stare at him, and suddenly it all made sense. Well, not *all* of it. I still didn't understand why reporters thought you wouldn't understand the concept of bad weather unless they stood outside and showed it to you. But at least the part about Curt's impromptu audition made sense.

"Do you have time for this?" I asked him.

"Not really. But it's only for one or two shows." He slid his arm around my waist and pulled me against him. "Now about those high heels and low-cut tops."

A shiver started at my toes and worked its way up.

"Could someone hose down the old people?" Maizy practically yelled. "I'm trying to do a job here. *God.*"

The shiver flatlined in the vicinity of my kneecaps.

Maizy turned back to TJ. "Where does Bones live?"

Oh, right. The possible killer who'd gone underground. That was important, too.

TJ shrugged. "I've never been to his place, but I don't think he lives too far from here." He glanced at us in turn. "You don't think Bones did anything wrong, do you?"

"Doubtful," Maizy said.

"You don't know until you know," Curt said at the same time.

That was usually Maizy's philosophy. It sounded strange coming from Curt. Even stranger *not* coming from Maizy.

Mike's pocket buzzed. He pulled his cell phone out and glanced at the screen. "Archie's been tied up," he said. "He's not going to make it here today."

Well, that was awfully convenient, considering we were planning to check Mike's alibi with him. Made me wonder if that text had truly come from Archie or if it was an easy way to be rid of us.

Mike dropped his phone into his pocket. "Sorry to rush you guys, but we really need to get broken down." He looked at me. "Come in and audition when you get that vomiting problem under control."

Just the thought was enough to make me race for the bathroom.

CHAPTER EIGHT

———

We were halfway through the bar on our way to the exit when someone whispered, "*Pssst!*"

Maizy glanced over her shoulder at me. "What?"

"I didn't say anything," I told her.

"*Psssst!*"

We all stopped and looked around. Behind the bar, Plop slowly rose to come into view. He glanced side to side before leaning forward on his elbows to whisper, "TJ lied to you."

Maizy's eyes narrowed. "I *knew* it!"

"What about?" I asked.

Plop held a finger over his lips. "*Sssh.*"

"What about?" I whispered.

"He was *really* ticked off about Nicky stealing his songs," Plop whispered back. "He played it cool, but I heard him tell Nicky he'd be sorry for ripping him off."

"What do you think he meant by that?" I asked.

"You guessed it," Plop said, although I hadn't. "Don't let his size fool you. TJ's got a wicked temper. He was especially cheesed about Nicky stealing 'Puddle of Drool.' He thought that would be our breakout song. Nicky didn't even like it at first, said it was too mainstream. And then he put it on his CD."

Right. Nothing said mainstream like "Puddle of Drool."

"Just thought you ought to know," Plop whispered. "Oh, and something else." He glanced side to side again. His paranoia was making me nervous. "You might want to talk to Hank from the two Susans if you want inside info. He's engaged to Susan One."

Curt frowned at me. I did a palms-up who-knows? shrug.

"He don't come inside much," Plop said, "but he follows her to all the shows, waits in the parking lot to make sure she leaves alone. Check out the parking lot at the Golden Grotto. Or head over to Max's Garage. You can't miss him. I got a Buick smaller 'n him."

Oh, good. A jealous giant. We'd have to take reinforcements. I eyed the width of Curt's shoulders. Not ginormous, but not bad. While I was at it, I eyed the taper of his waist and parts farther south. Then I raised my eyes to find him staring at me with a crooked little grin, like he could read my mind.

"Why should we talk to him?" Maizy asked. "If he doesn't even come inside?"

"*Much*," Plop said. "Last night was one of those times."

"What'd he do?" Curt asked.

"He just stood there and stared," Plop said. "He stared at her, and then he stared at *him*. Dude is off the rails *scary.*"

"You never told us what *you* were doing between sets," Maizy said.

"Me?" He blinked innocently. "I was catching some Zs. You'd be surprised how tired the digits get." He waggled his fingers at us. They seemed perfectly alert to me.

"Were you alone?" I asked.

He seemed surprised by the question. "Sure I was alone. Nobody else was tired." He shrugged. "I gotta jet." And he sank down into a low squat and stayed there.

We all looked at each other.

Maizy hoisted herself onto the bar on her forearms. "You're still here, dude."

Without looking up, Plop duck-walked away and out of sight.

Maizy shook her head. "Doofus."

I had to wonder if Plop was a doofus by accident or design.

CHAPTER NINE

———

Maizy used an ancient *Yellow Pages* at the bar, and twenty minutes later, we rolled to a stop at Max's Garage. It was strictly a repair facility, without gas pumps or niceties such as squeegees and snack foods. The door to its single service bay gaped open like a screaming mouth. A car sat on the single lift inside. A couple of tree trunks wearing denim and steel-toed boots stood working beneath it.

No one got out of the Jeep.

"So are we done here?" I asked.

"We should talk to him," Maizy said.

No one moved.

The behemoth that had to be Hank stepped away from the lift to plunder a giant rolling tool chest. Cannon ball shoulders beneath a flannel shirt. Big shaggy yeti head. Hands the size of catcher's mitts.

"Who knew Plop was a master of understatement," Curt said.

"I didn't know blood could pump that high," Maizy said.

"I have to go to the bathroom," I said.

"I'm sure there's a bathroom here," Curt said.

"At home," I said.

"I read about people who can't use strange bathrooms," Maizy said. "You're a shy urinater."

"Pretty sure I'm not," I said. "In fact, I'm doing it a little right now."

Curt's head jerked around. "I hope you're kidding."

I rolled my eyes. "Maybe we should wait until next Thursday night to talk to Hank. At the Golden Grotto. When there are lots of people around." Also known as witnesses.

"And lose this opportunity?" Maizy opened her door. "Who's coming with me?"

Curt let out a pained sigh.

"Are you sure?" I asked him.

"Who else is going to do it?" he asked.

Implicit in that response was *there's certainly no way a ninety-eight-pound weakling like you can stand up against Mechanic Yeti in there.*

How insulting. But I was willing to overlook it.

"Come on, guys." Maizy shifted from leg to leg, impatient. "Don't let his freakish ginormousness scare you. I bet he helps little old ladies across the street and collects kittens."

"Probably to make stew," I muttered. But I wasn't going to be the only one who sat in the car, safe behind locked doors, with my fingers twitching over the ignition key and my foot hovering over the gas pedal. I had my pride. I got out of the car and followed Curt and Maizy at a safe distance of roughly ten feet.

I didn't have *that* much pride.

When we—and by *we* I mean Curt and Maizy—got closer, Hank lifted that grizzly bear head of his to glower at us (them) under his unibrow. His voice was like an echo in an oil drum. "Help you?"

"Are you Hank?" Curt asked him, not sounding intimidated at all although Hank had a good six inches and probably fifty pounds on him. To be fair, Curt had a secret weapon. Maizy. She'd marched right up to Hank with the world-weary bearing she'd mastered watching *Columbo* on Antenna TV. World weary wasn't easy for a seventeen-year-old to pull off, but she managed.

"That's my name," Hank said without a trace of good nature.

"I'm Alana Winkelrod," Maizy said. "I'm investigating the death of Nick DiBenedetto from Virtual Waste."

Hank's head drew back, his jaw drew down, his eyes dropped, and there, finally, at knee level, he found Maizy. "Your hair is blue," he told her.

"It is?" She clapped a hand on top of her head. "How'd that happen?"

One corner of Hank's mouth twitched for a millisecond. Probably as close as he got to smiling.

Maizy narrowed her eyes at him. "Guess that makes me a blue-haired girl."

Oh, no. I didn't even want to *think* this giant was the killer.

His expression remained stony. "You're who?" he asked. "Doing what?"

Maizy flashed a business card at him. "Alana Winkelrod. Private eye." She stuck the card back in her pocket. "About Nick DiBenedetto."

"I couldn't see that," Hank said.

"Then you'll have to come down the beanstalk," she said. "I'm doing the best I can here."

Hank's glower transferred to Curt. "Who're you?"

"He's my partner," Maizy said. "Vin Diesel. No relation."

"No kidding," Hank said. His attention shifted to where I was cowering behind Curt. "Who's this one? Beyoncé?"

For some reason, I sensed skepticism.

"No idea," Maizy said. "We picked her up hitchhiking. What was your relationship with Nick DiBenedetto?"

"Him again." Hank blew out a sigh. "I got no relationship with him. All I know, he's a guitar player or something for that band plays over at the Pinelands."

"Drummer," Maizy said.

He shrugged. "Whatever."

"Did you ever watch them perform?" Curt asked him.

"I don't like music," Hank said flatly. "My girl likes it enough for the both of us."

"Does *she* watch them perform?" Maizy asked.

He snorted. "She ain't missed a show in a year. You ask me, she's making a fool of herself."

"I *am* asking you," Maizy said. "Why'd you say 'him again'?"

"Because how many times does she have to see the same lousy band play, that's why." He shook his massive head. "It's like it's her job or something. What, I ain't good enough for her? I'm working six days a week so we don't have to live in a tent, and she's all the time going on about that Nicky D. 'Isn't he cute, Hank. Isn't he something, Hank. Isn't he—'"

"I don't get it, either," Maizy said. "Insecurity is so attractive in a man."

My ears perked up. I knew bitter when I heard it. Here was my opening to ingratiate myself with Hank so I could charm some more information out of him.

"I know what you mean," I said. "My job doesn't pay much, either. You should see the car I drive. Well, I mean, you probably *should* see the car I drive, you being a mechanic and all. It makes some weird noises, but then who doesn't? Not like I can afford to get it fixed. I should probably ask for a raise, but I've got this thing about asserting myself. My mother says that I—"

Curt said, "Ahem."

Oops. "At least I'm not covered in grease and motor oil," I finished.

Hank looked me up and down. "You wanna be?"

"Hey," Curt said sharply. "Have some respect."

Hank put up his hands. "Sorry, man. Didn't know you and the hitchhiker had it going on."

I blinked. Did we have it going on? I guess that depended on what *it* was.

"It's like they've known each other for years," Maizy said. "It's really something. So I hear you wait outside for your girlfriend when the band plays."

"Who told you that?" Hank asked. "That Susan broad tell you that?"

"I don't like that word *broad*," Maizy said. "And my sources are confidential. Are you afraid she's doing nicky-nack with someone from the bar?"

"What'd you hear?" he asked immediately. "It's that drummer, isn't it? I knew that guy was up to something again, the way she talked about him. Always 'Oh, he's so talented. Oh, he's so cute. Oh, he—'" He stopped short, his cheeks going red.

We stared up at him.

"Dude, get a grip," Maizy said. "*God.*"

He regrouped with a shrug of the shoulders that caused a slight breeze. "A man can only take so much," he said. He glanced at Curt. "You know what I mean."

"Everyone's got a breaking point," Curt said. The way he was standing there, dead still, laser focused, grim faced, made me think he'd just about reached his.

"That's it," Hank agreed. "Breaking point."

"What's yours?" Maizy asked.

"Ain't reached it yet." He glared at her. "But I'm getting close."

"Yeah, me, too," she said. "One more *broad* and I'm there. Where were you last night?"

Hank stared out into the parking lot. "I was replacing a clutch. And a set of plugs."

"Were you here alone?" she asked.

"I'm always here alone," he said. "Unless I'm not."

Oh, that was helpful.

"The clutch picked up around seven," he said. "Worked out good."

Especially if he wanted to head on over to the Pinelands for a quick murder before heading home to dinner.

"And then you went to the bar, right?" Maizy prompted him. "You might as well admit it. We already talked to someone who saw you there."

A thundercloud rolled across his face. "What if I did? Ain't no one gonna pick her up on my watch. I ain't having it."

"Nicky D tried to pick her up?" Maizy asked. "Did you teach him a lesson or what?"

"Had to," Hank growled. "He didn't understand the word *no*."

"Wait a minute." Maizy whipped out her cell phone and held it up with her arm fully outstretched. It reached Hank's chin. "Say that again, nice and loud into the phone so I can record your confession."

Hank's expression hardened, if that was possible. "What confession?"

"You taught him a lesson," Maizy said. "Everyone knows that means twenty years to life. So just say it again, right into the phone here, and we'll be on our—"

Hank ripped the phone out of her hand and slammed it to the ground at his feet with a malevolent smile. It wasn't hard at all for my imagination to substitute the phone for an amplifier and the ground for Nicky D's head.

"I think we're done here," Maizy said.

I would have voiced my agreement, except I was sprinting back to the car. I didn't need an amplifier to fall on *me* to put two and two together. Forget TJ. Hank was an evil giant who'd killed Nicky D out of pure jealousy. Case solved.

Now it was up to someone else to rope him and brand him and lock him up in a very big cage.

CHAPTER TEN

———

"That went well," Maizy said when we were back on the road.

My heart was more or less back in the right place, but my eyes, when I checked in the mirror, were still a little wild, and I couldn't stop shivering even though sweat trickled down my spine. "What are you talking about? He destroyed your phone!"

Maizy shrugged. "It's insured. I needed a new one anyway." She tapped Curt on the shoulder. "That was smooth, right? We got him to confess to murder even if it's not on tape."

"Not quite, Maize." Curt turned up the air conditioning. "The guy's obviously a jealous maniac, but that doesn't mean he killed anyone."

"Somewhere, somehow, sometime in his life," Maizy said, "he's killed someone. I guarantee it. I can read people. It's a gift."

"If you can read people," I said, "why'd you stick your phone in his face?"

"Be serious," she said. "It was nowhere near his face. Besides, he practically admitted it. Nicky D moved on Susan One, and Bruce Banner went all Hulk on his—"

"We should talk to Susan One," Curt cut in.

I stared at them. "What is wrong with you two? How can you be so calm after what just happened?"

"What just happened?" Maizy asked. "We have a prime suspect, and I have a broken phone. Don't be such a drama queen."

"Drama queen?" I yelled. "He could have killed us and buried us in the Pine Barrens, and no one would have ever known!"

"See? Drama," Maizy said sadly.

"It's not drama," I snapped. "You hear about it all the time. People disappear in the Pine Barrens *all the time*, and no one ever knows what happened to them!"

"He wasn't going to kill us," Curt said quietly.

"How do you know?" I demanded.

"I know." He brushed the back of his hand along my jawline. "He's a bully. And like every bully, he'd back down if he was challenged."

"Are you packing heat, Uncle Curt?" Maizy asked. "If I'd known, I could have been *really* forceful with him."

"I'm not packing heat," Curt told her.

"You should be," Maizy said. "You can't be too careful. I hear people disappear all the time in the Pine Barrens."

I turned to glower at her. She gave me a cheery smile.

"I can score you a bazooka if you're interested," she said to Curt. "Herbie Hairston's having a sale on account of his dad wants to use the shed again."

"I'll pass," Curt said. "Where did Herbie Hairston get a bazooka?"

Maizy shrugged. "I don't ask questions like that. I need plausible deniability."

We drove along for another mile or two while I wondered what my problem was. I had to have one. I mean, here I was, in the middle of the Pine Barrens, mired in yet another murder investigation, confronting the Unjolly Giant and backstabbing musicians and maniac drivers trying to run me off the road.

Speaking of which.

"Did either of you happen to notice the F-150 back at Max's?" Curt asked.

"The one with the baseball cap on the dashboard?" Maizy said. "Yeah, I saw it."

"Did it look like the truck from last night?" he asked.

Maizy gnawed on her lower lip, thinking. "I don't know. I'm not sure about the color."

Curt glanced at me. "What do you think?"

"You're kidding, right?" I said. "I was busy trying to stay on the road. Besides, even if it is the right truck, that doesn't mean it's Hank's. It could just be in for repairs."

"We could always go back and ask—" Maizy began.

"No," Curt and I said together.

Maizy shrugged. "Or we could sneak back after hours and look for the papers in the glove compartment. Older trucks are easy to break into."

Curt narrowed his eyes at her in the mirror. "Are they, now."

"They're left unlocked all the time," Maizy said. "I mean, what's there to steal?"

"The truck itself?" he said.

She did a dismissive wave. "It's a niche market. Not worth the time."

"Do not sneak back there," I told Maizy. "Under any circumstances. Ever. Even with a bazooka."

"How would I get there?" she asked innocently. "I don't have a car or a license. Remember I'm blacklisted from the DMV for six more months 'cause that doofus examiner fell out of the car during my test."

Because the car had been an Honest Aaron special, and the examiner had fallen out when the door had fallen off.

"What are you talking about?" Curt asked. Being under the impression that Maizy had failed for less nefarious reasons, like parallel parking, an antiquated maneuver that was completely pointless in a state where spacious parking lots proliferated like mold spores in a damp basement. Because that's the impression I'd given him. And yes, I did feel a twinge of guilt about that.

"I mean," Maizy said, "he tripped while getting out of the car after a completely uneventful road test."

Curt fell silent, the muscles of his jaw flexing and relaxing while he ground his teeth. "Maybe society is better off," he muttered. I was pretty sure the rest of that sentence was *without you having a driver's license,* but he wasn't about to say that. Not when he had Maizy's future car parked and waiting in his driveway for her to take legal ownership of it. Which didn't seem likely to happen so long as Honest Aaron stayed in business.

Maizy cheerfully ignored that comment. "What's next?"

"We should talk to the other guy from the band," I said. "Bones. Interesting that he hasn't shown up today. TJ said he was a terrible driver and might have had an accident." I hesitated. "What does Bones drive?"

"I'm not worried about Bones," Maizy said. "He didn't do it. It wasn't him going backstage. I'd know him."

"She's got a point," Curt told me.

"That person was all covered up," I pointed out. "Anyway, he could have seen something," I said. "Or heard something. Or at least be able to corroborate or refute alibis."

"Listen to you with the jargon," Maizy said. "Took you long enough."

"I was bound to pick up something at the foot of the master," I said drily.

"That's what I keep telling you," she said breezily. "Bones will turn up for the next show. We can talk to him then. He's kind of a loner anyway. He doesn't like to be bothered."

Sounded like a prima donna to me.

"Don't forget Archie Ritz," Curt cut in. "He hasn't been around for very long, but you never know."

"And the two Susans," I added. "If we can find them."

"That's easy," Maizy said. "They'll be at the next Virtual Waste concert. If they find a drummer. I should let my friend Walter Thistle know they're hiring. He can't play, but he looks like Roger Daltry, and that's got to count for something. Maybe he can fake it onstage. You know, like Milli Vanilli."

"That didn't end well," Curt reminded her.

"Walter won't care," Maizy said. "Why should we?"

"They've got a new drummer," I said. I glanced at Curt. "Right?"

"Only for a week or two," he said. "Until they find a permanent replacement."

Maizy squeezed herself in between the front seats with an alarmed expression. "You mean you were serious about that, Uncle Curt? You know they play at night, right?"

Curt sighed. "What's your point, Maize?"

"My point," she said, "is you're like Virtual Waste's median age plus thirty. You don't have any tattoos. And have you even heard of guyliner?"

"He can play the drums," I said. And he looked awfully good doing it. Hm. Maybe I had a little groupie in me after all.

"I'm sure you'll be there," Curt reminded her. "You can compensate for any lack of cool you think you see."

"I could," Maizy agreed, "but that's a heavy lift."

"That reminds me," Curt said. "I've got to put that Civic in my driveway up for sale. It's just taking up room."

Maizy's Civic, if she ever got tired of Honest Aaron's bargain junkyard.

"On the other hand," Maizy said, "I do like a challenge."

"Thought you might." Curt smiled. "Don't worry. I'll just keep my eyes and ears open. I won't interfere."

"I sincerely hope not," Maizy muttered. She'd gone into classic teen angst mode, arms and legs crossed, foot bouncing. "I've got it going on," she added.

Curt's lips twitched. "I know you do."

"I need room to operate," she said. "I won't be oppressed. You don't write my script."

"I wouldn't know where to begin," Curt said.

CHAPTER ELEVEN

————

It turned out that Maizy's Grandpa Ed showed up on Sunday for a visit, which gave me a reprieve from thinking about Nicky D. Instead, I spent the day with Ashley alternately napping and watching easily digestible movies. Between *The Breakfast Club* and *Fast Times at Ridgemont High,* I ordered a small pizza with pepperoni. Ashley was mostly interested in the napping part, although she did deign to nibble on some cheese.

Eventually my attention drifted away from Jeff Spicoli to Virtual Waste. More specifically, their various motives and alibis, which were less than ironclad. Plop, alone and sleeping, that was believable on its face, but how did we confirm it unless he was doing it onstage? Also, Plop had seemed awfully quick to throw his bandmates under the tour van. Someone with a psychology course in their background might call that deflection.

As for TJ, short of finding autographed cigarette butts, we had no way of knowing if he'd been telling the truth about his between-sets smoking break. It was possible someone had seen him outside, maybe even talked to him, but how did we find that someone? And TJ certainly had a clear motive in his stolen songs. Probably I should buy a copy of Nicky D's solo CD to determine how strong that motive was. I was pretty sure I could get through a few songs in the service of justice. But I didn't really want to. I had that ten bucks earmarked for better things than "Puddle of Drool."

Then there was Mike. We could confirm easily enough that he and Archie Ritz had been at the bar together between sets and maybe even that Mike had argued with Nicky D, as Bryn had said. But it would be helpful to know what they'd argued about. My guess was it had been something serious since Mike seemed the type who didn't suffer fools gladly. Everything about him seemed no-nonsense, except for that goofy unexplained arm movement at the Pinelands' back door.

The same apparently couldn't be said about Nicky D. Nicky D seemed to be all nonsense.

That left Bones, about whom I had no opinion since he had been conspicuously absent, and I knew nothing about him short of his penchant for silver jewelry. And that according to TJ, he was a terrible driver. Which made me think about the pickup with its round silver crucifix on the mirror. But there were probably plenty of terrible pickup drivers of faith. Maizy had given him a strong endorsement, so that would have to do for the moment.

And finally, massive Hank and his matching jealous streak. And that was as far as I planned to go with *that*. All this not knowing made my head hurt.

Curt called around five to invite me downstairs for some barbecue, followed by an untimely but heated discussion over which candy was best to give out at Halloween—he was in the Snickers camp, but everyone knows Hershey bars were the only way to go—after which I fell into bed just before eleven, thinking I'd just lived my version of the perfect day. Which meant something bad had to be looming on the horizon.

That something showed up when I got to work on Monday morning. I worked for a law firm called Parker Dennis, with no comma and no ethics, the sort of firm you see advertised during episodes of *Jerry Springer*. Ken Parker and Howard Dennis were the two survivors of a triumvirate which had included a self-aggrandizing shyster who'd filed his eternal brief but had left behind a less than Coppola-like suite of television ads. His partners didn't miss him, mostly because Ken only showed up at the office to have a quiet place to sleep—he'd flirted with the idea of retirement, but it was hard to retire from a perpetual nap—and Howard thought *he'd* invented the concept of specious lawsuits, although he let the Boy Lawyer, Wally Randall, chase all the ambulances. Because Wally worshipped Howard, he was only too happy to do it, even though he sometimes didn't know what to do with them once he caught them.

The support staff was a bit of tarnished brass, too. I held the lofty title of first executive assistant, only because I'd brought in a tidal wave of business after becoming a murder suspect. In reality I was a legal secretary along with Missy Clark, aiding and abetting the lawyers while they dodged disgruntled clients. And there were more of those than you'd think. Janice Iannacone still massaged the finances and somehow managed to find enough cushion to keep herself in a string of luxury cars. After a brief flirtation with assertiveness, the paralegal, Donna Warren, had rediscovered her essential mouse and ventured downstairs just long enough to snatch up a volume of *Superior Court Reports* or a weighty medical textbook before scampering back to the safety of her office.

The newest addition to the firm was an investigator named Eunice Kublinski. Eunice had initially presented herself as a recent graduate of the Harvard School of Law and Mortuary Sciences (Online), and while her enthusiasm for filing baseless lawsuits had thrilled Howard, it soon became clear that Eunice didn't know a tort from a tart. But she was useful because she thought outside the box, even if she dressed like one, so Howard kept her on in the role of investigator, with a pay cut and without a private office.

That's why I found Eunice at the empty desk in the secretarial area, frowning at a yellow legal pad while she read, her lips moving slightly. Eunice blended nicely into her environment, which is to say you hardly noticed her. Brown slacks, beige sweater, clunky brown Earth Shoes, no jewelry except for a wristwatch on a thin gold band, no makeup, threads of gray woven through brown hair. Don't let the *blah* fool you. Eunice could think on her feet.

It was when she was sitting down that she had problems.

She glanced up. "Do you know anything about the Pine Barrens?"

A shiver tingled up my spine. "I know the Jersey Devil lives there," I said. "What else do I need to know?"

She held up the legal pad, the page full of Howard's tiny precise handwriting. "One of Howard's defendants is fighting back. He lives there."

I stashed my bag in the desk drawer and sat down. "Counterclaim?"

Eunice nodded. "He rear-ended our client, and he claims her car was illegally stopped, so the accident wasn't his fault."

"Where was she stopped?"

"At a red light," Eunice said. "But she stopped on the yellow."

Yellow lights in New Jersey weren't cautionary as a rule. They were encouraging. Sometimes daring.

Eunice consulted the legal pad. "He claims he can't work because his back is out and he lost his ability to…um…" Pinkness washed across her cheeks.

"Got it," I said. A loss of consortium claim, kind of a while-we're-at-it count that found its way into just about every personal injury Complaint. "And Howard wants action shots to defeat the counterclaim."

"That's it," Eunice agreed. "But I'm not taking action shots of *that*. I've got my scruples."

She might be working in the wrong place.

I looked over my day's work while waiting for the computer to boot up. A few Complaints. A Motion for Summary Judgment. Two Notices of Deposition. Some checks to be distributed according to the Settlement Sheet from one of Howard's cases. Howard had already skimmed his percentage off the top. "So what's the problem?" I asked.

"Our client says he's got a temper," Eunice said. "He jumped out of his pickup and started yelling at *her* because she stopped for a light. Can you imagine?"

The shiver prickled at the back of my neck. "What color pickup was it?"

Eunice consulted the legal pad. "Doesn't say. Is that important?"

Couldn't be. "Probably not," I said.

"To tell you the truth," she said, "I'm afraid of the Pine Barrens. I had an encounter with the Jersey Devil while I was camping, and I swore I'd never go back." She shuddered. "At least it's not Halloween. You don't go to the Pine Barrens on Halloween. All those old cemeteries and ghosts."

I looked up. "What kind of encounter?"

"I'll never forget it," she said. "I was fifteen at the time. Or no, maybe I was sixteen. No, wait, my sister Patty was sixteen. Or was that Kevin? Anyway, it happened while everyone else was asleep. My dad took us camping every year, even though we didn't want to go. But he'd never let us stay home. He was worried we'd throw a keg party while he was gone. Never mind that I was a straight C student."

"The Jersey Devil," I prompted.

She blinked. "Oh. Right. Well, I never could sleep on the ground. I mean, if God wanted us to sleep outside, he wouldn't have invented vinyl siding, right? But I don't think anyone else had the same problem, because everything was real quiet, except for the wind. You could hear it way up in the trees. It would have been kind of peaceful, if it wasn't for the flapping."

"The flapping?"

"His wings," she whispered. "I saw the shadow first, on the other side of the tent flap, and it was *big*. And it had this goat head with *horns*. And a forked *tail.*" She'd gone pale.

"It was probably your brother, pulling a prank." My voice trembled.

She shook her head. "No way. Kevin was in the tent with my parents. He was still afraid of the dark then. Besides, he was only five feet tall. This thing was—" she rolled her eyes up toward the ceiling "—*big*."

I leaned forward, my work forgotten. "What did you do?"

"What could I do?" she said. "I screamed like an air-raid siren. I heard the wings flapping and saw the shadow as it lifted off the ground and heard it crash through the tree branches while it flew away." Her mouth twisted. "And then my dad came and yelled at me for scaring everyone. Isn't *that* rich. *I* scared *them*."

"Didn't you tell him what had happened?"

"Sure I did. And he told me I must have eaten too many hot dogs for dinner." She gazed morosely at the legal pad. "And now I have to go back there."

Yeah, I had to go back there, too, only now I got to do it with the details of her little bedtime story gnawing at my brain.

I opened a blank file to type my first Complaint. Wally was suing a jeans manufacturer because his client, Rory

Rohrbacker, had managed to get his junk caught in the fly and had kept right on zipping. He was claiming pain and suffering along with substantial loss of income, now that he was unable, due to a bruised winky, to pass out tokens at an arcade four hours a day. For good measure, and to cast a wider net, Wally had added the zipper manufacturer and the department store chain that sold the jeans as codefendants.

You couldn't make this stuff up.

"Maybe you could go with me," Eunice said suddenly. "You're not like me. You're brave."

I didn't know where she'd gotten *that* impression, unless Webster's had changed the definition of *brave*. Now, Rory Rohrbacker, forging ahead despite a superficial winky bruise, *that* was bravery.

"I don't know," I said. "I have an awful lot of work to do here."

"That's okay," she said. "I have to go take some pictures at the mall today. Wally's client slipped and fell on some gelato in the food court. And I have to take pictures of the client's injuries tomorrow. She's in a full-body cast."

"From slipping on gelato?"

"Wally insisted on it," she said. "But we could go tomorrow."

"I don't think Howard would appreciate that," I said. "He likes me to be here during the workday."

"Oh. Howard. Right." Her mouth twisted while she thought. "How about Wednesday night? I don't really want to go at night, but we should be okay so long as we stick together."

Should be wasn't the kind of ironclad guarantee I would hope for.

"It won't take long," she assured me. "We'll just get a quick shot of him—I don't know— taking out the trash or walking the dog or something, then come right home."

That seemed harmless enough. Not much chance of being attacked by some giant, horned, goat-headed, fork-tailed flying beast while in the flower of our middle age.

Eunice brightened. "Maybe Maizy could come, too. She's pretty resourceful."

That was like saying Usain Bolt was pretty fast.

"Well…" I hesitated. "We *are* kind of involved in a case at the Pinelands Bar and Auditorium."

Her eyes got wide. "That place is still open? I thought it closed years ago, after that little incident they had."

"What incident?"

"Someone died there," she said. "I don't remember much about it, but everyone said the place was haunted after that. It used to *look* haunted."

"Still does," I said. "Was it a bar fight or something?"

She shook her head. "I heard it was murder. And that the killer was never caught." She lowered her voice. "They say that every summer, someone gets killed at the Pinelands."

"That's an urban legend," Missy Clark said. She stood in the doorway, wearing a traffic-stopping white pantsuit with sky-high heels, her hair full and loose down her back, a $600 rag & bone leather tote bag on her arm, and a white Leonetti's Bakery box in her hands. Because I could appreciate beauty as much as the next junk food addict, my eyes locked on to the box. Leonetti's had the best doughnuts and pastries in the tri-state area. "You don't really believe that, do you?" Missy asked.

"She's not wrong," I said. "Someone *was* killed there Friday night."

"Have you seen the Pinelands Bar?" Eunice asked. "There's something wrong with that place. Someone tried to burn it down a couple of years ago. It wouldn't even burn. And people report hearing strange noises coming from there at all hours."

"That's just the house band," Missy said. "I hear they're not very good."

"Does Howard have a depo today?" I asked her. Depo was legal slang for deposition, which was the civil litigation equivalent of a criminal interrogation, with all lawyers in a case present along with the plaintiff, defendant, expert or lay witness, and a court reporter to commit the testimony to written form.

Missy nodded. "You don't think he'd splurge on Leonetti's for *us*, do you?"

Eunice licked her lips. "Any chocolate frosted in there?"

"Yes." Missy shifted the box to her other side, farther from Eunice. "And you can't have any until Howard's done."

"There might not be any left by then," Eunice said.

"That's a chance you'll have to take," Missy said. She disappeared into the conference room to off-load.

Eunice ripped the top page off the legal pad, folded it into quarters, and stuffed it into her bag. "What do you think, Jamie? We can help each other. Remember, we had a hoot before, when that old guy with the naked David statue was killed."

Oxnard Thorpe, the Adult Diaper King of New Jersey. Maizy and I had found him facedown in his swimming pool on his wedding night. And *hoot* was hardly the word I'd use.

On the other hand, there was safety in numbers. Especially if Curt was one of the numbers. "Alright," I said. "We'll catch Howard's defendant in action Wednesday night. Sound good?"

"It'd sound better if we didn't have to go into the Pine Barrens to do it," Eunice said.

CHAPTER TWELVE

At six o'clock Tuesday night, while a Big Mac, fries, a chocolate milkshake, and I were sitting at a window table of the nearest McDonald's watching darkness shroud the world on the other side of the glass, Maizy dropped into the chair across from me. "I found Susan One. We should go talk to her."

I never knew whether Maizy followed me, had planted a GPS tracker on my car, or just had a well-honed spidey-sense, but she was always able to find me. She was usually able to read my mind, too, and that was more disturbing.

I washed down a fry with a mouthful of milkshake. "I thought you were going to lose the blue hair."

"I will," she said, a little impatient. "I'm just giving it a proper mourning period first. We have to hurry."

"Can I finish my dinner first?"

She assessed the spread in front of me. "You call this dinner?"

"Not tonight, Maize," I said. "I had a rough afternoon." Wally had dumped an urgent Response to Request for Motion for Production on my desk at four thirty then offered his assistance by refusing to copy any documents for attachment. Apparently pushing a button was beneath Wally's pay grade.

"Me, too," she said. "Herbie Hairston sold the bazooka. And I had it on layaway."

I stared at her. "He offers *layaway*?"

She did a dismissive wave. "Unimportant. The point is we're going to have to buy a morning star instead if we want to protect ourselves. Herbie's having a sale on morning stars."

Who didn't like a sale. And "morning star" sounded kind of pleasant.

Except.

"Why do we need to protect ourselves from Susan One?" I asked.

"We don't," she said. "Probably. But it never hurts to be prepared." She pilfered a fry. "Although I doubt we need a medieval weapon to do it."

The last piece of Big Mac slipped from nerveless fingers. "Medieval weapon?"

Maizy grabbed it and snarfed it in seconds. "What'd you think I meant by 'morning star'?"

I did an I-dunno shrug.

Her fingers danced on her smartphone, and she stuck it in my face. My breath caught in my throat. Think that kiddie toy with the ball attached to the paddle, only on steroids and made of metal, with spikes.

"Why would you want one of those?" I asked her.

"Because Hank might be home," she said.

"I'm not going anywhere near that guy," I said. "Forget it. We can talk to Susan One at the next Virtual Waste concert."

"Be serious," she said. "You can't talk during a Virtual Waste concert. It's not done."

I rolled my eyes. "Because it's blasphemy?"

"Because it's *loud*," Maizy said. She put the phone on the table and stole another fry.

I pointed. "That's a nice phone. You didn't waste any time."

"Are you kidding?" she said. "I wasted twenty whole minutes downloading all my stuff from the cloud." She polished off my fries, thinking. "Maybe if we hurry, we can catch her at work," she said. "The store closes at eight. You're not busy, right?"

Well, I had planned on folding some socks, just as soon as I got around to washing them.

"Depends," I said. "Where's she work?"

"In the Pine Barrens," she said.

I shook my head. "I'm busy."

"You don't look busy," she said. "What, are you going to bed early or something?"

"No, Maizy," I said wearily. Suddenly I thought of Eunice. "Hey, do you remember Eunice Kublinski?"

"The fake lawyer Howard hired?" she said. "Sure, I remember her."

"She has to chase down a defendant in the Pines," I said. "And she doesn't want to go alone. She asked if we could help tomorrow night. We could talk to Susan One then."

"Cool," Maizy said. "But why doesn't she want to go alone? There's nothing scary down there unless you're afraid of trees and cedar water. And spiders and snakes. And the Jersey Devil."

"Bingo," I said. "She saw the Jersey Devil when she was a teenager."

"No way!" Her eyes lit up. "How'd that go?"

"It wasn't a date, Maize," I said. "It was traumatic."

"Why?" she asked. "Sounds pretty lucky to me. I'd like to see the Jersey Devil."

"There was nothing lucky about it," I said. "She's *still* afraid of the Pines."

"I hear that happens to old people," Maizy said. "They're afraid of everything. My Gramma is afraid of her bedroom slippers. And Cheez-Its."

I crumpled up the Big Mac wrapper and tossed it with the empty French fry sleeve on the plastic tray. "I'm going home."

"Maybe I can come over," she said. "They're having a *Match Game* marathon on GSN tonight. You can drive me home later." With great casualness, she studied her nails. Blue now, with a puffy white cloud motif and two dark storm clouds on her middle fingers. Hopefully that wasn't prophetic. "Or I can take your car. Whatever."

"Nice try," I said. "I'll drive you."

"I don't want to be in the way or anything," she said.

I unlocked the car, and we got in. "In the way of a *Match Game* marathon?"

"In the way of nicky-nack," she said. "I read that the endorphins released during nicky-nack can improve your mood. You seem a little tense."

"Thanks for the thought," I said. "But nicky-nack needs two people if you want to do it right."

"Not necessarily," she said. "I read that—"

"I'll stay tense," I said sharply.

She shrugged. "Whatever. They're your endorphins. You want to hoard them, that's your business. I just thought you might want to spend some quality time with Uncle Curt later, when he's done learning Virtual Waste songs. He's wearing a red shirt tonight."

I hesitated. Curt was dark and dangerous looking even in pink, but in red, he was killer hot. Red might just be worth letting Maizy take my car.

Wait.

"How do you know what he's wearing?" I asked. This was beginning to sound suspiciously like a setup.

"Because that's what I told him to wear," Maizy said. "And I told him to leave it unbuttoned, like on those book covers. Except the guys always have long hair on those covers, and Uncle Curt doesn't."

"He doesn't need it," I said, picturing Curt in a red shirt. And without a red shirt.

"Because he's *smoldering*, right?" she asked.

He sure was.

"This conversation's getting a little weird, Maize," I told her.

"Tell me about it," she said.

CHAPTER THIRTEEN

———

My endorphins didn't get released, Curt didn't wear red, and there was no *Match Game* marathon. Story of my life.

Wednesday night, we were back in Curt's Jeep, plus Eunice, cruising past a scenic landscape of trees and more trees and still more trees broken in sporadic patches by sluggish cedar water streams. Which, thanks to Maizy, now had me thinking of water moccasins, because worrying about the Jersey Devil apparently hadn't quite wrung all the anxiety out of me. I shrank into my seat, arms crossed, in mild pout mode. I'd rather be home watching summer reruns and eating ice cream. Curt kept glancing at me without saying anything. Typical behavior from the male of the species when he sensed displeasure in the female but was unsure of its cause.

Eunice smiled at her own reflection in the glass, bright and happy since she wasn't alone. Maizy's forehead rested against her window, lost in thought as she watched the landscape roll past.

Until we came to a familiar opening and Maizy reared back. "Stop the car! This is our chance!"

Curt braked, threw it in reverse, and backed up.

"This isn't the address," Eunice said, sounding confused.

"This is it, alright." Maizy pointed to the Max's sign. "And there's the pickup."

"How do you know?" Curt asked. "You said you didn't see it well enough to describe it."

"Call it a hunch," Maizy said.

"Not good enough," Curt said. He put the Jeep in gear.

Maizy rolled her eyes. "How many ginormous pickup trucks can there be around here?"

A horn blasted behind us, and a ginormous pickup truck roared past.

"Wasn't that odd," Eunice said.

She'd better get used to *odd* if she planned to spend time in Maizy's orbit.

"That wasn't him," Maizy said. "That sounded normal." She pressed her nose to the window. "We have to blow that horn. Then we'll know for sure."

I had a thought. "Does it have front end damage?"

"From pushing you?" Maizy said. "I doubt it. But I can't tell from here." She tapped Curt on the shoulder. "Come on, Uncle Curt. Five minutes."

Curt scanned the yard. "Doesn't look like Hank's there."

"Who's Hank?" Eunice asked. "Is he single?"

I felt my hackles rise. Whatever hackles were. "I don't want to do this," I said.

"You don't have to." Maizy bounced around in her seat. "If it's got an air horn, I'll find out who it belongs to from the registration, and we'll be on our way. Don't you want to know who tried to run us off the road? It might have been the person who killed Nicky D making his getaway."

"Why would he try to run us off the road if he was making his getaway?" I asked. "Why not just drive around us like everyone else does?"

"Maybe he didn't mean to," she said. "He could have had an incoming text or something. There's a lot of distracted driving going on out there." She glanced at Curt. "I hear."

I shook my head. "I was there. He meant to." Because he knew Maizy had seen him?

"Who's Nicky D?" Eunice asked. "Is he single?"

"He's dead," Maizy told her. "That's what happens when someone is killed."

"Then I'll stick with Hank," Eunice said.

Curt swung into Max's lot and backed into an open spot near the driveway. "Hurry up, Maize," he said. "If you set off an alarm, don't take the time to disable it. Just get back here."

"She can disable alarms?" Eunice asked.

Maizy snorted as she slipped out of the Jeep.

"She's very gifted," I told Eunice.

The pickup truck was parked nose first between a wood-paneled station wagon and an old Beetle. I couldn't tell from our distance in the dark whether anything hung from the mirror or sat on the dash. It was entirely possible that truck had been sitting there for days.

It was also possible it hadn't.

We watched as Maizy tried the door. It wouldn't open. When she glanced at us, Curt did a come-on-back gesture, which she promptly obeyed by pulling a pair of latex gloves from her pocket and going to work. A minute later, the door swung open.

"She really is gifted." Eunice sounded awed. "Do you think she can teach me how to do that? I lock myself out of the house a lot. I gave a spare key to my next-door neighbor, but I want it back. I think he sneaks in and tries on my unmentionables when I'm at work."

Curt bit his lip to keep from laughing.

A shadow shifted inside the office area. A large shadow.

Immediately a vise squeezed my chest. "Do you see that?"

He nodded, his ghost smile gone. "I see it."

"I see it, too." Eunice pushed up between the seats, her face bloodless. "It's huge. What *is* that? Does it have wings?"

"That's a Hank," I said.

"Really?" Eunice pushed her glasses up her nose. "Well, isn't he a lot of man. He's more man than Antoine from the Twining Valley Country Club." I heard her pull in a breath. "Wait a minute," she muttered to herself. Papers rustling then another small gasp. "Hank, Hank, Hank," she muttered.

I kept my eyes on the office. "What are you doing?"

"That's him," Eunice said. "That's Howard's defendant. Hank Sedgwick. Max's Garage. That's *him.*"

"Are you sure?"

She'd gone pale. "Our client said he's enormous. And this is where he works. Only he isn't supposed to be working since the accident. He *lied.*"

Not exactly a novelty in the land of litigation.

The shadow in the office had gone still.

"What's he doing?" I asked.

"He's watching," Curt said.

But who was he watching, us or Maizy? Either way, the thought gave me the shakes.

"I have to get some pictures," Eunice said. "Right?"

"Right," I said.

"I've got him dead to rights," she added. "He's not incapacitated, right?"

"Right," I said.

The large shadow moved some more, and the pale jutting square of Hank's jaw appeared in the window, faintly illuminated by the light of a nearly full moon.

"Oh, my," Eunice said. "He *is* a big man."

Another shift, and the tire iron in his hand became visible.

"Eunice." Curt's voice was level and sharp. "Behind your seat is a toolbox. It's unlocked. Get me the hammer."

"What are you going to do with that?" Eunice asked him. "Are you going to hit him?"

"I'm going to help him hang a picture," Curt said.

I kept my eyes on the pickup. No sign of Maizy. No interior light. No sign of movement from the office. Everything felt wrong.

"There's no need for violence," Eunice said disapprovingly. "I can handle this. I used to be a fake lawyer, remember?"

And not a very good one. Public speaking tended to make Eunice faint. And by public speaking, I meant speaking in public. I turned to discourage whatever scheme she was cooking, but she was already gone. When she neared the office, the door opened, and Hank stepped out of the shadows.

Immediately Eunice stopped and swayed a little on her feet.

I forgot all about using my indoor voice. "What is she doing?" I practically yelled.

Curt's cell phone buzzed with an incoming text from Maizy. *What is she doing?*

Across the lot, Hank moved fast to snake an arm around Eunice's waist, keeping her from going down. Her head lolled back, her knees gave way, and she sagged into him.

"She fainted," Curt said. "We need to—"

"We sure do," I said. I grabbed his phone and texted *Stay put* to Maizy.

She replied, *Duh.*

Curt and I reached for the door handles.

Hank hoisted Eunice over his shoulder and turned to tote her into the office, her backside bumping around six feet off the ground. Not a good look for her.

Suddenly Eunice turned her head to us and gave us the thumbs-up.

"She's got this," Curt said with wonder.

His cell phone buzzed. *She's got this.*

The office light came on to show them sitting with their backs to the window, Eunice slumped over and Hank trying to foist a paper cup on her while doing some useless there-there back patting.

I texted Maizy, *Now.*

She replied, *Duh.*

Maizy was starting to get on my nerves.

The pickup's door cracked open, and she slithered out, rushed across the lot, and slipped into the back seat.

"So?" I demanded. "Whose truck is it?"

She shrugged. "Beats me. There wasn't any paperwork. Not even an insurance card. The worst part is I couldn't even blow the horn, with the giant doofus over there." She pointed her chin at the office. "What's with her? That wasn't very smart."

"You're right about that." Curt's voice was grim. "You won't be doing this again, will you?"

"I didn't mean *me*," Maizy said. "I meant Eunice. She went in without a plan. You need to have a plan. Now we'll have to do an extraction."

That sounded painful. And potentially dangerous. And, as it turned out, unnecessary, since Eunice abruptly stood up and handed over a piece of paper, which Hank read, nodding, before stuffing it into his breast pocket. Then she walked out and back to the Jeep. When she got in, we all turned to stare at her.

"What?" She patted her head. "Have I got pine needles stuck in my hair?"

"Did you just give him your phone number?" I asked.

"Did he threaten you?" Curt asked.

"Did he confess?" Maizy asked.

Eunice blinked at us. "No. But he offered to fix my car in exchange for a home-cooked meal."

"With who?" Maizy asked.

Eunice smiled. "With me. I'm going to home-cook that man straight to the altar."

"Do you give lessons?" Curt asked her.

I ignored that. "What happened to 'he lied'?"

"It was just a little lie," she said. "I'm sure he had to use a heating pad after the accident. Maybe take some aspirin."

Whatever. That was Howard's fight, not mine.

"I hate to tell you this," I said, "but he's got a girlfriend."

"He mentioned that," Eunice said. "But she's too busy chasing after musicians to pay much attention to him. He's really mad about it, and I don't blame him. Can you imagine ignoring a hunk of man like that? He said he'd taken care of the problem, but now he needs a good woman. That's me."

"Wait a minute," I said. "What does that mean, taken care of the problem?"

Eunice shrugged. "He didn't say, and I didn't ask. I wasn't about to risk turning him off when I'd just turned him on."

Disturbing on so many levels.

Eunice tapped Curt's shoulder. "Can you break my car?"

He frowned. "Excuse me?"

"Hank agreed to fix my car," Eunice said. "My car's not broken. You don't have to do anything dramatic. Just…break it somehow."

"I know what we can do," Maizy began.

"No," Curt said. "I'll loosen a plug," he told Eunice. "Easy to fix, no lasting damage."

She sat back, satisfied. "I should get a picture of his house," she said. "Show Howard that I did *something* so he won't fire me. It's 106 Third Street. Did we pass Third Street?"

"They have names?" Maizy lowered her window, ushering in a flood of steamy air and a few thousand buzzing and flapping insects. "They barely have streets," she said. "Or signs."

"Do you mind?" I asked. "I'm getting eaten alive."

"More drama," Maizy said. She rolled up the window. Which only trapped seven hundred bugs inside with us and treated them to air conditioning.

"There's a sign." Eunice pointed to a three-foot wooden stake driven into the ground. Curt slowed so we could read it. "The letters are a little faded, though."

"You think?" Maizy cocked her head. "I can't make out anything but a *T* and an *r*."

"But the letters are in the right place," Eunice said. "Turn here."

Here was a tiny, no lane, rutted dirt road leading to utter blackness at the end of the earth. That road had horror movie written all over it, even though Curt was with us. That was small comfort when everyone knows the man always gets it first in those movies, leaving the women to fend for themselves.

He rolled down his window and hauled in a big breath of tree-scented air and all the relatives of the seven hundred bugs who must have sent out invitations. "It's great down here. We should come camping some time."

"Sure thing," I said. "I look good in big red welts. Roll up the window."

"You don't have to worry about these." Curt flicked at some tiny winged horror that had landed on his forearm. "It's the no-see-ums that'll drive you crazy."

Just that name made it so much worse.

I rubbed my arms. "I'm chilly."

"It's 85 degrees," Curt said.

"It's probably ghosts you're feeling," Maizy said. "There's bound to be a lot of them in the Pine Barrens."

Well, *that* didn't help.

"You think they're hitching a ride?" Curt asked.

"You don't know," Maizy said. "They have places to go, too."

"Why wouldn't they just fly there?" Eunice asked.

Maizy snorted. "Maybe they're saying the same thing about you."

"Where do they have to go?" Curt asked. One of his dimples twinkled at me. He wasn't buying it for a minute. I wasn't too sure. I'd been in the Haunted Mansion. I knew for a fact that ghosts hitched rides.

Maizy shrugged. "Different places. You ever see an abandoned psychiatric institution? You can't tell me there are no ghosts in there. There's all kinds of stuff going on in those places."

"How would you know that?" Curt asked her. "Have you been on the Herbie Hairston Delinquency Tour again?"

"That's not bad," Maizy said. "Okay if he steals that?"

"Why not?" Curt said. "He steals everything else."

Maizy tapped me on the shoulder. "Maybe we should expand into ghost hunting. I saw it on TV. It's a growing field."

"That's a good idea," I said. "No."

"Think about it," Maizy said. "It doesn't seem that hard. Practice saying 'Did you hear that?' a lot, and you've pretty much got it."

"I'll do it," Eunice said, "only I'll have to buy some running shoes first."

Maizy poked me. "See? And *she* faints at *everything*."

Curt grinned at me. "Camping sounds a little better now, huh?"

"Yeah," I said. "That's just what I was thinking."

Maizy snorted.

"You don't want to go camping," Eunice said. "You're better off ghost hunting."

"She's right," Maizy said. "This place is a dead zone for cell phone service."

"That's kind of the point," Curt said. "No phones. No TV." He scowled into the mirror. "No teenagers."

"You can beg all you want," Maizy said. "I'm not coming. Hey, look. A house. Sort of."

The house was a cheerless one-story stone box with a patched roof, sagging porch, wooden steps, and one set of shutters for two windows. The dirt yard was strewn with car parts and litter. No grass, garden, driveway, or pavement of any kind. The address had been scrawled in heavy black marker above the door.

"That's not it," Eunice said with relief. "It can't be far, though. It says 100, and we're looking for 106."

We drove until we came to another house. 202.

"That doesn't make sense," Curt said. "We couldn't have missed that many houses."

"Maybe they were set back in the trees," I said. "But I didn't see any driveways."

"You know what?" Maizy asked. "I bet they're tree houses."

"Be serious," I said. "Nobody lives in a tree house."

"The Swiss Family Robinson does," Eunice said.

"The Papua Tree people do," Maizy said.

We all leaned forward, looking up. No tree houses.

"Either we have the wrong street," Eunice said, "or the house doesn't exist."

"Couple of things," Maizy said. "First, this isn't a street. Second, these aren't houses. And third, you're going about this all wrong."

"I usually do," Eunice said. She slumped in dejection. "What am I going to tell Howard? I don't have any pictures."

"Yeah, that's a problem," Maizy said. "Now can we go talk to Susan One?"

"We agreed to help," I said.

Maizy rolled her eyes. "*Fine.* You know what you should do? You should ask around at the Pinelands Bar, see if anyone knows where this house is. Those people know everyone. It's like a high school clique there, only with a cover charge."

"I wouldn't know about that," Eunice said. "I wasn't part of any high school cliques. I was what you'd call a loner."

"Me, too," Mazy said. "Only I call it being an individualist 'cause I'm not a doofus."

Eunice smiled. "I like that. An individualist. Maybe that's what I am."

"Nah," Maizy said. "I'm pretty sure you're a—"

"She found the dink," I cut in. "It's Hank."

"Seriously?" Maizy asked. "That dude's a walking nuclear plant accident. You better get a telephoto lens so you can keep your distance."

"Oh, no," Eunice said. "You've got him all wrong. He didn't make me faint or anything."

"You need to raise the bar a little," Maizy told her.

"Did anyone hear that?" Curt cut in.

We all got still.

"Hear what?" Maizy asked.

"I'm not sure." Curt stared hard at the dirt road unfurling in front of us. "It almost sounded like a scream."

"I knew it," Eunice whispered. "It's still out there."

Icy fingers clawed their way up my spine.

"I doubt anything's out there," Curt said. "Except maybe campers and animals."

"Yeah," I said. "Let's go with that."

"The Jersey Devil is kind of an animal," Eunice said.

"She's right," Maizy agreed. "It's got horns and wings and claws and a forked tail. But it didn't start out that way. It started out normal. Well, as normal as a kid can be whose father's the devil. Come to think of it, maybe it's Herbie Hairston."

"That's not nice," I told her.

"Have you *met* Herbie Hairston?" she asked.

"Whatever it was," Curt said, "it's gone now. I think we're done here." He executed a crisp K-turn on the dirt road and headed back the way we'd come. "What's next? Susan One or the Pinelands?"

"Susan One," Maizy said immediately. "The store closes soon." She looked at Eunice. "You'd better wait in the car, since you're trying to steal her boyfriend."

Eunice shook her head. "No way. I want to know what I'm up against. I might have to up my game."

"What does that look like?" Maizy asked.

"Steak tartare instead of spaghetti," Eunice said.

CHAPTER FOURTEEN

———

It took fifteen minutes to find the store nestled in a clearing along Route 206 and two seconds for me to turn on Maizy. "You didn't mention that she works at a lingerie store!"

"She works at a lingerie store," Maizy said.

Curt's expression was pure delight. "Let's go. Time's wasting."

I rolled my eyes. I could just imagine what Susan One looked like, and I was bound to come up short in comparison since I had a body like a fishing pole. What was a lingerie shop doing in the middle of a forest, anyway? Susan One couldn't have found a job selling rock crawlers or digging up bait worms like a normal woman?

"I *could* use another flannel nightgown," Eunice said. "Plus it'll give me a chance to get a look at Hank's soon-to-be ex."

"Good idea," Curt said. "Let's go."

"You've got an awful lot of faith in that home-cooked meal," I told her.

"I've got a can't-fail recipe," Eunice said. "I use lots of gravy. What man doesn't love gravy?"

Curt glanced at his watch. "She'll be closing up soon. We ought to get inside."

"Why don't you go in," I said to Maizy. "If we all go, it might intimidate her."

"She's got a point," Eunice said. She opened her door. "Come on, everyone."

I could see Eunice and her gravy meant business. We got out and followed her into the store.

Maizy paused to take it in. "I think I've seen this before. In those catalogs that come in plain brown envelopes."

She was right. The place was ho-hum on the outside and va-va-voom on the inside. Lots of mannequin busts wearing lots of lingerie of the racy, lacy, and complicated variety, like bodysuits made of shoelaces held together by silver rings or rhinestone clasps. White lacquered tables and faux dressers held panties and bras. Short silk nighties and camisoles hung in staggered rows from silver racks. The walls shone in soft mint green and white stripes under recessed lighting. A jazz saxophone recording played softly in the background.

"I don't see any flannel," Eunice said, looking around.

"I don't see Susan One," Maizy said.

I didn't see any point in being in a place where the mannequins were built better than I was. It wasn't exactly a confidence booster.

Curt handed me his credit card. "Go buy something."

As if. I was wearing perfectly comfortable cotton underwear from the 2012 Hanes collection. "Don't try to change me," I said.

He grinned. "Maybe I'll just browse around, see what catches my eye."

"I knew we should have left you in the car," I called after him.

"Maybe he can help me find the flannel," Eunice said. She followed him.

"Isn't that cute," Maizy said. "Uncle Curt wants to do nicky-nack with you."

I watched him move through the store. "How can you tell?"

Maizy shrugged. "He's buying you the uniform."

I turned. "What?"

"Black lace," she said. "It's so clichéd it's almost funny. Why can't men just accept women who wield their feminine power in untraditional ways?"

"Pretty sure I don't have feminine power," I said.

"Sure you do," she said. "You just need some black lace to bring it out of hiding."

I stared at her.

"I'm sorry. I'm getting ready to close. Can I help you?"

We turned to find Susan One standing behind us. She was pretty, but not stunning. Athletically built, not voluptuous. She smelled faintly of cigarettes and wore black-framed glasses with no lenses in them.

Across the store, Eunice pretended to browse a rack of camisoles with her eyes locked on Susan One.

"Hey, I saw you at the Virtual Waste concert Friday night," Maizy said, as if our being in the store was by accident rather than design.

"Yeah, I saw you, too." Susan One's gaze floated up to Maizy's blue nimbus of hair. "You're pretty memorable."

"I'm special," Maizy agreed. "Did you hear what happened to Nicky D?"

She nodded. "It's awful, isn't it?"

"Being bashed in the head with an amplifier?" Maizy asked. "Yeah, you could call that horrible. You could also call it murder."

Susan's lower lip started to tremble, and her eyes welled. "You mean he was right?"

"Who was right?" I asked.

"My boyfriend, Hank." She sniffled. "He'd heard a rumor that it was no accident. But I didn't want to believe it."

It occurred to me that could have been less rumor, more confession on Hank's part.

"Did he tell you where he'd heard that?" I asked.

"I don't think so." Another sniffle. "Does that matter?"

"Everything matters to us," Maizy said. "We're detectives. Your boyfriend is that ginormous no-neck who sits in the parking lot during the shows, right?"

"That's him," Susan said. "How'd you know that?"

"We're *detectives*," Maizy repeated with great patience. "Why doesn't he go inside with you?"

"He doesn't like music," Susan said. "And Hank thinks if he sits outside, I won't leave with another man and cheat on him."

"Do you?" Maizy asked.

"Not regularly," Susan said. "Besides, it was Nicky D. It didn't count."

I could just imagine Hank hearing *that*. Sounded like he had a reason for his suspicion, and it wasn't born out of simple jealousy. But maybe his motive was.

"Were you there when they found Nicky D?" Maizy asked.

"I'd just left," Susan said. "I had to open up Saturday morning. In fact, I drove past the paramedics, but of course I didn't know where they were going." She blinked a few times to staunch the tears. Call me cynical, but that seemed like a strong reaction over someone she'd claimed to fool around with only occasionally.

"What do you mean by 'just left'?" I asked. "Just left after they found him? Before they found him?" *After you killed him?* No, I couldn't see it. It was easy to see she'd cared for Nicky D. She wouldn't have had any reason to kill him.

But Hank would.

"I guess a few minutes before," Susan said. "Don't get the wrong idea. I don't make a habit of cheating on Hank, even if the only thing Mr. Romance is good for is reaching the top shelves."

"Then why stay with him?" I asked her.

She seemed surprised by the question. "I use the top shelves."

Eunice stopped pawing the camisoles, took a deep breath, and headed for us. She stopped short just behind Susan, dragged in another deep breath, and demanded, "Can you cook?"

Susan turned with a start. "I'm sorry. I didn't notice you before. Can I help you with something?"

"I'm an excellent cook," Eunice said. "Is that your natural hair color?"

Susan's mouth fell open.

"This is my natural color," Eunice said. "I'm a *real* woman."

Susan's stare shifted from Eunice to Maizy. "Am I being punked?"

On the far side of the store, Curt held up a little black lace number smaller than a wallet. I couldn't handle that much feminine power. I shook my head, ignoring his crestfallen expression.

"About Mr. Romance," I said.

Eunice whipped a pad of paper and pen from her bag, poised to take notes.

"The man is a complete slob," Susan said. "He leaves his dishes in the sink and drops his clothes everywhere. Does he even *understand* the concept of a hamper?" She shook her head. "Not that he could hit it anyway. You should have seen the shirt he *almost* put in the waste basket Saturday morning. Ketchup stains all over it from his dinner Friday night."

"Ketchup," Eunice muttered. "How pedestrian."

Ketchup? Maizy and I traded glances.

"Are you sure it was ketchup?" I asked gently.

Susan smiled. "Hank always puts an inch of ketchup on his burgers. What else—" She broke off, her smile dropping away. "No," she said. "No, no, no. Hank would never do that. He's not that way."

"What did you do with the shirt?" Maizy asked her.

"I washed it," Susan said. "Twice, if you must know. And then *I* threw it out."

"Where?" Eunice cut in. "Does it smell like him?"

Susan ignored her. She shook her head again. "It's just not possible. How could anyone want to hurt Nicky D? He was a *god*."

"If you like that type," Maizy said. "Of course, he made a move on anything with an X chromosome. I even saw him try to pick up the bartender one night."

Susan blinked. "Tommy?"

Maizy shook her head. "Hannah. And Bryn, the security guard. And your friend Susan Two. And—"

"I *knew* it!" Susan practically shouted. "She told me she was going to the ladies' room, but no one can powder their nose for that long. And we agreed we'd stick together, too."

"Stick together for what?" I asked.

Maizy glanced at me. "Seriously?"

Oh. That.

I wondered why Susan One seemed more upset about the possibility of Susan Two hooking up with Nicky D than with the thought of her boyfriend giving him an amplifier hat.

"What we had was real," Susan moaned. "I could have been Mrs. Virtual Waste someday."

If I had a dime for every time I'd heard that.

"Did Hank know?" I asked.

"Not yet," Eunice muttered under her breath.

Susan gave a little shudder. "I certainly never told him. But it doesn't matter. Hank wouldn't kill anyone."

I didn't hear a whole lot of conviction in that statement.

Curt did an over-here wave and held up a red fishnet bodysuit with cutouts for the yippee and the yahoos.

I turned my back on him.

"Is it possible he found out?" I asked.

Susan considered it. "People do talk. I wish they'd've talked a little louder about Susan and Nicky D." She rolled her lips inward as if stifling some dirty words. "I feel like an idiot," she said finally.

"Better an idiot than a murderer," Maizy said.

"I'm not ruling it out," Susan said. "If Hank hurt a hair on Nicky's head, I'm going to kill him."

CHAPTER FIFTEEN

————

"I'm not wearing that," I said for the third time.

"That whole store," Eunice said, "and not a single flannel nightgown. What's up with that?"

"I just thought of something," Maizy said. "Maybe the pickup is Hank's. He probably keeps the registration and insurance card in his wallet. I need to check out his wallet."

"Don't rule it out," Curt said. "Take it upstairs, keep it with you, feel it once or twice. It might grow on you."

It was the short black silk nightie he'd just bought for me. Compared to the alternatives, it was as conservative as a pinstriped suit. I still wasn't wearing it. Silk wasn't a good look for me. Nighties weren't a good look for me. He should've gone to the Disney Store and replaced the Mickey Mouse T-shirt that I usually slept in. *That* would have been money better spent.

I stared gloomily out the window as we headed for home. What a wasted night. We still didn't know who owned the pickup or even if that pickup was the one that had tried to run us off the road. We'd found out that Hank was a slob and potentially a killer. And we'd found out that Susan One had a rich vein of jealousy of her own, especially when it came to Nicky D. And we hadn't even gotten a photo for Howard's case.

"What am I going to tell Howard?" Eunice asked. "He'll make me come back here. I know it."

"I wonder where Hank leaves his wallet at night," Maizy said.

"You need to push your boundaries," Curt told me. "Try sleeping in it one night—see how you like it."

"I'll slide right out of bed," I said.

He laughed. "You won't slide out of bed."

"Well, I'll be cold," I said peevishly. "And it'll get twisted all around me every time I roll over and probably wind up strangling me in my sleep." And that would be better than having him see me in it.

"That can happen," Maizy said. "It happened to some lady in Teaneck like a month ago. Only her nightie was polyester. And brown."

"Not helpful, Maize," Curt said.

"Are you kidding?" Maizy asked. "It's nothing *but* helpful. If she'd been *wearing* it, her husband couldn't have wrapped it around her neck and strangled her." She tapped me on the shoulder. "You might want to rethink this whole thing."

"I wonder if we can sue the nightie manufacturer," Eunice said. "It seems to me it should have ripped before it strangled her."

"That depends on how many foot-pounds of torque her husband applied," Maizy said. "It takes at least a thousand to break someone's neck."

Eunice went a little green.

Curt glanced at me. "You don't like it. I'll take it back."

I thought of Maizy's theory on black lace being the uniform for nicky-nack. Black silk was probably the backup uniform. Clichéd or not, I was pretty sure I was ready for some nicky-nack. I just wished I could wield my untraditional feminine power in sweats.

I sighed. "No, don't do that."

"She shouldn't be alone with it," Maizy said. "It could be dangerous. You should sleep over, Uncle Curt."

"What she needs—" Curt began, and then something hit the Jeep, bounced off the roof, and careened away into the darkness.

I ducked down instinctively. "What the—"

"It's the Jersey Devil!" Eunice shrieked. She dove onto the floor behind my seat.

"Hit the brakes!" Maizy yelled. "I want to see!"

"It wasn't the Jersey Devil," Curt said, his expression grim. He pulled as far out of the travel lane as possible. "Stay here," he told me.

That went without saying.

Maizy was already out of the Jeep, circling it and jumping up and down to try to see the roof. Curt got out, looked around at the darkness, and then did a slow pass around the Jeep, checking for damage.

I rolled down the window about an inch and put my mouth to the opening. "Is anything out there?"

"Not right here," he said. "Out *there*, it's hard to tell."

"Are there hoof marks?" Maizy asked him. "Did his claws scratch the paint?"

"Hooves," Eunice moaned. "Claws."

"It was probably just a tree branch," I told her. "It's been awfully windy lately. These trees are pretty old."

"Trees don't fly," she said. "It flew away. It tried to attack us, and then it flew away."

"Nothing tried to attack us," I said. "It just bounced off the roof and landed out there in the dark somewhere."

"Then why doesn't he see it?" she asked. "It's because it flew away. I *knew* I shouldn't have come back here again."

"You didn't have a choice," I said. "Howard needs proof."

"Let Howard get his own proof," she said. "I'll quit if he tries to make me come back. Or I'll hire my own private investigator. I'll hire *you*."

Yeah, like *that* was happening. No way was I running around in the dark trying to take pictures of a phantom. The firm could do with one less lawsuit. It could only help its reputation.

The back door opened, and Maizy climbed in. "He's gone." She sounded disappointed.

Eunice lifted her head. "Is it safe?"

Curt slid behind the wheel. "Where's Eunice?"

I jerked my thumb over my shoulder.

He leaned between the seats. "All clear," he told her.

"That's what he wants you to think," she said. "He's probably out there right now, hiding behind the trees, waiting for his opportunity."

I stared hard into the darkness. No red eyes stared back, so that was reassuring.

"He just had his opportunity," Curt said, "Nothing happened."

"Is there any damage?" I asked him.

He shrugged. "Can't really say. I didn't feel any dents, but it might be scratched. It was probably a deer. That does happen occasionally." He put the Jeep in gear, and we headed out.

I waited ten minutes before I said, "About that camping trip."

He raised an eyebrow in question.

"I'd rather wear the nightie," I said.

CHAPTER SIXTEEN

———

Two nights later, I stood in front of the full-length mirror in the black silk nightie. The color was right for preserving some modesty. The length was right for hiding some of my chicken-wing legs. The drape was right for softening straight lines. If you ignored the socks, the effect was more or less what you aimed for when you wore a black silk nightie.

I swallowed hard, looking at the cell phone in my hand. It had been one step forward, one step back for Curt and me since he'd become my landlord, which left us stuck in neutral, romantically speaking. It wasn't Curt's fault. It wasn't anyone's fault, really. If he was less of a gentleman and I had any confidence in myself, we'd have made real progress by now. But he was, and I didn't, so the next move would have to be mine.

I knew Curt was downstairs. I'd heard him come home about an hour earlier. It would only be fair to let him see the nightie. He'd bought it, after all. And I'd made an implicit promise to try it on when I hadn't let him return it. I hadn't promised to let him *see* it, but black silk deserved an audience, and Ashley was sound asleep.

My hand shook. Maybe it wasn't a good time. Curt probably tired after working all day. He had Virtual Waste music to learn. He had eight hours to sleep.

On the other hand, I might not get a better chance. I was alone, the moon was high, the stars were bright, Maizy was nowhere in sight.

My heart pounded behind my eyeballs.

I peeled off my socks and brought up my Contacts list.

Someone knocked on the door. "Jamie?"

Curt.

Courage is fleeting. I grabbed for a towel to wrap around myself. It slipped right down my silk-clad body and puddled on the floor.

I'd *known* that was going to happen.

"Give me a minute," I yelled. I needed a bathrobe. Why didn't I have a bathrobe like a normal woman? I should put on my clothes and drive right to Walmart to buy a nice opaque floor length bathrobe. Who was I kidding, thinking I could pull off a grand seduction? I couldn't even interest my cat in looking at me.

"I've got something for you," he called.

That something had better be chocolate chip muffins. Where was that so-called feminine power Maizy had lied about? If I had any, I'd be slinking right over to open the door and lead him in by his tongue instead of looking in the hamper for a semiclean shirt.

My feet were cold. Terror did that to me. I pulled my socks back on.

Another knock. "Jamie?"

"On my way!" I yelled.

Over on the sofa Ashley lifted her head, cracked open one eye to look at me, yawned hugely, and went back to sleep.

That's the reaction I'd been afraid of.

My fingers closed on the familiar soft cotton of my Mickey Mouse T-shirt. I gave it a shake, pulled it over my head, and went to the door. But I didn't open it. "Is everything alright?"

"Why do I think I should be asking *you* that?" Curt asked. "Are you going to let me in?"

I rested my forehead on the door. "That's complicated."

"What do you mean, it's—" His voice trailed off. Then, "What are you wearing?"

I didn't answer.

"Jamie? Are you wearing the nightie?" he asked without a bit of lecherousness but as if the idea surprised him. Good to know I could surprise him. Now if only I could surprise myself by opening the door.

Except I couldn't.

"Maybe," I said. I closed my eyes. *It's only a nightie, for crying out loud.* Sure. Except *I* was underneath the nightie. And I wasn't ready for primetime. Curt had probably dated women much more…womanly than me. Women with unfrizzy hair who knew how to apply makeup and walk in heels and had some fashion sense. *Those* women wouldn't be cowering behind their door in a Mickey Mouse T-shirt when a hottie like Curt was waiting on the other side.

He wasn't saying anything. Probably wondering what was wrong with me. He wasn't the only one.

"Jamie, open up," he said quietly. "I won't come in unless you want me to. At least let me give you what I brought."

I bit my lip and opened the door.

True to his word, he didn't make a move. I didn't, either. I'm not even sure we breathed. We just stood there looking at each other. His gaze took in the T-shirt, the socks, and the portion of black silk visible between the two. It might have been a trick of the light, but I thought his expression softened. Then, very slowly, he leaned in and kissed me softly on the forehead. "Here." He handed me a bulky shopping bag. "I thought you might need this." And he turned and went back down the steps. A few seconds later, I heard his back door open and close.

I reached into the bag and pulled out a floor length terry bathrobe.

CHAPTER SEVENTEEN

———

"Will you stop staring at me?"

I couldn't help it. I'd never seen Maizy like this before. Un-blue. Her hair was now a middle-of-the-road shade of dark brown, albeit with a single purple streak that paid homage to her indomitable essence. She must have spent hours with a flat iron, straightening it into a gleaming sheet. Her eyes seemed bluer and softer without the heavy Jack Sparrow eyeliner. Forget the crazy disguises. *This* was a Maizy no one would recognize.

I shook my head to snap out of it. "Sorry. I'm not used to seeing you looking so…"

"The word is boring." Her nose wrinkled. "I look like a nine-to-five drone. I look like *you*."

Hardly. My hair never looked that good.

"This isn't working for me," Maizy said. "I feel like I should be wearing support hose."

I rolled my eyes. "Your hair is *brown*, Maize. Not gray."

"Well, it's just an experiment," she said. "I might go with black. It's more *me*. Maybe swap out the purple for pink. What do you think?"

"Stick with brown," I said. "It blends."

"Blending goes against everything I stand for," she said. "My whole life is about *not* blending."

Then it was a life well lived so far.

A week had passed since I'd endured a trip to the Pine Barrens. It was Thursday night, with a bright moon hopscotching between high patchy clouds, and we were on our way to the Virtual Waste show at the Golden Grotto to watch Curt in action. I still had warm feelings about the bathrobe, and a new resolve to model the nightie for him. Just as soon as I gained ten pounds.

Easier said than done for me. By the time that happened, he might not want to see it anymore. But I had a plan, and it was sitting in my lap. I stuck my hand into the bag of caloric Hershey's Kisses and grabbed a few more.

"What's with the sugar overload?" Maizy asked. She was behind the wheel, having finally regained some of her mojo after the DMV blacklisting. She hadn't lost any of her skills. As usual, Maizy drove like the wheelperson of a getaway car. She'd lost the summer motif on her nails and gone with pure black with a grinning silver skull on each middle finger. Silver nose stud and Lord only knew what other studs in place. She wore a black leather vest as a shirt, torn-up jeans, and scuffed Doc Martens. The blue hair would have been right at home.

I'd gone with my usual jeans and T-shirt combination, heavy on the insect repellant. I smelled like a chemical bath, and next to her, I looked like I was on my way to the local Walmart to buy some white bread and whole milk.

"I'm trying to gain some weight." I popped two Kisses into my mouth. "So my clothes fit better."

"You're kidding, right?" she said. "You wear sweatpants half the time."

"My other clothes," I snapped.

"Why don't you just buy smaller clothes?" she asked.

I glowered at her. "Why don't you—"

"Oh, I get it," she cut in. "You're talking about the black thingy Uncle Curt bought you, right? What's the big deal? He gave you a blanket to cover yourself up, didn't he?"

"It was a *bathrobe*," I said.

"Whatever. I thought Uncle Curt had more game than that."

"His game is fine," I snapped. It was *my* game I was worried about. I didn't have one.

"The only way that black thingy'll fit better is if you buy some boobage," she said. "But you don't want to do that. You have a perfectly serviceable body."

"'Serviceable'?" I repeated.

"That's not an insult," she said. "It does what it's supposed to do, only with no bells and whistles. Like a manual lawn mower."

I closed my eyes.

"There are other ways to close the deal with Uncle Curt," she said. "I can help."

"Kind of wish you wouldn't," I told her.

"Wait," she said. "I know. This girl at school sticks chicken cutlets in her bra to get extra boobage. I saw it in gym class. I can ask her where she got them if you want."

I ate another Kiss. "Chicken cutlets?"

She nodded. "They're not real. They're made of rubber or something. But the way *you* cook—"

"Never mind," I snapped. "How do they look?"

"Bodacious," she said. "Except once the clothes come off, you're on your own."

"That's false advertising," I said.

"So what? Men have been doing that forever, right? I mean, why do you think tube socks were invented?"

"For women," I said. "We get cold feet."

"Men have been doing *that* forever, too," she said. "My mom's friend Winnie has been left at the altar six times, four times by the same guy. Winnie's a slow learner. Hey, you know what? You should sleep in the nude. Skin always fits."

"I'm not ready for nude," I said. "Do you sleep in the nude?"

"Me? No." She shook her head. "I sleep fully dressed. I never know when I'll have to deploy. But if I was as old as you, I might think about it. I mean, how many good years have you got left? Might as well make the most of them."

"I'll give it some thought," I said sourly.

"If you're ready for nicky-nack," she said cheerfully, "you're ready for nude. Your decision. Remember, you can always use the horse blanket Uncle Curt bought you."

"You're being unfair," I said. "It wasn't like that. It was really sweet."

"Is that what women want?" She hung a left and floored it. "Sweet?"

I thought about it while I massaged the whiplash from my neck. "Sometimes."

"What about the other times?"

"I'll tell you when you turn 18," I said.

"No, don't," she said. "I'm not that interested. I've got an agenda of my own. Gilbert Gleason turned up."

"The band's old agent?" I popped another Kiss. My supply was starting to dwindle. It was almost time to move on to the Kit Kat bars. "How'd you find that out?"

"Talked to his ex," she said. "He's staying at a trailer park not far from here. He's not very smart for a fugitive."

"Maybe he's not a fugitive," I pointed out. "Maybe he came back because he missed his family."

"Sure," she said. "That happens. You and your sister have lots of kumbaya moments."

"That's not fair." My sister and I couldn't have been more different. While I'd followed a high-powered career path of kowtowing to lawyers with dubious ethics, Sherri worked at a bridal shop and spent her spare time husband hunting. Her criteria were male and blond. She'd even dated Wally briefly, before his roots grew out, and then she'd gone back to Frankie Ritter. Frankie was a human troll, but he apparently had an endless stockpile of bleach.

"Maybe you've got a point," I conceded.

"I usually do," she agreed. "Anyway, the ex had plenty to say. Turns out Gilbert didn't give her a lot of 'sweet.' I think we should talk to him."

"And say what?" I asked. "Did you come back to town to kill Nicky D?"

She rolled her eyes. "You're embarrassing yourself. We just make strategic small talk while he does the neighborly thing and fixes our stove. He'll never suspect a thing."

Yeah, like I'd never heard *that* before. Wait. I shifted to face her. "What stove? We don't have a stove."

"Not *with* us," she said. "That would be weird. That's why we're going to borrow the one in the trailer across the street from his for a little while. Don't worry. I did some checking, and the place is empty. I think the owner is gone for eighteen months to five years."

"I don't like the sound of this," I told her. "We're supposed to be going to the Golden Grotto. Curt will be worried if we aren't there."

"He won't have time to worry," Maizy said. "He'll be busy with the old ladies stuffing money down his pants. He's just their type."

"Old ladies go to Virtual Waste concerts?" I couldn't see it.

"Only a few," Maizy said. "But they're real go-getters. That reminds me, I should've warned him to wear two pairs of underwear. I hear they can get kind of handsy."

I let out a snort. "What are you talking about? We're going to a concert, not a male strip show."

"Don't be such a noob," she said. "Women throw themselves at musicians all the time. Especially Susan Two. She's a legend."

I'd forgotten about Susan Two, but I doubted that she'd filed for Medicare yet. Every muscle in my body went rigid with indignation. "We have to get to the Golden Grotto *now*."

"We'll catch the second show," she said, unconcerned. "We've got important work to do."

Nothing was more important than keeping old women's hands out of Curt's pants. "Does the band have security?" I asked. "You know, to keep women from running onstage?"

"Oh, sure," Maizy said. "Flagler runs a tight ship. He moves pretty quick for an eighty-year-old, too."

I stared at her. "That's it? One eighty-year-old man?"

She shrugged. "Those women aren't animals."

I relaxed a little. "That's good to hear."

"They sneak backstage between sets instead," she said. She glanced at me. "Don't you trust Uncle Curt?"

"I don't have to trust him," I said. "We're not exclusive or anything."

She rolled her eyes. "You're delusional. What does he have to do? He gave you a horse blanket, didn't he? In some cultures that's as good as an engagement ring."

"I doubt that," I told her.

"Well, it means *something*," she insisted. "He gave you a horse blanket to put *over* a black silk nightie. You two might as well be married."

"I'm not having this conversation," I said. "And I don't think we should be doing this alone. It doesn't feel safe."

"Safe is relative," she said. "Two minutes from now, some doofus could try to run us off the road again. How safe would that be?"

I checked the side view mirror. Clear. Wish I could say the same for my head.

"Here, if it makes you feel better." She shoved a container of spray paint at me.

I hefted it in my right hand. "What's this for?"

"Self-defense," she said. "Spray it, throw it. Your choice."

"Is that legal?"

She made a right onto yet another dirt road, this one less bumpy and hole-riddled than the one we'd been on a few nights earlier. Still, plumes of dust spun up from the tires and fanned out behind us like a train on a wedding gown.

"Is legality a concern?" she asked.

I couldn't swallow. "Let's just go to the Golden Grotto. We can talk to Gleason when Curt is with us."

"Too late." She pointed. "We're here."

Here was the Whispering Pines Mobile Park, a couple of acres of pine-needle-strewn ground carved out of the forest with trailer homes plunked down in rows meant to suggest careful urban planning. Each had a single parking slot. Many had potted flowers out front and American flags tethered to makeshift flagpoles. No sidewalks. No paved streets. No street lights. Just flickering ambient lighting from television sets or overly optimistic landscape lighting.

It was very quiet. Too quiet. The sort of quiet you get right before that hand shoots up from the grave to grab you by the ankle.

"Gilbert's on C Street," Maizy said. "That should be the next one."

Street was a grandiose description for a dirt path without curbs wide enough to accommodate a car.

A black cat darted out from our left, slinked across in front of us, and disappeared between two mobile homes.

"Uh-oh," Maizy said. "That can't be good."

"Nothing about this is good," I muttered. Right that very minute, Susan Two could be moisturizing her hands.

Maizy stopped in front of a trailer on the right and pointed. "Gilbert's place is over there. I don't see a van, though. His ex said he had a van."

The vehicle of choice for homicidal maniacs everywhere.

"And this one's ours," Maizy added.

Our trailer had the look of vacancy, with no lights and no decorations.

An open ladder sat in front of the door.

"You have got to be kidding me," I said. "I'm not walking under that."

"Me, either," Maizy said. "It's bad mojo."

We sat there looking at the ladder.

"It's not the mojo," I said. "It's a safety issue. That ladder could fall at any moment."

"Agreed," Maizy said. "Plus it's the mojo."

I turned to her. "I guess we're going to be able to make the first show after all. It starts in fifteen minutes. You can turn around right up there."

"Go move the ladder," Maizy said.

I frowned. "*You* go move the ladder."

"I've got to park the car," she said, "while you move the ladder."

"I'm not moving it," I said. "Someone put it there for a reason."

"They put it there to make it look like someone's working on the place, which they're not. Go on, before someone notices us just sitting here."

I didn't know who that someone could possibly be. I'd seen cemeteries with more activity than the Whispering Pines Mobile Park. Then I thought of the maybe-a-deer-but-probably-the-Jersey-Devil attack earlier in the week and figured we'd be safer in the trailer, so I heaved a sigh and got out of the car, slashing through the predictable fog of insects that swarmed me.

A few minutes later, we were standing in Felon X's living room while I scratched a half dozen new bites. It was too dark to distinguish detail, but I didn't get the impression he watched a lot of HGTV. The place was kind of a mess. It even smelled dusty. Trust me, I knew that smell.

"Here's the story," Maizy said. She'd moved away from me while I'd been admiring the décor, her voice coming from off to my left. "I'm the girlfriend. I just came by to check on the place, and I found the stove broken."

I squinted into the darkness. "But what if it isn't broken?"

I heard a snap.

"It is now," she said. "Where's the light switch?"

"Are you sure you want to actually see this place?" I asked.

"It'll be hard to explain to Gilbert Gleason why we're in the dark," she said.

Not necessarily. Being in the dark was a way of life for me.

I heard Maizy toggling a light switch. A light bulb flashed, popped, and sizzled faintly into blackness.

"Slight complication," she said. "Do you happen to have any light bulbs?"

"It's probably for the best," I said. "Listen, how do we know that the guy who lives here doesn't have a real girlfriend that Gleason might have seen?"

"Fine," Maizy said. "Then I'm the cousin. But I have to tell you, I'm not comfortable being related to a felon. It doesn't comport with my life code."

That's what I needed, a life code. Or a new pastime. One that didn't find me groping around a stranger's smelly trailer in the dark and questioning murder suspects. My eyes were gradually starting to adjust, although I wished they weren't. Darkness was much kinder to the place than the light.

"Can we go now?" I asked.

"Not yet," Maizy said. "Let's wait a few minutes. Gilbert might've just run out to buy cigarettes."

"Well, let's leave the door open," I said. "And I'm going to open the windows, too."

"Be careful moving around," Maizy said. "We don't want to knock anything—"

Something bounced off my hands and crashed to the floor.

Maizy activated the flashlight app on her phone and directed it downward. "Uh-oh."

A pepper shaker lay there, which didn't bother me, except its companion salt shaker lay right beside it, and that did. The cap broken, a little mound of salt bleeding from the top.

"*That's* bad mojo," Maizy said.

"I wish you'd stop saying that." I grabbed a few pinches of salt and tossed them over my shoulder.

"This is starting to feel creepy," Maizy said.

Starting to? When it wasn't itching, my skin had been in full prickle since we'd turned into the Whispering Pines. The whole neighborhood was too quiet and still. It was unnatural. I could hear the breeze soughing high in the trees, just the way Eunice had described it right before the Jersey Devil's appearance.

"Listen, Maize," I said. "I don't think Gilbert Gleason is coming back anytime soon."

"Yeah." She was quiet for a second. "It might be a good opportunity to check out his *real* trailer."

"I'm not stepping foot in another trailer tonight," I said.

"But there might be evidence," she said.

"Like what? A picture of an amplifier?"

"Like a written confession," Maizy said. "Lying on the night table next to the open bottle of sleeping pills."

I must have missed something. "What sleeping pills?"

"The ones he used to kill himself," Maizy said. "On account of he was riddled with guilt over killing Nicky D."

"Now there's a dead body in there, too?"

"Not necessarily," she said. "He could have spontaneously combusted."

Oh, for Pete's sake.

"Forget it," I said. "I'm not going in his trailer."

"You don't have to," she said. "You can wait outside and give me the signal if anyone shows up."

I didn't want to wait outside. Outside was where you-know-who lived.

"Then you can wait in the car," Maizy said.

"Will you *please* stop doing that?" I blew out an exasperated sigh. "*Fine*. What's the signal?"

"Blow once on the kazoo."

"What kazoo?" I asked. "I don't have a kazoo."

"You don't?" she said. "You left it home?"

"Yes, Maizy," I said. "I left my kazoo home."

"Then just blow the horn," she said. "And have the car running. We may need to make a quick getaway. You should probably wait in the passenger seat."

"You know," I said, "Just because his van isn't here doesn't mean *he* isn't. Maybe he traded it in for a pickup that just happens to be in the shop right now."

"Good point," Maizy said. She painted a circle around our feet with the light. I didn't look. I didn't want to know what was down there. Then she swept it quickly over the walls, where I caught quick glimpses of NASCAR posters as wall art. "We need to find out who owns that, too," she added.

"Tried that," I said. "It didn't go so well."

"But now we have a secret weapon," she said. "Eunice. Ask her to cook something, and we'll go see Hank again."

"Okay, fine." I'd offer to hand-feed him if it got me out of that dingy little trailer. "Now let's get to the Golden Grotto."

"Did you forget already?" she said. "I'm going to check out Gilbert Gleason's trailer."

"*Fine*," I snapped. "Then let's get to it."

"Wait." Her voice was hushed. "Look at that penny."

It wasn't doing anyone any good lying there on the ratty indoor/outdoor carpeting. I reached for it.

She grabbed my arm. "Don't. It's heads down."

"So? It spends the same either way."

"Heads down is bad mojo," she said.

"Will you stop saying *mojo*?" I threw her off more forcefully than I'd intended to, knocking her arm upward. Her cell phone flew out of her hand and smashed into the mirror above the sofa. A splinter appeared diagonally across the face of the mirror.

"Oh, come *on*!" Maizy yelled.

"That's seven years of bad mojo," I said kind of snidely.

"For *you*," Maizy said. "You broke it."

"It was *your* phone," I said.

"But you knocked it out of my hand," she said. "I was just trying to save you from yourself."

"Don't do me any favors," I snapped. "If I'd had my way, I'd be at the Golden Grotto right now watching Curt perform instead of in this dark, smelly—"

"Look out!" Maizy yelled, shoving me out of the path of the giant black bird that had just soared in through the open door. It settled on the back of the sofa, shook its head, spread its wings, stretched its legs, and sat there staring at us with beady little black bird eyes.

Maizy and I looked at each other.

"We'll check out Gilbert Gleason's trailer another time," Maizy said.

"Last one to the door pays the cover charge," I said. And I'm proud to say it wasn't me.

CHAPTER EIGHTEEN

———

Twenty minutes later, after we'd finished calculating the ninety-two years of bad luck that were headed our way, Maizy said, "It was a good plan."

I had my doubts about that, but I was so happy to have the Whispering Pines behind us that I said, "It got a little weird back there is all."

She nodded her agreement. "We'll do surveillance and wait for our chance at Gilbert Gleason's trailer. I'll get an old pickup truck from Honest Aaron. Nobody will pay attention to another pickup truck. Do you have any flannel shirts?"

I'd stopped listening. I was busy watching a set of headlights in the side view mirror that seemed to be getting bigger in a hurry. "Maize, look."

She glared into the rearview. "Is that what I think it is?"

I sure hoped not. "Maybe it's just someone in a hurry," I said.

The high beams flashed on, lighting up our interior like a spotlight.

"I don't think so." Maizy scowled into the mirror. "Too bad for him *I'm* driving this time."

"What does that—" I was hurled forward against my seat belt when Maizy suddenly slammed on the brakes. All my breath left me in a *whoosh*. The Escort zigged left and zagged right, squealing madly. I heard tires screeching behind us, and then the interior abruptly went black and the pickup roared past us with its headlights dark and its deafening air horn blasting.

"Not bad," Maizy said with grudging admiration. "The doofus has good reflexes."

"Are you trying to get us killed?" I yelled.

She straightened out the car and gave it some gas. The car lurched forward with hesitation, as if it couldn't understand what we were asking of it.

"Don't you get it?" Maizy asked.

Oh, I got it, alright, if *it* was nausea.

"He's been watching us," Maizy said. "He must have followed us to the trailer park."

I swallowed several times, until the oily taste of panic slid back down my throat. "I don't care," I said. "And I don't care who killed Nicky D. Maybe the amplifier *did* fall on him."

"Maybe the doofus lives there," Maizy said. "On C Street."

"I never even met Nicky D," I muttered. "So he was good-looking. Big deal. There are lots of good-looking men in the world."

"No, I don't think so," Maizy said. "We'd have seen it."

"One of them's playing the drums right now," I said. "At the Golden Grotto."

She chewed on her lip, thinking. "Wish I had the plate number. Then we could go on offense."

I wasn't sure what that meant, although I was sure I didn't like it. But I had nothing useful to contribute, so I stayed quiet and tried to rub the seat belt imprint off my stomach.

"We need to go back to the garage," she said finally. "See if the pickup is still there. Don't worry. We'll have time to do it later."

Oh, good. I was afraid we might not be able to make it.

"Might as well take a break," Maizy said. "That should be the Grotto up there where that yellow sign is. Looks a lot busier than the Pinelands."

A lot nicer, too. The Golden Grotto had a hole-free sign with a picture of, what else, a cute little golden grotto fed by a sparkly golden waterfall. The building itself was more log cabin than nightclub, with a big stone chimney at one end and a porch stretching across the front. The lot was nearly full. Curt's Jeep was parked in the far corner next to the Virtual Waste van, near a paver stone walkway leading down the side of the building, probably to a rear entrance.

I waited until she'd fitted the Escort into a spot. "You know, you never told me what Gilbert Gleason's ex said. Does he have a temper?"

"The guy who put a bullet through a snare drum while trying to shoot someone? Gee, she didn't mention that."

"Very funny," I told her. "What *did* she mention?"

"She mentioned Gilbert was disbarred," Maizy said.

"Probably that anger-management problem of his," I muttered.

"It's not that," Maizy said. "He did nicky-nack with a client."

Geez. Even Howard and Wally hadn't sunk that low. That prohibition was practically on the front cover of the ethics handbook. "That's despicable," I said.

"According to his ex," Maizy added, "it was bound to happen anyway. She said it was just a matter of time, that if he wasn't suing them, he was—"

"The client wasn't related to Nicky D, was she?" I cut in. If so, that polished up Gilbert's motive to a high gloss.

"We can ask her," Maizy said. "Her name's Miranda Law. I've got the goods on her right down to the Social Security number."

I couldn't hide my suspicion. "How?"

"Not like that. From her file." Maizy shrugged. "Gilbert's ex worked in his office. And she's not the forgiving type. She's still furious that Gilbert didn't keep his junk where it belonged. But then my friend Haley says men never really grow up."

Haley, the Samantha Jones of Maple Grove High.

I scanned the lot for a homicidal pickup. "Do you think maybe he'll be here?"

"If we're lucky," Maizy said. "Try to stop shaking, will you? I've got a reputation to maintain."

"I can't help it." I scratched my arms. "I do that when someone tries to kill me."

She fished an ID from her pocket. "Why? You should be used to it. Besides, it might have just been someone in a hurry."

"That's what I said!"

"Yeah, but it sounds better coming from me," she said. "You were a little hysterical when you said it."

I glowered at her. "That's because one of the people trying to kill me tonight was *you*."

"Yeah, we probably shouldn't mention that to Uncle Curt." Her gaze settled on something at the edge of the lot, near the Virtual Waste van. "Go ahead of me. I need a second to get in the zone."

I rolled my eyes. "What are you talking about? You're an expert at getting into bars illegally."

"That's kind of you to say." She gave me a little push. "Don't worry. I'll be there in a minute."

Someone was hovering near the Virtual Waste van, the tip of his cigarette flaring red in the darkness. Either he had a visor built into his forehead, or he wore a baseball cap. He practically dissolved into the night in a dark hoodie. And dark sunglasses.

"Who is that?" I asked.

"That's Bones."

"We should talk to him," I said. "We could ask him why he wasn't with the band last Saturday."

"I bet he had a good reason," Maizy said.

"Right. Like maybe he threw out his back picking up that heavy amplifier on that Friday night."

"They all pick up the amplifiers," she said. "They don't have roadies."

"You know what I mean."

"Besides," she said, "he doesn't have to sneak backstage. And I'd have recognized him anyway."

Unless...

"Maybe he used that to his advantage," I pointed out. "He knew no one would question his going backstage."

"That's not bad," she said.

That sounded vaguely like an insult. But I was too busy detecting to take offense. "Why's he wearing sunglasses? Does he have something to hide?"

"He's got an image," Maizy said. "Don't be so judgmental. *God.*"

"Wait a minute." I stopped walking. "Didn't you say the guy you saw was wearing a hoodie and work boots? And didn't TJ say Bones always wore a hoodie and work boots?"

"That doesn't mean anything. Everyone wears hoodies and work boots."

Yes, but in the summer, in the northeast, when you could not only breathe the air but bathe in it?

"I bet Uncle Curt's waiting for you," Maizy said. "You'd better get in there."

She was up to something. I could feel it in my bones. The thing was, I didn't know what, and I didn't care to stick around to find out. Despite the creepy woods, the abandoned trailer, the reappearance of the maniac driver, and the cornucopia of bad-luck omens, I'd been unable to shake the image of Susan Two chasing Curt around the stage with bad intentions and well-lubed hands.

I went inside.

CHAPTER NINETEEN

———

After handing over ten bucks for the privilege of being grilled by the security guy at the door, I knew what Maizy was up to: finding another way inside. I had to lay out enough personal information to gain national security clearance before I was free to look for Curt. Two indecent proposals and one fanny pinch later, I found him backstage, deep in conversation with Mike and TJ. Plop was sitting on the floor nearby, back to the wall, eyes closed, very Zen. I didn't buy it. I wasn't sold on Plop's outward cluelessness, even though he hadn't given me any useful argument against it.

Bones stood alone near the open side door, hands stuffed in his pockets, staring at the floor. His baseball cap and hoodie now sat on an equipment trunk. His shoulder-length black hair was pushed back behind his ears, showing an assortment of silver hoops, barbells, and studs in both ears. Multiple silver chains around his neck. Broad leather straps around his wrists. Still with the sunglasses.

And something else about him caught my attention. Deep bruises and a small cut on the inside of his right bicep. Strange place for bruising.

I knew opportunity when I saw it and when it was standing alone ten feet away from me. I hurried over to him. "You're Bones, right? Can I talk to you for a minute?"

He may or may not have looked at me. It was hard to tell since I couldn't see his eyes. Either way, he said nothing.

"My name is Hortense Doe," I said. "I'm a private investigator looking into Nick DiBenedetto's death." If it worked for Maizy, it would work for me.

It wasn't working for me. Still nothing from Mr. Charisma.

I gestured to his arm. "Those are some nasty bruises. Did you get those lifting all this heavy equipment?" *Especially the amplifier?*

The sunglasses settled on me for a long, unsettling, silent moment. Then finally: "Car accident." His voice was surprisingly deep and rich. A voice made for telling bedtime stories. The adult kind.

Back on point, what a convenient excuse.

"That's too bad," I said. "What do you drive?"

Another pause. "Truck."

The kind of truck that tried to run women off the road? Probably not a prudent question, since I had others that needed answers. "When did that happen?"

"Couple Fridays back."

Friday? Run-me-off-the-road Friday? No, that couldn't have been Bones. Not unless there were two maniac drivers out there. Because even if it had been Bones on that Friday night, he didn't seem psychotic enough to show up at the Golden Grotto, calm and unflappable, minutes after running us down a second time.

I struggled to keep my voice calm. "I guess that's why you weren't around to help the band pack up the morning after Nicky D died, right?"

A tiny shrug.

"TJ tried to call you, but he said you didn't answer," I added.

"Broke my cell," he said. "In the accident."

Wow. Almost a full sentence there.

"No landline, huh? Lots of people are getting rid of those. It's the prices. I'm keeping mine, though. Can't get enough calls from telemarketers." I attempted a smile.

He shifted and glanced over my shoulder. He was growing impatient.

Okay, fine.

"I need to ask you about Nicky D," I said.

Not surprisingly, he said nothing. I'd had more satisfying conversations with Ashley.

"Where were you between sets on the night he died?" I asked.

Long silence. You could time an egg by this guy. "Talking to my mother," he said at last. "Outside." His head swiveled toward me so that I saw my own reflection in the mirrored glasses. I should've worn a different color. And used more anti-frizz cream on my hair.

"Your mom comes to your shows?" I asked him, surprised. "You don't see too many people that age going to clubs anymore. I'm sure she fits right in, though. It's nice that she supports you like that."

This time I was convinced he was staring at me. "On the *phone*," he said flatly.

Oh. Of course. That would be another way to do it.

"You must have seen TJ outside, too," I said. "He stepped out to have a cigarette between sets."

Was that a smirk?

"TJ doesn't smoke," he said.

I blinked, not sure I heard him correctly. "Excuse me?"

"He doesn't smoke. It affects his singing."

"But he said..." I trailed off. It didn't matter what he'd said if he'd lied.

"That it?" he asked. "Hortense *Doe*?"

Well, there was no need for snark. "I'll be in touch if I have any more questions," I said.

That time I *knew* it was a smirk when Bones brushed past me. That had gone spectacularly. Rather than clear anyone, I'd added another suspect or two. I took a moment to reflect on my lack of interrogation skills before turning to track down Maizy.

I found her perched on a stool backstage, watching everyone and everything as if she had to describe it all to the police after the show. She grinned at me, unconcerned that she'd exposed me to an admission process that had stopped just short of a cavity check.

But I'd have to deal with that later. At that moment Curt was making it hard for me to breathe. There was something different about him. His dark hair seemed even thicker. His eyes seemed even blacker. His chest seemed even...chestier. He had a five o'clock shadow that made his teeth practically glow when he smiled.

And I hadn't even gotten to the good stuff yet.

As if he could read my mind, he glanced over while I was blotting drool from my lower lip. Immediately he broke away from Mike and TJ to join me. "You missed the first set. Where've you been?"

Maizy materialized behind him, shaking her head. In the background Mike drifted off, melting into the crowd on his way to the bar. TJ started scribbling on a piece of paper. I couldn't help but wonder if he was writing another note to "Blue-haired Girl."

"The killer driver struck again," I blurted. Hey, I'd never made any promises. Besides, at that instant, I would have given Curt just about anything he wanted, including my last Butterscotch Krimpet. And everyone knows how I feel about Butterscotch Krimpets.

Oh, boy. That sounded an awful lot like groupie-think.

Maizy rolled her eyes and did that annoying *tsk* sound perfected by teenaged girls the world over.

"I don't want to hear it," I told her. "You couldn't bring me in the back way? They did everything but give me a gynecological exam out there!"

"What's your point?" she said.

"Hold it." Curt's smiled vanished. "The pickup? Did he hit you again?"

"No, he didn't hit us," Maizy said. "*I* was driving."

"But she tried her best," I said snidely.

"Are you sure it was the same one?" he asked.

No. I shoved the thought aside. No one could be so unlucky as to have two nut jobs chasing them around South Jersey.

"Sounded like it," Maizy said. "But I was busy maneuvering, and Jamie doesn't see too well at night because of the cataracts."

I ignored that.

"Maneuvering," Curt repeated. "What does that mean?"

"It means he got away again," Maizy said. "Turns out he drives almost as well as I do."

"You failed your driver's test twice," Curt said.

She shrugged. "Hate the car, not the driver."

Curt turned to me. "Did you get a partial plate this time?"

I shook my head. "Same MO as before. He kills the lights before he flies past us, blaring that deafening horn."

"It's okay, though," Maizy said. "We're going to check out Max's Garage later and see if the truck is still there. We can at least run the plate."

"How do you plan to do that?" Curt asked her.

"You don't really need me to answer that, do you?" Maizy said.

He gestured to her hair with a sigh. "I'd hoped that meant you were finally going straight."

"Don't do that," she said. "You're doomed to disappointment."

"By the way," I told her, "I just talked to Bones. He's quite the conversationalist. I practically had to use pliers to find out he was on the phone with his mother when Nicky D was killed."

Maizy frowned. "Are you sure that's what he said?"

"He didn't say much else," I said. "Why?"

"Because they had a huge fight like two years ago and haven't talked since." Her brow creased. "She wanted him in college, not in a band. She even threw him out of the house."

"Maybe they reconciled," Curt said. "It happens."

Maizy shook her head. "Not the way he feels about it. He was really hurt. Bones is a sensitive soul."

Yeah. I could tell. Apparently he was also a liar. Maybe worse.

I glanced around. "How's it going here? Seen anything unusual?"

"Maybe." He put his arm around my shoulders and steered me out the side door. Maizy followed behind, close enough to clip my heels. Sure, *now* she didn't want to let me out of her sight.

Curt kept his arm around me and lowered his voice. "I talked to TJ about the night Nicky D died. He said he tried to meet with Mike between sets about recording their next CD."

"What's so unusual about that?" I asked. "I'd expect them to do that."

"Except they didn't," Curt said. "TJ couldn't find him. He even asked Archie Ritz if *he'd* seen him."

"Wait, what?" Maizy ducked under Curt's elbow and elbowed her way between us. "Mike and Archie were supposed to be at the bar together. That's what Mike said, right?"

"Mike might have lied to us," Curt said.

"That's a given," Maizy said. "Everyone lies to us. I thought you knew that. What else did TJ say?"

"Next time he saw Mike was when Mike yelled for help," Curt said. "When he found Nicky D backstage."

"Maybe he didn't *find* him so much as *leave* him," I said.

Curt nodded his agreement.

Maizy's mouth twisted. "I never liked Mike. His hair's too short. What about Archie? Did he disappear, too? Maybe they were in it together."

"According to TJ," Curt said, "Archie left between sets. Said he was in kind of a rush. He's supposed to be here tonight. Be a good chance to talk to him, see if he's got a motive. Or an alibi."

Maizy chewed on her lip. "Does Archie drive a pickup truck?"

"You think Archie tried to run us off the road?" I asked. "Why would he want to do that?"

"Why would you want to put pineapples on a pizza?" Maizy asked.

"But he doesn't even know us," I said.

She snorted. "Like that's stopped anyone from trying to kill us before."

Curt's arm dropped from my shoulder. "*What?*"

"She's exaggerating," I told him. "What she meant to say was it hasn't stopped anyone from *wanting* to kill us."

"Yeah, that's better," Maizy said.

"That is *not* better," Curt snapped. "You're grounded."

"You can't ground me," Maizy said. "You're not my father."

"You're right," he said. "If I was your father, I'd arrest you."

"What about *her*?" She pointed at me. "They want to kill *her*, too!"

I stuck my fists on my hips. "What did *I* do except pay the full cover charge and submit to a thoroughly intrusive wanding at the door?"

"You're never going to let that go, are you?" she said.

"If you two have a minute," Curt said, "I'd like to set up a game plan for tonight."

"Way ahead of you," Maizy said. "You're going to play. I'm going to talk to Archie when he shows up. And Jamie's going to surveil the room."

"Why can't *you* surveil the room?" I asked. "And *I* can talk to Archie."

"Be serious," Maizy said. "You don't know enough about Virtual Waste to pull it off."

I rolled my eyes. "What do I need to know? That TJ wrote 'Puddle of Drool'?"

"Impressive," Maizy said. "Now what's Bones' real name?"

"I have no idea," I snapped. "What is it?"

"Got me," Maizy said. "But that's not important. We all have our jobs to do. Oh, and Uncle Curt, stay away from Susan Two. She's like an octopus."

"Don't worry about me," he told her. "I'd better not see you at the bar."

"I go where the investigation takes me," she said.

"It might take you to your room for a month," he said. "Stay where I can see you."

"Good idea," she said. "That way you can learn something."

Curt and I watched her make her way through the crowd, blending in effortlessly without the blue hair. Maybe I *was* better off letting her do the heavy lifting while I surveilled the room. Except what did surveilling a room mean, exactly? Did I have to take notes or pictures? Where should I stand? What was I supposed to be looking for, and how would I know it when I saw it?

Something occurred to me. I turned back to Curt. "What did TJ do when he couldn't find Mike?"

"He went outside for a smoke. That's where he was when Nicky D's body was found."

At least he was consistent, even if he was lying. That's what he'd said before. "But I just talked to Bones," I began, "and he said—"

"Hey, man." Plop was at the door. "Showtime."

I glanced at him and drew back in surprise. Plop had a bandana tied around his head with the number 20 above his right eye.

"Be right there," Curt told him.

"Curt." I moved closer to him so I could whisper in his ear. Or smell his cologne. Whatever. "What's that number 20 on his head mean?"

He looked over at the doorway, but Plop had already gone back inside. "IQ?" he suggested.

I wasn't smiling. "What does he drive?"

"He came in the van with Mike." Curt's eyes met mine. "Plop's been here the whole night, Jame. He's not our guy."

"No, I guess not." If Bones wasn't our guy, and Plop wasn't our guy, who *was* our guy? This thing seemed to be turning into a process of elimination. "But that bandana," I added. "I think I saw something like that in the video Maizy took that first night. Something on the dash of the pickup. I saw a number 20, anyway, I'm sure of it." As sure as I could be while simmering in a stew of terror.

"I'll get a look at him onstage," he added. "I've got to go." He touched the ends of my hair. "While you're surveilling the room, check out the new drummer. They say he's pretty good."

A smile tugged at my lips. "I don't know. I've got my eye on the keyboardist. I'm a sucker for a guy named Marion."

That breathtaking smile again, meant just for me. My breath caught for a second. He took advantage of my silence to grab my hand. "Come on," he said. "Showtime."

He was telling *me*.

"Excuse me," someone said behind me.

I turned to find Mike trying to make his way back to the stage. He seemed surprised to see me. "Hey, it's Hortense, right? How've you been?"

"Good. Great." I tried to step aside, but I could barely move. Since we were nose to chest, I might as well make the most of it. "Can I ask you something?"

He took a drink from the glass in his hand. "Sure."

"I know you said you weren't arguing with Nicky D the night he died," I said. Not that I believed him. "But we were told you gave some kind of signal at the door right after what they *thought* was an argument, and then you propped the door open. Like maybe for someone in the parking lot to come in."

His expression grew dark. "What kind of signal?"

"Like this." I tried to mimic Bryn's demonstration, but we were packed so tightly, I wound up smacking two people in the back of the head and one in the shoulder.

"Knock it off, will you?" someone yelled.

"Sorry." I holstered my arm again. "Like that," I said.

Not sure what I expected from him, but it wasn't laughter. Still, that's what I got. You'd think I was used to that, but not so much coming from a relative stranger. I felt my temper rising.

"I'm not kidding," I told him. "It's a serious question."

"I'm allergic to bee stings," he said.

"Sorry to hear that," I said. "What about the signal?"

"You got some bad information." He tipped an ice cube into his mouth and crunched on it. "Hate to disappoint you, Nancy Drew, but that was no signal. I was trying to get a bee away from me."

"You didn't tell Ma—Alana that when she asked you," I said accusingly. "You played dumb then."

His eyes drilled into mine. "Maybe you have better technique than she does."

If that was some kind of come-on, it was my turn to play dumb. Even if I'd been interested, he wasn't my type. My mouth twisted in disappointment. "Only a bee?"

He bent to speak in my ear. "Not *only* a bee. That bee was a spy, and my buddy the CIA beekeeper was waiting outside for my signal."

Funny. Of course, it might have been funnier if his necklace hadn't fallen out of his collar right into my face. A silver cross, in a silver circle. Just like the one hanging from the mirror in the pickup. Up close I could see the little shield and bar on the bottom of the cross. I wasn't sure what it meant, but I knew it was unique enough to be unmistakably identical.

"Yo, Mike!" Plop yelled from onstage.

Mike gave me a sly smile. "I've got to go play. Thanks for the laughs." And he was gone, heading back to the band.

Swatting at a bee. Good grief.

It took me a few minutes to find a suitable spot from which to see the whole room, mostly because I was being pinballed around by a rowdy crowd to whom I stood at armpit level. When I spotted an empty chair, I dragged it over against the wall and climbed on top, glad to have a little breathing space. I wasn't a pub crawler; the only bar I'd seen apart from when Maizy and I had pursued a skinny green man (no, I wasn't tipsy; it had really happened) was on *Cheers*, where the place was always clean and bright and frequented by well-mannered customers.

The Golden Grotto was no episode of *Cheers*. It was nicer than the Pinelands Bar and Auditorium, but that wasn't saying much. One large room, dark, noisy, and smoky, with the stage at one end, the bar running along the far wall, pool table, air hockey table, and pinball machine at the other end by the fireplace, none currently in use. I scanned the room, noticing a familiar face with black-framed glasses but no lenses. Susan One, her attention riveted to the band. I was surprised to see her, given that it had seemed Nicky D had been the object of her obsession rather than the band at large. I'd been wrong.

Or maybe it wasn't the band at large that absorbed her attention. Maybe it was Curt. Her head hadn't moved to follow TJ or Mike around the stage. She wasn't watching Plop behind the keyboard. Bones might as well not exist for her. She'd stayed trained on one person. Unless she was lost in a standing meditation, she was ogling Curt.

I didn't like that one little bit. She might have already killed once by proxy, through that human sequoia that she was dating. Was she planning to add to the tally?

A curvy blonde in heavy makeup appeared at her side. They exchanged a few words while keeping their mutual focus on the stage. Was that Susan Two? I forgot all about surveilling the room. *This* was important. And my question was answered when Susan Two reached into her bag and pulled out a tube of moisturizer, which she proceeded to squeeze liberally onto her hands.

The girl was shameless.

Suddenly the crowd shifted, and I lost sight of the two Susans when more people pressed into the room. But I immediately recognized another familiar face. Bryn, the bouncer from the Pinelands. She was striking in a windblown kind of way, imposing but feminine with a red sweater and red lipstick, standing a head taller than the tide of women who had washed in with her. She scanned the room in bouncer mode, alert for trouble. Occupational hazard, I supposed, the same way Wally scanned the floors of public spaces for spills and sidewalks for uneven concrete. Bryn's eyes settled on Maizy. Although I was standing on the chair, she hadn't noticed me. In fairness, I was eminently unnoticeable.

Snippets of conversation floated over to me from a nearby group of girls.

"...it happened at the Pinelands..."

"...any idea who..."

"...outside with Plop when they found him..."

That came from a petite redhead, and it wrenched my focus off Bryn. Outside with Plop? But Plop had told us he'd been napping between sets on the Friday night while Nicky D was getting himself killed. I studied the girls as surreptitiously as I could, which wasn't easy since I towered over them on the chair. None stood out as accessories to murder, but if I'd learned anything about killers, it was that they didn't fit into neat archetypes.

"...Nicky D was cute but..."

Maizy was right; we'd been lied to plenty of times, and it wouldn't surprise me if it had happened again. It *would* surprise me coming from Plop. He didn't seem like he had it in him to be deceptive. He didn't seem like he had *anything* in him except fumes.

Of course, that white number 20 on his bandana...

"...the new guy's pretty hot for an older man..."

Well, I wasn't about to stand there and listen to *that*.

Someone tapped on my kneecap. "Excuse me. Can we use this chair?"

I looked down into the mesmerizing pale green eyes of the redhead. She was striking in a way that left me uncomfortably aware of my boring clothes. Maybe I should make more of an effort. Boots instead of sneakers. Sweater instead of gym wear. Skinny jeans instead of mom jeans.

The redhead waited, oblivious to my eternal struggle for a sense of style. "We're one short. Would you mind?"

Plenty of time later for self-loathing. I shook my head, climbed off the chair, and found a crumpled tissue in my pocket to wipe the seat while I considered the best approach. "Were you diddling Plop two Fridays ago?" I asked.

Okay, maybe that wasn't the best approach.

She took hold of the chair, but I was still polishing the seat, holding it firmly in place.

"What are you, his girlfriend or something?" she asked. "You trying to kiss up to him after what you did?"

What I did? Did I lose his favorite socks in the laundry? Dye his favorite T-shirt pink? Wake him up before noon?

"I'm not his girlfriend," I said. "But let's pretend I was. What did I do?"

She gave the chair a tug, but I wasn't finished with it or her.

"If you don't know," she said, "I'm not going to tell you."

Wow. Now I knew why Curt got irritated when I said that. It was the third leg in the trinity of guilt, along with "I shouldn't have to ask you" and "You could have at least called if you were going to be late."

"I'm asking because I'm a detective," I said. "Hortense Doe. And you are?"

"I'm Tiffany," she said. "I've never met a detective before. You must be undercover, right?" She did a quick head-to-toe appraisal. "*Really* undercover."

I stifled a sigh. I got it; I was only a few pegs above Plop on the worst-dressed list. Mr. Blackwell wouldn't even waste ink on me. I bought my underwear in six-packs and my T-shirts in the irregular bins. I didn't even know the meaning of *ruching*.

And it mattered about as much as bedtime mattered to a narcoleptic.

"Tell me about the girlfriend," I said. "What did she do?"

"What do all girls do around Nicky D?" she asked.

Stare? Drool?

She rolled her eyes at my blank expression. "She messed around with him."

Of course she did.

Wait. That sounded like a possible motive.

"Do you know where she lives?" I asked.

Tiffany shook her head. "Plop said she flew off to Cancun with her sister. I think her sister has a condo there or something."

Too bad I didn't have a passport and a bikini body. Sounded like someone we might have wanted to talk to.

"And Plop told you this? How long have you known him?"

"I just met him that night," she said. "I've been to almost all their shows, though. I like to watch him."

I couldn't imagine why.

"So between sets, you went outside with him?" I prompted her. "And he told you all about his girlfriend, right?"

She didn't notice my biting sarcasm. "I finally got my chance. He was wonderful."

I *really* couldn't imagine it.

"And he was awake?" I asked.

"Sure, he was awake," she said with a frown. "He wouldn't be able to talk to me if he was asleep."

Oh, *ick.* Plop was a talker. That was *way* too much information.

"He just pretends to be out of it half the time," she said. "Don't let him fool you. That's the character he plays."

I thought about his performance at the Pinelands, both while Curt had been auditioning and afterward behind the bar. Oscar worthy.

"Plop is maybe the smartest guy up there," she said. "Like that Friday night? He said we'd better go outside because things were going to get ugly." She shuddered. "Boy, was he right."

Ugly? What did that mean? Ugly as in he was about to kill Nicky D, or he already had and knew his handiwork would be discovered soon enough?

"How did he seem to you?" I asked. "Was he agitated in any way? Upset?" *Guilty?*

"No, not really. He seemed as happy-go-lucky as ever."

The band launched into a cover of "Move It On Over" by George Thorogood. Plop stood intensely focused on his keyboard, looking neither happy-go-lucky nor particularly smart. Curt, on the other hand, looked magnificent, head bobbing in time to the music, occasionally grinning at Mike or TJ when they made some comment to him. He was easy to watch (just ask Susan One), but my gaze was drawn to Bones, to the side of the stage, playing his guitar, looking at no one, saying nothing. Even with the sunglasses concealing his eyes, you could tell he was utterly lost in the music. I watched him for about twenty seconds while it slowly dawned on me that his total, uninhibited immersion in his craft was maybe kind of sexy.

I forced my focus back to Tiffany while I polished the back of the chair. "What about Bones?"

"What about him?"

Good question. "Does he get along with the rest of the band?"

She shrugged. "I guess so. I feel kind of bad for him, to tell you the truth. Nicky D was always so mean to him. He was a real bully, but he didn't seem to treat anyone else the way he treated Bones."

"How do you mean?"

"I'll show you." She brought up YouTube on her cell phone and handed it to me. It was Nicky D, clearly unaware he was being recorded because he was laying into Bones like a mean girl, ridiculing his looks, his musical inadequacy, his lack of charisma, and if the recording had been longer, probably the way he breathed. It was awful to watch, and I was glad when it ended and I could give her back her phone.

"He did that a *lot*," Tiffany said. "Nicky D didn't think he had the rocker vibe, whatever *that* means. That's the phrase he used, 'rocker vibe.' He said they'd have to replace him if Virtual Waste was going to go global."

Global? They'd be lucky to go to the next county. Still, it seemed worth following up on that.

"How do you know all this?" I asked her.

"I know a lot about Virtual Waste," she said. "They're big around here. Besides, these aren't exactly secrets. *Everyone* knew Nicky D hated Bones."

Had the feeling been mutual? Bones didn't seem like much of a fighter, but maybe he'd made his stand one time and made it count, lashing out in revenge.

Tiffany glanced around, scoping out another free chair, tired of waiting for mine.

"About Plop," I said quickly. "You're sure about when you met him outside?"

She nodded. "I know because I had to give my friend Gina a ride home. I only had him to myself for ten minutes, though, before...well, before everything happened."

Ten minutes? "That doesn't really seem worth getting undressed," I muttered.

"Excuse me?"

Had I said that out loud? My face grew warm. "Sorry," I said. "Your love life is your business."

"My *love* life?" she repeated. "You think I *slept* with him the night I met him? What kind of girl do you think I am?"

Uh-oh.

"But you said you went outside with him between sets," I said. "I guess I assumed..."

"To *talk* to him," she said. "About getting together for a jam session. What kind of detective are you, anyway?"

I thought that was fairly obvious. I gave the chair one last swipe and stood back while she snatched it up and stormed off with a fire-breathing glare.

"I see you've made another friend," Maizy said from behind me. "You have a real gift."

"I'm investigating," I snapped. "I had to keep her talking."

"I know a better way to do that." She whipped out a crumpled ten. "Works every time."

I didn't make enough to go passing out cash. I'd wasted my last ten on the cover charge so I could get in and polish up the furniture. And if Maizy had been handing out counterfeit bills, I *really* didn't want to know about it.

"It's not counterfeit," Maizy said, shoving it back in her pocket. "Herbie Hairston gave me a refund on some equipment."

"The death star?"

"*Morning* star," she said. "Not death star. Turn off your TV once in a while. *God.*"

"Look who's talking," I shot back. "You can name the cast of *What's My Line?* and it was on fifty years ago!"

"That's different. I use that show to sharpen my skills."

"You can stop watching," I said. "They're sharp enough."

"That's not possible." She blew some hair out of her eyes. "And just so you know, the morning star is a multipurpose tool."

I sighed. "It's in my trunk right now, isn't it?"

"Right next to the bag of lime," she said. "And the shovel. And the do-it-yourself embalming kit I bought at the flea market. I've got my doubts about that one."

"You really worry me," I told her.

"You can't be too prepared," she said.

For what, a DIY burial?

We stood watching the band play.

"Remember that necklace from the pickup truck?" I asked. "Mike's wearing it."

"Yeah, I noticed that necklace." Maizy sounded thoughtful. "Bryn's got one, too. I've seen her wear it a couple of times. I think it's a Harley thing."

Were they giving those things away?

"Does Mike ride a motorcycle?"

She shrugged. "I guess he might. I've only seen him drive the van. Maybe I should find out. I don't trust anyone with hair that short."

"Your Uncle Curt has short hair," I said.

"Yeah, but he probably has enough chest hair to make up for it," she said. "I think Mike shaves his chest. He's a girly man."

Curt was no girly man. He had just the right amount of chest hair.

We listened some more.

"Maybe all Mike's hair is on his butt," Maizy said. "I hear some guys are like that. Cue ball up top, Koosh ball down below."

Eww. I was *not* going there. "I don't want to talk about Mike's butt hair," I said. "Watch the band."

We watched the band for a minute.

"The two Susans are here," I said. "Two brought her moisturizer with her."

"Uncle Curt's safe while he's playing," Maizy said. "She always makes her move between sets."

Oh, well, then there was no point in worrying, so long as the band played until Monday.

"Did you know that Bryn is here, too?" I asked.

"Hard to miss her," Maizy said. "Guess she's a fan."

"Or she's still trying to help us solve Nicky D's murder," I said.

Maizy snorted. "Amateur."

Well, *that* was rich.

"Did you talk to Archie?" I asked her.

She shook her head. "I haven't seen him. He was supposed to be here." She chewed her lip, thinking. "So what'd that girl say?"

"Plop wasn't sleeping between sets like he said. He was outside with her. She said the clueless thing is an act."

"Wonder why," she said.

"Maybe it's easier for him that way," I said. "No expectations, no chance of failure."

Her eyebrows rose. "That's pretty insightful."

"Sometimes I surprise myself," I said. "Also, his girlfriend wanted to take Nicky D to Bermuda with her."

"There we go," Maizy said. "Back to earth."

There had to be more to it than garden-variety cheating. Plenty of people cheated, and their significant others didn't go around knocking them off. Of course, it only took one nutcase to skew the odds. Was Plop a nutcase?

"Could be," Maizy said. "I'll look into it."

"I asked you not to do that," I said.

She shrugged. "Then don't make it so easy."

I didn't make *anything* easy. Ever.

How could we find out about Plop's relationship with Nicky D without asking him directly and potentially ripping off old scabs? Maybe Curt could find out. Plop would probably open up to another guy more easily than to me or even to Maizy and her maddening mind-reading skills.

The band hit the opening chords for "Free Bird," which would probably stretch all the way to the two a.m. closing time. After all, it was already eleven o'clock.

I scanned the people nearest the stage for the two Susans. No sign of them. Maybe Hank had picked up One outside and she was long gone, leaving Two to lotion her way backstage solo.

I turned to Maizy. "Did you know Nicky D wanted to ditch Bones?"

Her expression darkened. "The redhead tell you that?"

I nodded. "He thought Bones kept the group from going global."

"Global." She snorted.

Yeah, that's what I thought.

"She showed me a video of Nicky D bullying Bones," I said. "It was pretty bad. Nicky D wasn't a good guy."

"He was a doofus," she said flatly.

I hesitated. "Maybe we should leave well enough alone with this investigation."

Maizy was quiet for so long, it seemed she was ignoring me. Finally, she pulled a piece of paper from her pocket and handed it over. Drawn on the paper was the old Hangman game, complete with rickety oversimplified gallows and a hanging stick figure. Then I noticed the stick figure had poofy blue hair. And the answer to the not-so-subtle puzzle had been filled in at the bottom: A-L-A-N-A.

I went cold. "Where did you get this?"

"Bones found it under the wiper of the tour van earlier," she said. "When he went outside to smoke."

"And you didn't tell us?" I yelled.

Tiffany's posse turned to scowl at me.

I lowered my voice. "Why didn't you say anything?"

"What for?" Maizy asked. "So you could freak out?"

"I think I'm entitled to freak out," I snapped. "Someone threatened you again!"

"Alana," she said. "Not me."

"Pardon me if I don't see the distinction," I said. "You have to tell Curt."

"I will." She shoved the paper back in her pocket. "When the time is right."

"When would that be, Maizy?" I demanded. "Should I show it to him at your funeral?"

"Don't be so dramatic," she said. "It's just a flimsy attempt to scare us off."

It was inartistic, yes. Crude, sure. Unsubtle, definitely. Not sure I'd call it flimsy.

Something occurred to me. "Does Bones know you're looking into Nicky D's death?"

"Who's to say what anyone knows?" Maizy said. "But I don't see how he couldn't. Like I said, people talk. What, you think Bones drew it?"

"Why not?" I asked.

"Because it wasn't Bones who went backstage," she said.

"It was just someone wearing his clothes," I said.

She stared over my shoulder. "Jamie, look."

"Nice try," I said, "but we're not done talking about this."

"No, seriously," she said. She took me by the shoulders and spun me around. "*Look.*"

Even from across the room, I couldn't miss Hank. No one could miss Hank. He stood belly button, chest, shoulders, and head above everyone else in the bar. He'd swapped out his grease-stained work shirt for a slightly less grease-stained work shirt, and his hair had a little less bushiness to it. But the scowl was still there beneath the unibrow, and it was directed onstage. At Curt.

Oh, no.

A queasy feeling roiled in my stomach while I did a quick scan of the crowd. Sure enough, Susan One had made her way near the stage, all big hair and toothy smile, sights set on her next obsession. She'd lost Susan Two somewhere along the way, which was only more incriminating for her.

"What's he doing in here?" I asked. "He's supposed to wait in the parking lot."

"It's a giant's prerogative to change his mind," Maizy said. "Quick, go see if the pickup is outside. I'll provide a distraction."

Maizy had various methods of distraction, and I didn't want to know any of them. "Be careful," I told her.

She rummaged through her pockets. "Go. You've got five minutes."

I didn't waste them asking why. Thirty seconds later, I was standing outside in the dark parking lot. Plenty of cars, but no one in them. No people coming or going. I was alone. *Alone* worked for me in the safety of my own apartment. Not so much in the Pine Barrens. Problem was, I had only a partial view of the parking lot.

I took a tentative step. When nothing exploded, flew at me, or tackled my legs out from under me, I took another one. Before I knew it, the music had faded to a memory tease, and I had the full view from the middle of the lot. There were a dozen pickup trucks, but none was of the gargantuan variety. Which was a relief and a disappointment at the same time.

I wondered if ours was the truck at Max's Garage, picked up and dropped off like a taxi to accommodate bouts of road rage. Maybe it wouldn't be a bad idea to take a quick drive past while Hank was busy stalking Susan One. After all, he had access to any of the cars in the garage; he wouldn't necessarily have to drive the pickup. And I could get Maizy away from Hank before her *distraction* possibly became dangerous.

A hand fell onto my shoulder.

I screamed and ducked and swatted and bolted all at the same time. You'd have thought I'd seen a dust spider. When I came up for air, Bryn was standing a couple feet to my right, staring at me with her mouth open.

I waited until my heart descended out of my throat and back into my chest where it belonged. "You startled me."

"I didn't mean to," she said in that little girl voice. "I saw you come out here, and I wanted to make sure you were alright. Is Alana with you?"

"She's around here somewhere," I said then hesitated. "Is this what you do on your nights off?"

"You mean spend it in another bar?" She smiled. "Not usually, no. But I want to help, so I thought I'd come by and try to find that guy I'd spoken to at the Pinelands. Remember I told you he'd seen Mike and Nicky D fighting the night Nicky died?"

Don or Dan or Derek.

I nodded. "Did you?"

"Not yet, but it's still early. He *must* be a Virtual Waste fan, right?"

"Who isn't?" I said. "Do you know why Mike would have had issues with Nicky D?"

"Everyone had issues with Nicky D."

TJ ought to put *that* to music. I'd heard it often enough.

"Mike's the money guy," Bryn said. "And I think he found out that Nicky was using the band's money as his personal bank. You don't mess with Mike's money."

I could relate. "How much money?"

She shrugged. "Enough to have them fighting about it and for Nicky to wind up dead the same night."

I blinked. "Are you sure that's what they argued about?"

"Why would Don or Dan or Derek lie to me?" she asked.

Same reason everyone lied to *us*. Because they could.

Still, it sounded like Mike was something of a control freak, and things might go badly for anyone who ended up on what my mother called his "bad side."

On the other hand, Mike seemed like the most level-headed member of Virtual Waste.

"What do you want me to do next?" Bryn asked.

I had no clue. "Listen, Bryn. I appreciate that you're trying to help, but we kind of have our own—"

Suddenly it dawned on me that the music had stopped. And someone was shouting. People began streaming out to their cars, some laughing, some grim-faced. Oddly, they seemed wet. I reached out to a couple as they rushed past. "What's going on?"

"Sprinkler malfunction," the man said. "They're shutting the place down for the night. Show's over."

That had Maizy written all over it.

Instantly Bryn snapped to attention. "They might need help clearing the place out." And she sprinted away. Show-off.

I made my way back into the Golden Grotto, which was now living up to its name. Everything was wet. Including Maizy, who stood stage right, sipping a ginger ale while the band hurried to store their instruments and equipment in a dry place. Hank and Susan One were gone, as were Tiffany and her friends and Susan Two. There were no bartenders in sight, and a moment later I knew why. They emerged from the men's bathroom with fire extinguishers in hand, followed by an elderly white-haired, slope-shouldered man who had to be Flagler.

I angled up to Maizy. "What did you do?"

"Not much," she said. "Just held a flaming paper towel up to the fire detector in the men's bathroom until it activated the sprinklers."

I stared at her. "You set *fire* to the bathroom?"

"Not the whole thing," she said. "Worked pretty well, right?"

"Depends," I said. "I thought you wanted to distract Hank, not commit arson."

"Do you see him anywhere?"

He was probably on his way home to towel off.

She waggled her finger at me. "'Provide a distraction' is what I said. And that's what I did. You can question my means but not my results. What'd you find outside?"

"The truck wasn't there." I watched Flagler directing people outside. Then I watched Curt sling two guitar cases on top of a heavy wheeled case. Definitely more fun to watch Curt. He glanced over, spotted me, and mouthed *Call you later.* I nodded and mouthed back *Come upstairs around six tomorrow, and bring baked ziti with garlic bread.*

A siren wailed in the distance, quickly growing stronger.

Maizy frowned. "That would be the fire department. We should probably go now. We'll head to Max's."

I glanced at Curt again, wondering if it would be a good idea to fill him in, just in case a search crew had to be dispatched later, but Maizy yanked at my arm, and Curt was hard at work, so I followed her through the side door into the night.

CHAPTER TWENTY

————

It took a while to get out of the parking lot, with all the customers leaving at the same time, and when we did, we couldn't reach any kind of speed until the herd thinned. By then, Maizy practically vibrated with impatience, and I'd dozed off. Until we got to Max's. Then I came awake as if a jolt of electricity had sizzled through me, remembering the last time we'd been there, with Hank lurking in the dark office. That wouldn't be a problem this time around since Hank was with Susan One.

Maizy swung a looping left turn into the lot. "It's here," she said. She seemed disappointed.

"So it's not the truck that keeps chasing us," I said. That wasn't entirely bad news because it made Hank seem less likely to be the main suspect. I wasn't at all sure we could handle that much suspect.

We sat silent for a beat.

"Hey," Maizy said. "It's been moved."

I frowned through the windshield. "Has it?"

Maizy put the Escort in park and leaned over to scrounge in the glove compartment. "It was nose-in last time we were here. Now it's tailgate in."

"Are you sure?"

"You know I am."

"That doesn't mean anything," I said. "Hank probably drove it into the garage to work on it."

"That would be one explanation," she agreed.

I moved my knees out of her way. "What are you looking for?"

"Something to write on. Scrap of paper. Bank envelope."

"You won't find one of those," I told her. I pulled a wad of napkins out of my bag and peeled one off. "Will this do?"

She took it and got out of the car. "Wait here."

"What are you doing?" I called after her. "It's not the truck!"

"Information never hurts," she called back.

Maybe information didn't, but winged creatures of the night did, so I stayed right where I was, watching while she slapped the napkin on the hood to jot down the license plate number then immediately picked it up and pressed her hand to the hood instead.

I rolled down my window. "What are you doing? Hurry up!"

"It's warm." She moved her hand around. "It's been driven recently."

Oh, boy. My eyes went straight to the office to check for movement inside. It was hard to see. The only illumination we had was the Escort's rheumy headlights.

"Get the plate, and let's go!" I urged her. "It doesn't matter anyway. It's not the truck!"

"I need to hear the horn!"

Oh, right. The air horn.

"Give me a second," she called.

I heard the drone of an approaching vehicle. "Someone's coming!" I yelled.

Maizy scribbled the plate number on the napkin, shoved it into her jeans pocket, and rushed back to the car. As soon as she slid behind the wheel, a decrepit white van wheezed past, the pale oval of a face turned in our direction.

"That's him!" Maizy gunned it, sending up a spray of dirt and cinders behind us.

I grabbed for the dash. "Who? Who is it?"

"Gilbert Gleason!" She peeled out onto the blacktop and took off after the van. "I bet he's going home. Talk about luck!"

I could talk about a lot of things, but luck wasn't one of them. "How do you know it's him?"

"I recognize him." She tossed her pen onto the dashboard. "Bar association photo. News article about the disbarment. You don't think I waste time sleeping all night, do you?"

Certainly not. I'd spent the night with her.

"Let him go," I said. "We know where he lives. We'll talk to him another time."

"*This* is another time," she said. "The universe wants us to talk to him tonight. Didn't you see how guilty he looked? I bet he'd confess if we gave him a little nudge."

I narrowed my eyes. "Define nudge."

"Make him think we've got something on him," she said. "Make him sweat."

"That sounds dangerous," I said. "Especially if he *did* kill Nicky D." And by the way, when had we decided that he had? Sometimes Maizy's reasoning gave me whiplash.

"Danger is relative," she said. "A peanut is dangerous if you're allergic. Where'd he go?"

She stomped harder on the gas, and the Escort leaped forward like an arthritic deer. "You really need a new car. We should've caught up to him by now. He was only doing like five miles an hour."

I stared out into the darkness. "I don't see anything. Maybe he took a shortcut."

"Good thing we know where he's headed," Maizy said.

Oh, no. Not the Whispering Pines Mobile Park. Anywhere but there.

I had a flash of inspiration and doubled over, clutching my belly. "I think I'm going to be sick."

"You're just saying that." Maizy switched off the headlights. It was like being summarily dumped head first into an oil vat.

My pulse hammered in my neck as I sat up. "What'd you do that for?"

"So I can see." She hung over the wheel like a vulture. "Feeling better already?"

I crossed my arms. "Fine. If you insist on going back to the trailer park, let's just get it over with so we can put an end to this dismal failure of a night."

"That's the spirit," she said cheerfully. "Now if I could just see—"

Suddenly a big white box loomed out of the darkness right in our path. It took a second to recognize the van, straddling the road. Immediately Maizy yanked the wheel hard to the left. The Escort went into a sickening fishtail, lurched off the pavement onto the sandy shoulder, and died.

"I thought you turned off the lights so you could see!" I yelled.

Maizy shrugged. "I miscalculated."

Gilbert Gleason leaped from the van and raced toward us, cackling madly. My first thought was *Albert Einstein is a very bad driver.* That didn't make any sense, so I refocused while he pounded on the Escort's windshield. My next thought was *Albert Einstein is a very bad driver.* I couldn't help it. Gleason's hair was white, wiry, wild, and too long. His mustache was white, wiry, wild, and too bushy. His nose was a little too large. It wouldn't have surprised me if he'd started reciting the theory of relativity.

"Hey!" Maizy yelled. "Hey! He's beating up your car!"

Gleason abruptly stopped pounding. He leaned closer to the glass to stare in at us with wild eyes. "You thought you'd get away with it, didn't you?" he shouted.

"What's he talking about?" Maizy asked.

I didn't want to make eye contact, but I couldn't look away. "No idea. This is the guy whose trailer you wanted to break into?"

Maizy shrugged. "Who knew he was a few nanoparticles short of a quantum dot?"

I thought *everyone* knew that.

"Lock your door," I said.

"You should sue him," Maizy said. "He's going to dent your hood if he keeps that up."

"He killed my car!" I shouted.

"Is all the drama really necessary?" Maizy asked.

Gilbert was still ranting. "When is it enough?" he yelled. He was getting worked up again; I saw his hands bunching into fists ahead of another windshield pummeling.

"Where's the nearest urgent care center?" Maizy asked. "We have to document some personal injuries to support our lawsuit. You should know this stuff."

"Just start the car," I said. "Let's get out of here before he breaks the glass."

She started the car and stomped on the gas. Nothing.

"Stop messing around," I said.

"I'm not," Maizy said. "We must be stuck in the sand. I *knew* this would happen if some demented ex-lawyer forced us off the road. I just always figured it'd be Wally."

Gleason leaned close to the windshield again, shaking his head and waggling his index finger back and forth at us. "You're not getting away from me that easily!"

"We need to weaponize," Maizy muttered.

"I'm pretty sure there's an armory in my trunk," I said.

"Let me rephrase," she said. "We need to weaponize without getting out of the car. What've you got?"

"Anxiety," I said. "High blood pressure. Cramps."

She just looked at me.

"Well, what've *you* got?" I asked peevishly.

Gleason started pacing back and forth, waving his arms wildly. "It's never enough! You want me to open a vein?" He spun toward us, arms extended, palms up. "You want blood? Is that it? You want *blood*?"

Maizy watched him raptly. "This guy is seriously skewed."

"Why are you doing this?" Gleason yelled. "It's not my fault! I told you it's not my fault!"

Maizy did a calm-down air pat. "Okay," she yelled back. "It's not your fault! *Doofus*," she muttered.

"Not helpful, Maize," I told her. "Don't antagonize him. We have to find something to protect ourselves."

"Are you open to improvisation?" she asked.

"I'll sue you!" he shouted. "I'm still allowed to do that much!"

Maizy snorted. "That's rich. *He's* going to sue *us*?"

I'd seen it before. He'd find some bottom-feeding lawyer somewhere who'd be willing to front him the filing fee to clog up the court docket. With my luck that bottom feeder would be named Wally Randall.

"Why's he so agitated with us?" I asked. "He couldn't have even known we were following him."

"It's probably a misdirected expression of hostility vis a vis erectile dysfunction," Maizy said.

I looked at her. "Yeah. That must be it." I snapped my fingers as a thought occurred to me. "That morning star you bought from Herbie Hairston, is it still in the trunk?"

"Do you really need to ask?" she said.

I speared the air with my finger. "I *knew* it! Why do you always have to keep your psycho starter kit in *my* car?"

"You never know when you're going to need a ball gag and a fireplace poker," she said calmly.

My jaw went slack.

"Maybe we should just ask him nicely," she said. She rolled down her window, hoisted herself upward to sit on the door, and banged on the roof of the car to get his attention. "Hey, goober! What's your problem?"

That was her idea of *nice*?

Gilbert Gleason paused his screeching medley about jurisprudence and a free press. "I'll sue you!" he yelled. "That's harassment!"

"I'll sue you back!" Maizy yelled. "That's intentional infliction of emotional distress!" She bent sideways to look in at me. "That's a thing, right?"

"Beats me," I said.

"That does it," she said. "I'm nominating you for Employee of the Year."

"Why are you following me?" Gleason yelled. "Haven't you people done enough?" He stormed toward the car.

Maizy pointed a can of spray paint at him. A second later a splotch of lime green appeared on his sweatshirt.

"How much of that did you buy?" I demanded.

She did another sideways bend to show me innocent eyes. "*I* didn't buy any, 'cause I'm underaged. That wouldn't be legal." She straightened again, muttering, "And you'd already know if you cleaned your back seat once in a while."

What was the point? It would only get dirty again.

"Hey!" Gleason shouted. "That's battery! I'll sue you for that!"

"It's getting old, dude," Maizy told him.

He wouldn't be stopped. "I'll throw in harassment, too. You'll be facing some pretty stiff fines, I can tell you *that*!"

Well, that wouldn't be good. I couldn't afford fines, stiff or otherwise.

"Chill," Maizy said. "We only wanted to ask you some questions."

That stopped him cold. His face relaxed, his hands unclenched, and his shoulders dropped away from his earlobes. "About time you showed up," he said.

Maizy slithered out the open window onto the ground. With a sigh, I opened my door and got out, too. We stood at the trunk of the Escort, Gilbert Gleason a few yards away. Maizy slipped the key into the trunk lock but didn't open it; still, I knew she was keeping the morning star option open if things got out of hand. Which gave me a small measure of comfort. Not as much comfort as, say, a seven-foot poison-tipped flaming lance, but it would have to do.

"You should have come sooner," Gleason said. "I warned you people a month ago something bad was going to happen, and no one believed me. And now it has." He squinted at the purple stripe in Maizy's hair. "You *are* FBI, right?"

"We're not—" I began.

Maizy shifted a little to stomp on my foot. And not accidentally, either. I knew that because she elbowed me at the same time.

"The hair threw you, right?" she asked. "It's part of a new initiative at the DOJ. About Nicky D's murder."

"What?" His eyes got comically wide. "Nicky D was murdered?"

"That was impressive," Maizy said. "Next time try less exaggeration. You know he was murdered. You just said you warned the Bureau about your plan a month before you carried it out."

"My plan?" he repeated.

"So you admit it," Maizy said. She nudged me. "Go get the camera. I want to film his confession."

"Confession?" he repeated.

"Camera?" I repeated.

"I didn't expect this to be so easy," Maizy told me. She turned back to Gleason. "What happened between you and Nicky D?"

"Nothing happened," Gleason said.

"And then you killed him!" Maizy said.

I frowned at her. She gave me a what'd-I-say? look back.

Clearly it was time for a gentler approach from a more reasoned mind. Unfortunately, Curt wasn't available, so it was up to me.

"You're a lawyer, right?" I asked him.

His face wrinkled as if he'd tasted something sour. "*Was* a lawyer. I had a decent practice before…" He trailed off.

"Before you killed Nicky D and became a fugitive?" Maizy asked. "Tell us all about it."

"Give it a rest," I told her. "Before what?" I asked him.

"Before I represented Virtual Waste," he spat. "It was the worst thing I ever did. And I've done a few questionable things in my life, I promise you that."

"Like killing Nicky D?" Maizy asked.

Enough, already. I jabbed my elbow at her. She made a casual *ole!* move, and I wound up elbowing the car, sending a jolt of pain up my arm, which made me lose track of my searing line of questioning. And pretty much everything else except the thought that I'd better get to the local hospital for some x-rays.

"How did that happen?" I asked through clenched teeth. "Becoming the band's agent?"

"I represented Nick in a personal matter," he said. "Unfortunately, we didn't prevail, but when the band was looking for an agent, they hired me on his recommendation."

"What kind of personal matter?"

"That's irrelevant," he said. "Next question."

Maizy stuck out her chin. "Bet the job description didn't say anything about dropping an amplifier on the drummer's head."

Gleason's mouth twisted. "Is that what happened to him?"

"Like you don't know," Maizy muttered.

"Lighten up," I whispered.

"He's jerking our chain," Maizy whispered back.

"Excuse me," Gleason cut in. "Hello? I can hear you." He shook his head. "The FBI sure has relaxed its standards."

"Let me guess," Maizy said. "He did nicky-nack with your wife."

Gleason stared at her. "Why would you say that?"

"He did nicky-nack with *everyone's* wife," Maizy said. "You just maybe took the revenge thing a little too far. You can admit it. You're among friends."

"I didn't kill him," Gleason said. "But I wish I could send flowers to whoever did. Nick cost me my livelihood and my marriage and my home."

"Yeah, we saw it," Maizy said. "Lovely place."

"Not *that* home," Gleason snapped. "The home where my ex now lives with the pool boy. Twelve rooms and a tennis court on four acres. Everything but a pool."

Geez.

"And that," Gleason added, "is after he made me untouchable *and* stiffed me on my fee. Don't I deserve to be paid for my work?"

I had no experience with that concept, so I kept quiet.

"What does *untouchable* mean?" Maizy asked.

"For all his faults," Gleason said, "and God knows there were many, Nick was media savvy. He slaughtered me. And I didn't realize it was happening until it was too late."

"How'd he cost you your livelihood?" Maizy asked. "Sounds like he gave you a better job than you had chasing ambulances in a graveyard."

"Theft by deception," Gleason said. "That six-figure salary he promised became a couple hundred bucks a month real fast. What'm I going to do with that? I can make more than that staging slip and falls." His face reddened. "I mean, I made more than that cutting grass when I was twelve."

Note to self: price lawn mowers.

"Sounds like you had a lot of grievances with him," Maizy said. "So you killed him, right?"

"Wrong," Gleason said. "I quit. I've got my pride."

Yeah. That was evident in the rattletrap van he drove and the palatial cracker box he now called home.

"That's not what I read," Maizy said. "I read you were fired."

Gleason snorted. "That's ridiculous."

"Then why leave the area?" I asked.

"I didn't," he said. "I took advantage of an offer from a friend to move across the street until the pressure died down."

Maizy and I exchanged glances, and I could tell we were thinking the same thing. The Norman Bates trailer was across the street. The least Gleason could have done was clean up after himself before he left. He'd probably left the toilet seat up, too. No wonder his wife had taken up with the pool boy.

I did a now-what? eyebrow raise.

She shrugged. "I think we're done here. Don't leave the area. We may have some more questions for you."

"Oh, shucks," Gleason said. "I'll have to cancel that trip to St. Tropez."

CHAPTER TWENTY-ONE

———

Five minutes later, after Gleason had driven off, Maizy and I were back in the Escort. The engine was running. The wheels were spinning. We were going nowhere, still stuck in the sand.

"We have to stop doing this," I said.

"Hey, you know what?" Maizy asked. "We never found out why Gleason called the FBI."

"You're right," I said. "Let's get him back and ask him. Then he can push us onto the road."

"Wonder if he filed a police report, too," she said. "I could probably acquire that."

"What about your shovel?" I asked. "It's in the trunk, right? We can dig ourselves out."

She shook her head. "Lent it to someone. He needed it for an important meeting."

That didn't seem like a question I wanted to ask.

Maizy drummed her fingers on the wheel, thinking. "Have you got anything we can put under the back tires for traction?"

"You tell me," I said. "My trunk is your storage unit."

We got out of the car. As soon as we opened the trunk, we heard the rumble of an approaching motorcycle. Immediately I closed it again. There were things in my trunk best left unseen, even if I wasn't sure what they were.

Seconds later, a hulking mass of black and chrome rumbled to a liver-quivering stop behind my car, its headlight pinning us against the trunk like butterflies to a bulletin board.

Maizy yelled, "Bryn!"

I took a closer look. "Bryn?" How did she always manage to turn up at opportune moments?

"She's *fierce*!" Maizy whispered. Clearly she was full-on awestruck. It irked me. Throw a little training and forty pounds on me, I could be fierce, too. Although I'd have to lose that perfectly rational fear of spiders. And learn to ride a Harley. Maybe get a few tattoos and buy some leather pants. Of course, leather pants and Walmart sneakers didn't go together, so I'd have to add biker boots, and I didn't think Howard paid me enough for leather pants *and* biker boots. Plus a ratty tee didn't exactly complement the whole leather ensemble, so I'd have to spring for one of those leather vests and probably a leather jacket, too.

Oh, forget it. I didn't have the budget for *fierce.* I could only afford *ill-tempered.* I didn't need an expensive leather wardrobe for *ill-tempered.* I could manage that stark naked.

Bryn lowered the kickstand, removed her helmet, hung it on the handlebars, and got off the bike. "Hello, Alana." She nodded at me. "Hortense."

And that was another thing. *Hortense* wasn't a fierce name. I'd have to pretend to be a Rocky or a Rusty instead, and that was bound to get confusing.

"Is everything okay?" Bryn asked. "Did you have an accident?"

I shuddered, remembering Gilbert Gleason's van in the middle of the street. "Almost," I said.

"We were tailing a suspect," Maizy said. "He made a countermove."

Countermove. Much better than admitting she'd driven off the road.

Bryn grabbed her by both shoulders and looked at her hard. "Did he hurt you?"

Maizy shook her head. "I'm indomitable," she said. "But the car's stuck in the sand."

"That's not a problem," Bryn said. "I've got a few minutes to help you out. I was just on my way home to my boyfriend's place anyway. The important thing is that you two are safe."

Standing there to the side, watching the two of them bonding, feeling as awkward as I had in high school, why didn't that *feel* like the important thing?

"Who was it, anyway?" Bryn asked.

"The band's old agent." Maizy pulled the key out of the trunk lock. "I'll get in and steer."

Bryn's eyebrow arched. "Gilbert Gleason's back in town?"

"He says he never left," Maizy said. "He squatted in a neighbor's place for a while. You push, okay?"

"That sounds like Gil." Bryn shook her head. "He's a piece of work."

Gil?

"Do you know him?" I asked.

"Not well," Bryn said. "He and my uncle knew each other for years from bar association functions, but I mainly saw him at the band's gigs. I know he didn't have much experience with agenting. They weren't very happy with him. That's how Uncle Doug got his job."

Maizy tapped impatiently on the trunk.

"Was Gil fired?" I asked. "Or did he quit?"

"Fired, I think," she said. "After he got disbarred."

"What do you know about the disbarment?" I asked.

"Hel-*lo!*" Maizy said. "While two of us are young?"

Bryn's face clouded. "I heard he slept with a client, that's all. He blamed Nicky D for being fired, but let's face it—Gil wasn't the spark Virtual Waste needed anyway." She paused. "I can tell you two are really serious about this. Can I help?"

"Yes," Maizy said. "You can help right now. How about a push?"

"We'll keep it in mind," I said. "But we usually work solo." And sometimes with Curt. Once with Eunice. Generally speaking, I liked as few witnesses as possible.

"Well, keep me in mind." Bryn turned her attention on the car, its back tires mired in the soft sand. "This doesn't look too bad. Let's see what I can do." She moved behind the car, bent to grab the bumper, hoisted the whole rear of the car into the air with a lot of groaning and creaking (from the car, not from Bryn), hauled it a few yards to the right, and put it down again with the rear wheels sitting on asphalt. "There." She brushed her hands together and smiled brightly. "Anything else I can help you with?"

I gaped at her.

"Fierce!" Maizy whispered. "That ought to do it," she said. "Thanks a lot. I'll catch you at the Pinelands next weekend."

Bryn gave us a wave, climbed onto her bike, kick-started it into life, did a tight U-turn, and roared away.

"Did I mention Bryn rocks?" Maizy asked as we got back in the car.

Too many times. Only this time, I had to agree.

CHAPTER TWENTY-TWO

"What do you believe when you don't believe anything?" I asked on Friday night. Curt and I sat at his kitchen table, sharing a fettuccini dinner with meatballs and garlic bread. A summer thunderstorm pounded at the windows. It was my first chance to fill Curt in on what I'd learned or, more appropriately, what I hadn't learned. This is what we did. I went out and made a mess, and then I brought it home for Curt to help me sort it out while he fed me. It was a pretty good system.

"I'm guessing that's not an existential question." Curt tore the last slice of garlic bread in two and put half on my plate. "What's on your mind?"

I shook my head. "The more people I talk to, the less I know. They're all lying to us. They all had a reason to want Nicky D dead. The question is who wanted it the most."

"Look at it another way," he said. "Who do you least suspect?"

I thought about it. "I suspect everyone."

He grinned. "And you suspect no one?"

"I wouldn't say that. *Someone* did it." I forked into my pasta. "You know more about the guys in the band than I do. What do *you* think?"

He ran a napkin across his lips. "I don't know how Virtual Waste stays together. Bones barely talks at all, to anyone. Plop wanders off on his own half the time talking to invisible friends. By the way, that bandana? He's a Tony Stewart fan."

That told me exactly nothing.

Curt noticed my expression. "NASCAR driver? Number 20?"

"Oh, yeah." I nodded. "Him."

He grinned at me. "TJ is always off in a corner, writing songs. And Mike." He quartered a meatball and sprinkled grated cheese on it. "I can't get a handle on him, other than he doesn't seem to like the guys in the band. And then there's that Archibald Dougal Ritz guy."

I looked up. "You've met him?"

He nodded. "He came to a rehearsal. At first he seemed perfectly normal. But he *cries*." His expression darkened.

"There's nothing wrong with a man who cries," I said. "It means he's sensitive." I hesitated. "What did he cry about?"

"What *didn't* he cry about," Curt muttered.

We ate in silence for a few minutes.

"Tell you the truth," Curt said finally, "I felt kind of bad for him. He's a widower, and I got the impression he doesn't have much in his life besides his work. Anyway, he's certainly been devoted to the band since he came on board. Maybe that's why Mike seems to really like him."

"Unlike Gilbert Gleason." I shook my head. "What an oddball bunch."

"And we haven't even mentioned Hank," Curt said.

That reminded me. "You know he was at the Golden Grotto. Inside, I mean. He was watching Susan One." I swallowed. "Susan One was watching you."

"You don't have to be jealous." He winked. "I don't date octopi."

"That's Susan Two," I said.

"Okay. Then I don't date Susans."

"I know that," I said irritably. "But does Hank?"

"I'm not worried about Hank," he said placidly. "I'm more worried about how you look in black silk."

My fettuccini almost got stuck halfway down my throat. Which didn't really matter because I had absolutely no idea what to say to that. Pretty sure that was my opening to come back with something flip and sophisticated, but all that came to me was "Urrggh?"

"One of these days," Curt went on, "you're going to shock me and show up wearing that little number, without the robe."

"One of these days" could have come and gone, and he wouldn't have known it. Too busy having a life when he could have been home, having—well…just *home*.

"You probably won't be here when I do," I said. "You'll be catering to your fan club."

He chuckled. "What fan club?"

"The octopi," I said hotly. "I can't compete with women like that."

His smile fell away. "You don't have to compete with anyone. You just have to call me."

My face grew hot. "And tell you what? Come home, big boy. I'm waiting at your back door in a little black nothing?"

"Yes, Jamie," he said. "That's all you have to do."

Oh.

I looked away, afraid my head might burst into flames from embarrassment. That must be the feminine power I'd heard so much about. Guess I had a little after all, and I hadn't even realized it. Even if I had, I never would have had the self-assurance to make that call, or the confidence to wait for him.

"Jamie," he said softly.

"It's just as well," I said.

"No, it isn't." He cupped the back of my head very lightly, and electricity sizzled southward. "Look at me."

"I'm out of moisturizer," I said. I'd have to remember to buy some…what was it again? Oh, right. Moisturizer.

"Look at me," he repeated, his voice a delicious vibration through my body.

I looked at him. "I'm sorry."

"Don't be." He stroked my hair. I pushed my head against his hand, the way Ashley did when she was being petted.

Thunder growled outside, followed by a vicious whip snap of lightning.

Curt slipped one finger under my chin to lift my face. "When you're ready," he said, "make the call."

CHAPTER TWENTY-THREE

———

Eunice waited for me outside the office on Monday morning. It was cooler but raining a little, the drops silvering the top of her head. She wore a shapeless beige raincoat that rustled when she rushed to open my car door. "Jamie, I need your help."

It took some work to get out of the car. I'd gone a little too far with the yoga, or whatever that was I'd been trying to do before I went to bed. I must have tweaked a kidney.

Eunice followed me inside. "You're a woman of the world, right?"

"Oh sure," I said.

"I'm having Hank over to dinner this weekend." She pulled out a lace hankie, patted the top of her head dry, and then pressed the wet hankie to her cheeks and forehead.

"That's good, right?" I said. "That's what you wanted."

"I thought so." She put away the hankie and began gnawing on her thumbnail. "But to be honest, I don't know if I can handle that much man. I'm not as sophisticated as I may seem."

"I don't think Hank's looking for sophistication," I said. "He seems more like a mud wrestling kind of guy." I thought about Hank watching Susan One watching Curt onstage at the Golden Grotto. Something told me Hank wasn't in the market for another girlfriend. But you never knew. Under all that grease, grime, and grimness, Hank might be a giant lovebug. Or he might be looking for a little tit for tat against Susan One. I didn't want Eunice to be his tit-for-tat tool. But I also didn't want to burst her bubble. After all, life played out in strange ways.

She switched to the other thumb. "I know Hank's not in the same league as Curt. But he might be the best I can do."

"I don't know about that," I said. "Don't sell yourself short. You're almost a lawyer, after all."

Her smile was as weak and fleeting as a peek of sun in the eye of a hurricane.

Something tugged in the vicinity of my heart. "What's going on, Eunice? Aren't you used to dating?"

"You could say that." She dropped both hands into her lap, where her fingers coiled and twisted around each other like small flesh-colored snakes. "I've never had a date."

My jaw went slack. "When you say never—"

"The opportunity never came up," she said. "I used to tell myself it was because some men are put off by career women, but let's face it, I'm not cover girl material." She sighed. "I guess I'm just looking for some advice. I've never seduced a man before."

She'd come to exactly the wrong place.

"Maybe you want to take it slow with Hank," I said. "Cook him dinner but then send him home. Make him want to come back again. Free milk and the cow, remember?"

She thought about it. "Am I the milk or the cow?"

"Don't overthink this," I said. "You'll be fine. You've got gravy, right?"

She brightened. "That's true. I do make fabulous gravy."

"Problem solved." I powered up my computer and turned to the files Wally had left for me. The usual assortment of Requests for Production and Complaints, a couple of Notices of Deposition. Forget courtroom drama. *This* was the real excitement of the legal world.

Wally came clicking in from the kitchen on knees wobbled by a semester of college football bench warming, dressed for Casual Friday and missing the point entirely in a double-breasted black suit, starchy white shirt, cobalt blue tie, and shiny black wingtips. The blond in his hair inspired by my sister Sherri had mostly grown out, and the orange-bronze makeup and guyliner inspired by the Mary Kay rep whom he'd dated after Sherri was gone. Which wasn't to say Wally was now handsome, but he *was* highly suggestible.

He lowered his Ray-Bans to mid nose and peered at us over the top of them. "Morning," he said in a way that was more statement than greeting. He turned to Eunice. "You're just the alleged investigator I wanted to see. Is our grievously wounded defendant hitting the dance clubs?"

Actually, yes, but for stalking, not dancing.

Eunice went pale and wobbled a little on the chair.

"She's working on it," I said. "We had a little trouble finding his house."

"Well, he has to live somewhere." No wonder Wally had made it all the way to Boy Lawyer. "What's your plan?"

"My plan?" Eunice repeated. She shot me a look of pure desperation.

I knew she didn't want to hand Hank over to a pack of legal jackals. Or to Howard and Wally.

"We're going to keep looking," I said. "Maybe we were on the wrong street. It's hard to read the signs."

"That's what we're doing," Eunice agreed.

Wally's frown encompassed both of us. "Well, do it fast. Howard wants to get this case moving."

Little beads of sweat dotted Eunice's forehead.

"We'll have a photo album for you by next week," I said.

"See that you do." Wally pointed his sunglasses at each of us in turn then pivoted sharply and headed upstairs.

Eunice's whole upper body sagged. "I'll get fired for sure if I don't get some pictures of Hank."

I thought about it. I was pretty sure Maizy would have a spymaster's tool kit in her arsenal, complete with telephoto lens. "Maizy and I will help you get your pictures. We have a meeting scheduled for Thursday night near there. You can come if you want."

"And Curt?" she asked hopefully.

"Curt can't make it this time," I said. Maizy claimed she wanted to talk to Miranda Law, the client who had precipitated Gilbert Gleason's career cliff dive, but things were rarely what they seemed with Maizy. I was convinced she had something else in mind, and if I was right, maybe I could distract her from it by arranging Hank's photo spread.

CHAPTER TWENTY-FOUR

———

The phone rang just before lunchtime, while I was in the middle of one of Wally's classic Wally Complaints. The plaintiff, proud owner of a brand new $40,000 Lexus, had applied very dark limousine tint to the windows, which was all well and good, until the moonless night when he'd parked in a dimly lit parking garage for a visit to his girlfriend's apartment. That visit had culminated in a heated argument and the plaintiff's hasty exit at midnight, at which time he'd backed both out of his spot and the garage itself since he'd had the visibility of a pilot in a haboob. Unfortunately, he'd parked on the fourth floor of the garage. Now Wally was suing the city for its shortsighted placement of a fire hydrant on the sidewalk below, along with the manufacturer of the tint as well as the installer, the girlfriend for dating an idiot, and the owner of the parking garage for failing to anticipate that one night some dimwit might use his facility as a runway.

Missy tapped the Hold button and cradled the phone. "Maizy's on the line."

I finished typing out the last few lines of Count III before taking the call.

"*Finally*," Maizy said. "I've been on hold for-*ever*. You've got to change that music, dude. What is that, Mantovani or something? I think it gave me blue hair just listening to it. *God*."

"You already had blue hair," I said. "What's up?"

"Have you taken your lunch break?"

On cue, my belly growled. "Not yet." But I had it all worked out. Takeout chicken parm from Giorgio's. If I played my cards right, I'd have enough left over for a night of weight gaining and channel surfing with Ashley.

I heard the kitchen door open and close.

"I've been thinking about Archie Ritz," Maizy said. "Everyone's pointing fingers at everyone else except Archie. Why do you think that is?"

"Because he's innocent?"

"There are no innocents," Maizy said. "Only suspects we haven't found yet. Maybe he's threatened everyone against dropping a dime on him."

"You're watching too much TV again," I told her.

"Possibly. But I still think we should talk to him. Thing is, he won't take my call. As soon as I said Nicky D's name, he hung up on me."

Wish I'd done the same.

"It's time for Plan B," Maizy said. "Hey, are there any saltine crackers in this place? I've got wicked heartburn."

"Wait," I said. "What do you mean 'in this place'? Where are you?"

"I'm in the kitchen," she said. "If you want to call it that. *Kitchen* usually implies food. There's no food here. Wait, here's a brown bag in the fridge."

"Don't touch that," I said. "That's Donna's lunch."

I heard rustling. "Smells like seafood," Maizy said. "I can't eat seafood anyway." More rustling, presumably as she rolled up the bag and put it back in the fridge. "Hey, are these Oreos?"

"Don't eat the Oreos!" I practically yelled. "They belong to Janice."

"You know that's called 'hoarding,'" Maizy said. "It's a whole psychological thing. They make shows about it and all."

"What do you want, Maizy?"

"I've got an idea," she said.

I knew I wasn't going to like it the minute she waddled into the room, her belly arriving three seconds before the rest of her thanks to the ginormous pregnancy pad under her maternity shirt. Clutching her low back, leaning at a forty-five-degree angle to compensate for the frontal overhang, she made her way to the empty desk across the room. After some groaning and sighing, she wedged herself into the chair. "I feel like an elephant. I must be retaining water. *God.*"

Missy's mouth fell open.

I eyed the hugely rounded mound. "Guess it's too late for The Talk."

"It's part of my plan." Grimacing, she put a hand behind her. "My back is killing me. This kid had better show up soon."

"You're not pregnant, Maizy." I hesitated. "Are you?"

"Not by the standard definition," she said.

"Is there another?" Missy asked.

My eye was twitching.

"Depends on your perspective." Maizy swung her legs up onto the desk. "Do my ankles look swollen to you?"

Hard to tell since they were encased in Doc Martens, giving her a weird Knocked Up G.I. Barbie vibe.

"That'll happen when you're fourteen months pregnant," Missy said.

Maizy looked down at her massive belly. "I'm just small boned. Here's the story. Nicky D took advantage of a young innocent girl and ran off after impregnating her. We have no choice but to go to Archie Ritz about this."

"Seriously?" I asked. "You couldn't have just made an appointment to talk with him?"

"I want to throw him off balance," she said. "You know how slippery lawyers can be when you give them time to prep."

"This ought to do it," I told her.

Missy chuckled.

The clock hit noon. I got up. "Good luck with that."

"What do you mean?" Maizy flattened her palms on the desk and leveraged herself out of the chair. "You have to come with me. You're my outraged mother threatening to sue the entire band."

I rolled my eyes. "Again, I'm the mother."

"Outraged mother," she repeated, louder. "Threatening to sue the entire band."

"Yeah, I got it the first time." I got my handbag from the bottom drawer. Missy kept staring at Maizy with an expression of one part sympathy, three parts incredulous.

"Go with her," Missy told me. "I'll cover for you. I've *got* to hear how this turns out."

I already knew. Not well.

"I've got a Caddy," Maizy said. "But only for a couple of hours. I promised Honest Aaron I'd ditch it at the airport before five. Oh, and it's probably best if you don't look in the back seat."

Been there, done that. Never again. I still had nightmares about it. "We'll use my car," I said.

"Yeah, right." She snorted. "*That'll* be believable."

I pointed at her hyperinflated belly. "You think *that's* believable?"

"It's the miracle of life," Maizy said breezily. She grabbed my sleeve. "Wait a minute. I need to pee. I swear this kid is sitting right on my bladder."

I opened my mouth and closed it again. That pretty much said it all.

CHAPTER TWENTY-FIVE

———

There were lawyers, and there were lawyers. Wally and Howard fell into the first category. Starched white shirts, polished wingtips, plenty of ego.

Archibald Dougal Ritz fell into the second. He was the human equivalent of a funhouse. For one thing, in eleven vertical inches of head, he had about three inches of actual face. His features were all packed together in a caricaturist's dream. Small eyes, pug nose, small round mouth, crammed beneath bushy eyebrows and layered stacks of white blond hair adding another three inches of height. I guessed him to be somewhere in his seventies, although he was in good shape for that age. Archie had been around the courthouse a few times, and it was clear that somewhere along the way, he'd planted his own flag. Instead of the traditional uniform of navy pinstripes, his wardrobe was by Crayola: hot pink sport coat with pink and green plaid pants. It wouldn't have surprised me a bit if he'd been wearing fuzzy bunny slippers. It was disappointing to see his tennis shoes, with neon green laces.

His office was less flamboyant. White walls, sand-colored Berber carpet, nondescript furniture, a couple of beige filing cabinets. An oak credenza behind his desk held a gold trophy, probably an ode to his golf game or some obscure bowling championship, a small crystal globe with a silver plaque affixed to its base, little bronze tennis rackets standing crisscrossed on a black base, and my personal favorite, a brightly colored toy-sized race car in a glass case. Alongside this homage to his athletic youth sat an array of family photos: A man in a Navy uniform. A woman in the Marine dress blues. Archie locked in a tearful embrace with an older bottled blonde woman, presumably his wife, with his arm slung around a man who bore a strong resemblance to the blonde, both gazing wetly into the camera, with his hands resting on the shoulders of two young girls holding frothy pink cotton candy while he wept gently upon their heads.

Good grief.

My attention lingered on that last photo for a moment. The girls were clearly sisters, probably the daughters of the small-featured man, but they'd escaped with a favorable face-to-head ratio. One wore a frilly white dress with a pink belt. Sparkling pink combs corralled her curls. She stood hand on hip, left foot angled prettily in front of the right. The other stood flat-footed and almost grim-faced in denim shorts and a baggy Speed Racer T-shirt, her hair scraped back in a high ponytail. It reminded me of my sister Sherri and me and how different two sisters could be.

The office lacked the visual impact of Parker Dennis, but it also lacked Howard and Wally, so it had *that* going for it. The overall effect was eminently forgettable, except for one feature. A giant stuffed brown bear towered on his hind legs in the corner, mouth frozen open in an eternal growl. Under a gray fedora.

Maizy took it in first with an expression of horror then one of deep disgust. "What'd he ever do to you?" she demanded.

Archie's tiny features reflected surprise. "I'm sorry?"

"You said it, not me." Maizy crossed her arms, her fingers drumming furiously on her forearms. "Give *him* a gun. *Then* we'll see what's what," she muttered.

I could already see this might not end well. Imagine my surprise.

"He came with the office," Archie said. His eyes seemed shiny. Was he crying?

"Like I haven't heard *that* before," Maizy fumed.

Archie Ritz perched on the edge of the desk, flicking a teary and uncertain glance my way.

"Pregnancy hormones," I said. "My daughter's usually very sweet."

Maizy bared her teeth at him.

"Yes. Well." He dabbed at his eyes while letting his gaze flick down to Maizy's belly and up again. "Please sit down, ladies."

I sat down. Maizy performed a parallel bars routine, grabbing the arms of the chair, simultaneously lowering herself and leaning backwards to accommodate her Hitchcockian girth while her legs went straight out in front of her, so that for a few impressive seconds she was suspended in midair, supported on her locked arms. I think they call it pike position.

When she'd stuck the landing, Archie tucked away his hanky and cleared his throat. "When you phoned, you mentioned that Mr. DiBenedetto…um…"

"Knocked me up," Maizy said. "You can say it. She knows."

His funhouse face swiveled my way.

"I know what you're thinking," I told him. "How could I possibly have a teenaged daughter when I'm only twenty-five myself."

Maizy snorted. "You forgot about ten years."

"I certainly did not," I said, indignant.

She rubbed her fake belly serenely. "So you had me at eight?"

The phone rang while I was sliding her a skin-melting glance.

He picked it up with a frown. "Doug speaking."

I looked beyond Maizy to the diplomas on the wall. Archibald Dougal Ritz had attended all the best schools. University of Podunk for undergrad. Hicksville Law School. Another shining star of the New Jersey Bar.

Maizy pounced as soon as he ended his call. "We're a very litigious family. Suing people is practically our family business. And we're going to sue the pants off you." She stared at his pants. "Well, maybe not off *you*, exactly. Your client."

"He can't seem to keep them on anyway," I said.

Maizy grinned at me. "Good one."

That was more like it.

Archie sniffled and reached for his hanky again. "Not another one."

"Another one?" I repeated. "You mean he's done this before?"

"I really can't discuss this." He blew his nose. "It would violate attorney/client confidentiality."

"But he's *dead*," Maizy said.

Archie sniffled and shook his head. "I'm sorry, but the confidentiality survives his death."

Just our luck. A lawyer with ethics. And possibly a summer cold.

"I'm sorry, too," Maizy said. "Let me tell you something." She tried to leverage herself out of the chair, but like Winnie the Pooh and the honey jar, it was easier getting in than out. The pad was wider than she was, and she wound up suspended on it four inches above the seat. Unfortunately, that hoisted everything upward so that she now appeared to have an esophageal pregnancy.

Archie had temporarily run dry. "Are you alright?"

"Why do you ask?" Maizy flattened both hands over her ribs and slid the pad down an inch or two. She rested her chin on top.

Archie glanced at me. I stared at my knees.

"But your belly," he said. "It *moved*."

Maizy blinked. "Did it? I hadn't noticed."

"Can we get back to the suing?" I said. "My daughter is a minor, Mr. Ritz. I'm sure you understand the ramifications of that. It would be a messy story if the newspapers got ahold of it."

Something flashed across Archie's tiny placid features. "Just a minute now."

"She's right," Maizy said. "This story's got legs. After all, I'm practically an orphan. I mean, sure, my mom is here *now*, but that's only because she smells money. Where was she when I was a ten-year-old sophomore, when I could have used her support?"

Hey, wait a minute.

Archie's eyes were damp again. "*Ten*-year-old sophomore?"

"When I could have used her support," Maizy repeated.

His wet gaze shifted to me.

"She was in AP kindergarten," I told him. "Very gifted."

"She should have been helping me prepare for my SATs," Maizy said, "but *no*, she was busy dancing on tables for lonely men near the airport."

Heat flooded my face. I'd just *known* something like this would happen. I practically had tire marks on my back, the bus had run over me so many times. *When* would I learn?

Archie's gaze flickered back to me. "Surely not."

This was doing magical things for my self-esteem.

"Would I lie to you?" Maizy asked. "But that was just nights. During the day, she chased the tour."

"Golf?" The clouds parted, and Archie's mini-face brightened at the mention of golf. "What's your handicap?"

I couldn't help it. I jacked my thumb in Maizy's direction. "Her."

Maizy pounced immediately. "See what I mean? Is it any wonder I turned out the way I did?"

I wondered every day.

"You poor child." Tears glittered in his eyes. He dabbed the hanky on his lashes and snuffled. By now that thing was wet enough to wash dishes. "What a tragic upbringing."

Oh, for Pete's sake.

"Don't pity me," Maizy said. "Help me. What do you know about Nicky D's death?"

Archie folded his hanky, tucked it away, crossed his legs, and clasped his knee with both gnarled hands. "It's not quite clear."

What was unclear about being gonged in the head with an amplifier?

Maizy's eyes got huge and wet and her lower lip trembled. How did she *do* that? More importantly, could she teach *me*? That could be a useful skill. "Were you there when it happened? Like maybe standing at the bar talking to Mike Crescenzo between sets?"

He frowned. "Not at all. I'd left long before the first set ended."

"Are you sure?" I asked him. "He seemed positive about it."

"Did he?" Archie drummed on his knee, thinking. "It's possible," he said finally. "When you get to be my age, you tend to become forgetful."

"Did you have to wait for him?" I asked. "Or did he go to the bar right from the stage?"

"I may have had to wait a minute or two," Archie said. "I'm sure he shook some hands along the way."

"Did he change his shirt along the way, too?" Maizy asked.

Archie blinked. "Why on earth would he do that?"

"Because of the bloodstains," Maizy said. "Duh."

Subtle.

"He might have removed his blazer," Archie said. "It was quite warm in there. But I'm certain I would have noticed bloodstains."

"Not if they were on the blazer," Maizy said.

Archie studied her for a moment before tipping his head in acknowledgment. He hesitated. "Forgive me, but it's not healthy for a woman in your condition to concern yourself with such a morbid subject."

"What condition is that?" Maizy asked.

Archie waggled his fingers gently in the direction of her belly.

She rolled her eyes. "Join the twenty-first century, Grandpa. We've got electricity and everything now."

A tear rolled down his cheek. Great. Now she'd gone and hurt his feelings.

"That morbid subject was the father of her child," I said gently. "It's only natural to wonder what happened to him."

He sniffled. "Of course. Well, I really wasn't there for long. I'd spent the day in meetings preparing for a church function, and I had to catch up on some paperwork the next morning. I'm a busy man with a thriving practice."

Sure. You could tell by the desk that was as empty as my skill set.

"Have you got indoor plumbing?" Maizy asked suddenly. "It's kind of an emergency."

Archie practically leaped off the desk to throw open the door. "Through the outer office, down the hall to your left."

Maizy wriggled and squirmed. Her ginormous pregnancy pad did not. It was cemented between the arms of the chair.

"What are you doing?" I whispered.

"Little help here?" she whispered back. "I'm stuck."

Oh, boy. I stood and grabbed her arms. It took a few tries and some rocking back and forth and a vow never to do this again before I hauled her to her feet and she tottered off to the bathroom.

Archie closed the door behind her, circled his desk, and sat down. I sat down. We looked at each other for a moment.

"I'm sorry for your predicament," he said finally.

"Thank you." I smiled. "It's not the best job in the world, but it pays the bills. Well, some of them, anyway. I mean, I don't have a car built in the last couple of decades, and I stole my cat, but no one's life is perfect, right?"

He stared at me. "With your daughter."

Oh.

We looked at each other some more. I wasn't great at small talk, but I'd never felt comfortable with silence. Still, probably the less said, the better, but I couldn't help myself.

"I met your predecessor recently," I said. "Gilbert Gleason."

Archie nodded. "Interesting fellow."

Interesting. That was one word. *Unhinged* would be another.

"Were you aware of his firing?" Gleason had played the I-quit card, but I didn't buy that for a second. It had "saving face" written all over it, especially after I'd seen him in action.

"I knew he'd been disbarred for having relations with his client." He shook his head. "I wish I could say his lack of discipline surprised me."

It had sure surprised *me.* "What do you mean?"

"I'm sure you've heard the term loose cannon." His eyes flicked to the door and, presumably, beyond it, through the front office and down the hall to Maizy. I felt a bristle of annoyance at the implication. "You could say I profited from the man's misfortune, so it might be hitting him when he's down..." He paused.

"But?" I prompted him.

"It was for the best. Mr. Gleason was ill equipped to deal with the group's internal machinations."

"You mean like Nicky D's shameless promiscuity?" Where had that come from? You'd think he really *had* impregnated my daughter.

A tear of sympathy moistened his eyes. "That, among other things."

"Let's stick with *that*." I glanced at my watch. Where was Maizy? "What did the rest of the band think of him?"

"There was consensus," he said. "They recognized that Nicholas was an opportunist and treated him as such. If only those poor young women had done the same." Another tear dropped onto his thigh, leaving a little round wet mark.

"Someone did more than recognize it," I said, thinking aloud.

His lower lip trembled. "It's terrible to say so, but he reaped what he sowed."

Spoken like a geezer, but I took his point. Archie seemed like an old-fashioned, overly emotional gentleman who'd had a front row seat to Nicky D's bad behavior. Despite his goofy wardrobe and Picasso features and inconvenient ethics, I kind of liked Archie Ritz. He reminded me of Ken Parker, without the sleeping disorder.

Someone yelled, "Mom!" from a close distance.

I reflected on reaping and sowing.

"Let's go, Mom!"

"Isn't that your daughter?" Archie asked.

Oh. Right. My daughter.

"I forgot she has a Lamaze class today." I scrambled out of the chair.

"You'll be late for your Botox injections!" Maizy yelled.

Archie and I looked at each other while I felt a surge of embarrassment heating my cheeks. "I don't actually… I mean, I don't have any… I'm much too young for—"

His eyes glistened. "I understand," he said. "Go tend to your child."

I went.

CHAPTER TWENTY-SIX

———

"Did you have to say that?" I demanded. "I was just getting him to open up!"

"If he'd opened up any more, I wouldn't need a shower tonight," Maizy said. "That man cries more than my Grammy Agnes. And let me tell you, that woman can cry."

"You don't have a Grammy Agnes," I said.

"Not anymore," she agreed. "You've heard that expression 'Cry me a river,' right? Well, she did, and off she went."

I rolled my eyes. "Don't be so dismissive. There's nothing wrong with a man who cries."

"Nothing right with it, either," she muttered. She was quiet, navigating the giant Caddy onto Route 206. "Check out the front pocket of my backpack," she said after a moment.

I shielded my eyes and felt around the back seat until my hand closed on the strap. I hauled it into my lap, unzipped the pocket, and pulled out a sheet of paper. "What is this?"

"You're kidding, right?" she asked.

It was the first page of a Complaint. Thomas John Pope, plaintiff, v. Nicholas Owen DiBenedetto, defendant.

I looked up. "TJ and Nicky D?"

She nodded. "I read the whole thing while you were schmoozing the Weeper. TJ was suing him for theft of intellectual property. So that thing he said about just writing more songs? Not so much."

"How'd you get this?" I asked. "Were you going through his files?"

"Of course," she said. "I knew *you* weren't going to do it. You didn't think I really had to use the bathroom, did you? By the way, I could hear everything you guys said. He's a pretty good guy, for a geezer. What'd you think of him?"

"I agree," I said. "And he has ethics."

"He dresses weird," Maizy said, "but he kind of reminds me of my Pa-Pa, you know? A waterlogged version. Anyway, I saw this commercial once with all these old guys who were taking some kind of miracle pill? In, like, two days they were old heads on Dwayne Johnson bodies. Freaky."

"I'd like to see that," I muttered. The Dwayne Johnson part, not the old head part. Dwayne Johnson had it going on.

"Not me." Maizy shuddered. "Too Frankenstein's monster for me. Hey, let me know if you see a bathroom. I need to lose this belly. I'm over it."

We drove on looking for a bathroom. Maizy occasionally shifted to scratch her belly. And her shoulder. And her belly again. "*God*," she said after a while. "How do women *do* this?"

"Do you think the band lied to us about their alibis?" I asked.

She thought about it. "You mean 'cause Archie says he didn't talk to Mike the night Nicky D was killed."

"I mean all of them."

"That's easy," she said. "Yes."

"They couldn't *all* have killed him," I said.

"You don't know that," she said. "But I see your point. All we can do is isolate them from the herd one by one and question them."

That wasn't much of a plan. Bones didn't talk. Plop *couldn't* talk. TJ *wouldn't* talk. And Mike...the jury was out on Mike.

"What else have we got?" Maizy asked.

The answer was absolutely nothing.

CHAPTER TWENTY-SEVEN

——————

I should've eaten more Hershey's Kisses.

On Tuesday night I stood barefoot in my bathroom, despairing over my less than voluptuous reflection in the black silk nightie. I should've known better. What made me think a week of snarfing Hershey's Kisses would make me a lingerie model? I'd been eating Butterscotch Krimpets by the box my whole life, and I didn't even have hips to show for it. And that was only my dribs. My drabs were another story altogether. I angled sideways to take in the profile, thinking about Maizy and her silicone cutlets suggestion. I could never pull it off. Could I? Maybe not in the nightie, but a nightie wasn't my only option. There were others. I could buy a bra made from something other than cotton, in a color other than white, in a size other than Prepubescent, to accommodate a couple of chicken patties.

I let my eyes drop, wondering if there were chicken patties for the gluteally challenged. No, I didn't want to go there. Things could get out of hand fast if I started cataloguing all the areas that needed reinforcement.

He'd gotten home late. I knew because I'd sat at the window, watching and waiting. The sun was just a radiant memory on the horizon, stretching water-colored orange and pink fingers into the twilight sky. Sultry breaths of warm breeze slid through my screens. It was a perfect night for a grand seduction. I'd already heard Curt's shower running, and I made sure to give him an hour or so to get dinner out of the way. I could picture him on the sofa, legs stretched out onto the coffee table, remote in hand. He'd be watching baseball, maybe the news. Hopefully shirtless.

It was time to shock him.

I slid into my new bathrobe, which was too warm for the season and too concealing for seduction, but I didn't plan to have it on for long. I'd knock, he'd answer, I'd let the robe drop to the ground without a word. Mission accomplished.

I left the lamp on for Ashley, in case she planned to do some light reading before bedtime, and opened my door.

Maizy was standing on the landing. "Hey, Jamie, I—" Her eyes got wide. "Are you on your way to the hospital? Is it food poisoning? Did you try to cook again?" She clapped a palm against my forehead. "You don't have a fever. Is it your duodenum?"

I slapped her hand away. "It's not my duodenum. It's your Uncle Curt."

"Where?" She looked down at the bathrobe. "Is he hiding under there?"

"Not tonight, Maizy. I've got plans." I stepped around her.

She clomped down the stairs behind me. "I hope your plans are to help me ditch the Caddy 'cause Uncle Curt's not home. He went to the Phillies game with my dad."

I froze. "He what?"

"Hurry up, and put on some clothes. I promised Honest Aaron the Caddy would be history by five, only I used it to run some errands and lost track of time. Now the drop-off point has changed, and I need you to give me a ride home."

I turned around and trudged back upstairs, each step weighted with an odd mixture of disappointment and relief. Might as well help Maizy. It wouldn't do me any good to sit at home eating Hershey's Kisses and feeling sorry for myself. I'd have much more fun watching Maizy drive a car into a marsh.

Thirty minutes later, I followed the big Caddy as it sailed onto Route 295 southbound toward the Delaware Memorial Bridge. Traffic was light as it passed through one of the few less developed areas left in the state. Twilight had surrendered to darkness, making it harder to keep Maizy in sight. That, and the fact that she'd floored it as soon as we'd hit the highway. I'd need wings to keep up with her.

And I wished I had them when a giant pickup roared past me in the fast lane. It could have been any giant pickup, but the tingling in my spine told me it wasn't. I hunched over the wheel, trying to pick out some identifying features. Dark in color. The driver sitting too high to get a good look at him. I squinted at the plate, but by that time it was too far away for me to read it.

Well done, Jamie.

Then I realized he must be going after Maizy. Who was surrounded by two thousand pounds of metal but was completely alone inside it. And he had the horsepower to catch up to her, while all I had was—

Morning star. I had a morning star. And I could have had a bazooka, if only Maizy had taken advantage of Herbie Hairston's clearance sale.

I mashed the gas pedal to the floor. I might not be able to catch up, but I would get there eventually, hopefully before any harm was done to Maizy. She was right; I needed a new car, a faster car. Maybe a bigger car. I needed the Batmobile.

There, up ahead, I caught a quick flash, like headlights reflecting off a metal bumper. I wasn't as far away as I'd feared. Probably Maizy had slowed down when she'd lost sight of me in the rearview mirror. But then I saw more lights, red lights, off to the right, at an odd angle, as if—

The Caddy had gone off the highway and into the marshy wetlands. The red lights were its taillights. And as I stared with my heart in my throat, they went out.

I didn't see the pickup anywhere, but I didn't care. Maizy was in that car, and I had to save her. I skidded to a stop on the shoulder of the highway, leaped out, and raced toward the Caddy, which was all but invisible now, settling into the murky marsh.

"Maizy!" My voice was high and thin with panic. Could you swim in a marsh? Or was it full of dangerous things like water snakes and old Cadillacs? I cupped my hands around my mouth. "Maizy! Are you alright?"

"I'm fine." Maizy stepped out of the darkness. "Took you long enough. Want to go for some gelato?"

I stumbled backwards, nearly falling onto the slow lane of the highway. "Don't *do* that!" I yelled. "Why aren't you in that car?"

"Should I be?" she asked mildly.

"Didn't you get run off the road?"

"By who? I did that on purpose. What part of 'ditching the Caddy' didn't you get?"

"But the pickup…" I trailed off. Had it been the same pickup? Maybe I'd been wrong. It was a crowded state. Plenty of people drove pickups. *Everybody* drove too fast. Still… "A pickup truck raced past me," I said. "I thought it was *him*, coming after you." I swallowed. "I was afraid I wouldn't get to you in time."

"You didn't," she said. "I've been sitting here for *five minutes*. I'm a busy woman. Why don't you let me drive? You seem a little freaked out."

I took some deep breaths. "I thought you'd gotten hurt. Or worse."

"You're not really made for ditching cars, are you?" She took my keys. "Next time I'll ask Herbie Hairston to—"

A deafening air horn tore into the night. Maizy and I spun around to watch the giant pickup truck speed past going the opposite direction, separated from us by the grassy median and too many yards to discern detail. We stood rooted while it disappeared into the night.

"What are the chances that's another pickup with a horn like that?" Maizy asked.

"No better than our detective skills," I said. "You know that's him. He must be following you." And we were nowhere near his home turf in the Pine Barrens, which meant he'd gone out of his way to do it. He might have been following Maizy for days. He might have followed her home. He might have followed her to *my* home.

That thought seriously freaked me out.

"That seals it." Maizy stuck her hands in her pockets and headed for the Escort. "Guess there's only one thing I can do now."

I followed her. "Call Curt? Call the police? Call the National Guard?"

She rolled her eyes at me. "Go back to blue hair."

Oh, sure. That should solve everything.

CHAPTER TWENTY-EIGHT

———

"What's his best side, do you think?"

Eunice had asked that question so many times since we'd left my apartment that I didn't care anymore. As far as I was concerned, Hank didn't have a good side. I'd agreed to help her get photos of him, not shoot him for *Playgirl*. Then again, it was entirely possible I was just in a mood from Tuesday night's romantic failure to launch. That hadn't been how it was supposed to go down. I'd seen enough Nicholas Sparks movies to know that not in one of them had the plucky if underweight heroine made a move on her man only to find he'd gone to a baseball game with his brother.

"Howard's not finicky," I told her. "Just so long as it shows Hank doing something he claims he can't do."

"Like bench pressing amplifiers," Maizy added.

"Oh, no." Eunice gave a vigorous headshake. "Hank's a gentleman. He'd never."

Maizy snorted. "What a noob."

On the plus side, Eunice had offered the use of her car, which was both good and bad. She drove a reliable Legume with a full tank of gas, but it was a little short on leg room. In fact, my legs were currently tucked in behind my earlobes. Maizy was sitting sideways across the back seat and still had her knees bent, resting on her backpack. And Eunice was driving, positioned close enough to the wheel to steer with her nose.

"I wish we could get a little closer to him," Eunice added. She had the telephoto lens already fastened to the camera to assure that we wouldn't. "There's no fun in lusting from afar."

Oh, ick.

"You're looking at it the wrong way," Maizy said. "It's like surveillance. Sort of like we do, only *you're* getting paid for it."

Eunice brightened. "I guess that's right, isn't it? And there's no reason Hank should have to know about it. I'll take my picture, and Howard will be happy, and I'll be able to keep my job, so I'll be happy. Plus I've already made a big pot of gravy, so Hank will be happy."

There was only one problem with that scenario. Howard was never happy.

Maizy tapped me on the shoulder. "About Tuesday night."

I sighed. I'd really been hoping she would forget all about that. I'd had trouble sleeping all night, replaying the Caddy sinking into the muck, this time with Maizy inside.

"What happened?" Eunice asked. "I bet it was more exciting than what I did. I sewed up some holes in my comforter. I want it to look nice, just in case..." Pinkness crept into her cheeks.

"That's what Jamie did," Maizy said. "Only her 'just in case' turned into 'not tonight' 'cause Uncle Curt went to a baseball game."

"That wasn't very nice of him," Eunice said.

"He didn't know," I said on a moan. I'd really been hoping Maizy would forget all about *that*, too. I know *I* wanted to.

"You two should work on your communication skills," Eunice said. "You make an adorable couple, but you'll never make it if you can't communicate."

This from the woman who fake-fainted her way into a one-sided relationship.

"She's working on other skills," Maizy said. She stuck her hand between the seats. "Here. This ought to help." She dropped two silicone chicken cutlets into my lap.

"You know you have to cook those first," Eunice said.

"They're not food," I told her. "They're..." I hefted one in each hand to chest level.

"Boobage," Maizy said.

"Really?" Eunice stared at them. "How do they work? Maybe I could get some. Do they come in different sizes?"

"Give them a try," Maizy said. "You're among friends."

I reached into my neckline and plastered one inside my bra. I shifted my shoulders around a little. "It feels like I'm being groped by sweaty hands."

"I want to try one," Eunice said immediately. I passed it to her. She stuck it in her bra and wiggled around some. Her face lit up. "You're right. It does. Where can I get these?"

"I have a source," Maizy said. "She's bound to buy another set soon."

I scowled at her. "You *stole* them?"

She shrugged. "It's not my fault she didn't wear them in the shower after gym class."

I squirmed around some more before yanking the cutlet out of my bra and tossing it back to her. "This feels terrible. I'd rather use tissues."

"Tissues cost less," Maizy said "but they don't offer the same mileage or quality. You want boobage that will stand up to inclement weather and be an eye-catcher in the summer months. Factor in cost per wear, and I think you'll find chicken cutlets are your best investment."

"Sold!" Eunice said. "When can I take delivery?"

"I'll get right on it," Maizy told her. She looked at me. "What do I have to do to put you in a set today?"

I shook my head. "Thanks, but I'll stick to Kleenex."

"Have it your way," she said. "But don't come running to me when you catch a cold and your bra size shrinks."

"I never have before," I said.

CHAPTER TWENTY-NINE

———

"I hope this isn't poison ivy," Eunice whispered a little while later, when we were huddled behind some unidentifiable flora or fauna (I could never keep those straight) with Eunice's telephoto lens trained between the leaves on Max's Garage. "I don't want to have poison ivy on my first date with Hank."

"It's not poison ivy," Maizy said. "Are we done here yet?"

"We've only been here for five minutes," I said.

"How many does she need?" Maizy asked. "He's not exactly a hard target."

Hank was talking to someone in the garage bay while they huddled under the hood of a vintage Corvette. I could tell it was Hank because his jeans-clad legs were a foot longer than the other set of jeans-clad legs and his work boots were three sizes bigger than the other set of work boots.

"That's a nice car," Maizy said. "I wish Honest Aaron would get one of those. I always wanted to drive a Vette."

"That Vette is broken down," I pointed out before realizing that observation added nothing to the conversation since it could be said of Honest Aaron's entire inventory.

"I wish my car would break down," Eunice murmured.

"That's not so hard," Maizy said. "Got any sugar? Maybe some marbles?"

"No, but Curt promised to break it," Eunice said brightly. She squinted through the telephoto lens, licking her lips. "I can't wait for Hank to fix my car." She shifted a little. "Are you sure this isn't poison ivy? I feel itchy."

"It's too soon to be itchy," Maizy said. "Maybe it's no-see-ums. Or spiders."

I looked up with alarm. "Spiders?"

"Probably not," Maizy said. "You'd know it if it was spiders. They're the size of saucers down here."

Great. Another fresh horror: saucer spiders.

Maizy stuck an elbow in my ribs. "The pickup's gone."

I'd already noticed. And I knew why. It was out trolling the interstate highway system looking for Caddys to terrorize.

"We'll never know," Maizy said sadly. "I never got to blow the horn."

"You can blow my horn if you want to," Eunice told her. She hesitated. "Why would you want to?"

"I wouldn't," Maizy said. "Your horn is irrelevant."

Eunice's mouth twisted. "I've heard that my whole life."

Hank's massive arm came up to rest on the upraised hood, the curl of his triceps bulging from beneath the sleeve of his T-shirt.

A little sigh escaped Eunice. "I should take some pictures of that. Of him. Pictures of him."

"Yes," Maizy said immediately. "Take some pictures. We've been here *forever*."

Eunice glanced at me with uncertainty.

"Might as well," I told her. "You only need a couple for Howard. You can keep the rest for yourself."

"I hadn't thought of that." Eunice smiled. "I'm going to use continuous shooting mode so I can make a whole album."

Nothing stalkerish about that.

Maizy checked her cell phone. "We're going to be late. Is the ginormous doofus that important?"

"Yes," Eunice whispered.

"It's a work thing," I told Maizy. "Why don't we go get the car while she finishes up here. I'll come with you." I nudged Eunice. "Make sure he doesn't see you." I turned. "Maizy, let's—"

Maizy was already gone.

CHAPTER THIRTY

Miranda Law would have been right at home on a college campus. She was cute and perky, with dark eyes and dark hair worn in a high ponytail. She wore denim shorts and a yellow top with spaghetti straps.

But she wasn't on a college campus. We'd met her at her apartment in an aging three-building complex tucked in beside a strip shopping mall.

And she was lying through her perfect white teeth.

"I don't know why you asked to see me," she said. "I don't know anyone named Gilbert Gleason." She rocked gently in a plush leather recliner, the very portrait of placidity. Despite the hard-luck exterior, the apartment was spacious, decorated with taste. It reminded me of cracking open a rock and finding sparkling amethyst inside.

"Sure you do," Maizy said. "Einstein with a JD? Used to represent Virtual Waste?"

"Sounds interesting." Rock, rock. "Doesn't ring a bell, though."

The small leather sofa we'd crowded onto might have been tasteful, but it certainly wasn't comfortable. And I was pretty sure I didn't look *placid*. I looked disheveled and sweaty, especially since I was balanced on my left cheek thanks to Eunice's cushion depression, our thighs practically heat-fused together. The apartment apparently predated air conditioning, and there wasn't a window unit or a fan in sight.

"That's strange," Maizy said. "Didn't he help you out once when you got arrested for—"

"Oh, *him*." Miranda took a sip of her iced coffee. "I'd forgotten."

I didn't like coffee all that much, but I would have killed for a sip from her cup. Or a glass of water. Or an ice cube to chew on. Despite the suffocating humidity practically dripping from the ceiling, Miranda seemed oblivious to the heat. She wasn't even perspiring. Eunice wasn't perspiring, either. She was *sweating*. Especially her thighs. But she was too engrossed in her pictorial retrospective of Hank Sedgwick to notice.

"I get it," Maizy said. "You've seen one arrest, you've seen them all, right?"

All? Miranda was a serial arrestee? But she looked like she could be a counselor at a summer camp for postulants.

"How do you know that?" Miranda snapped. "Who did you say you were again?"

"That's right," Maizy said. "So why did you do nicky-nack with Gilbert Gleason?"

"Why not?" Miranda shrugged. "He's a man, isn't he?"

Talk about low standards. Also, having seen Gilbert Gleason, I wasn't quite sure about that.

"Besides." Miranda's gesture encompassed the room. "What do you think paid for all this?"

If by "all this" she meant this Inquisition-worthy sofa I was melting into, I didn't care what she paid for it. I only cared how to peel myself off it without losing a layer of skin.

Wait.

"Gilbert Gleason's your sugar daddy?" I blurted out.

Another sip of iced coffee. A little cool trail of condensation trickled down the outside of the cup. I tried to imagine it splashing onto my forehead, but no, Eunice's moist and meaty thighs got in the way.

"He was that night," Miranda said.

That night? But that would make her…

"You're a sugar baby?" I asked.

Maizy rolled her eyes. "Better let me handle this." She looked at Miranda. "Who hired you?"

Hired her? But that would make her…

"What does it matter?" Miranda shrugged. "It was a business transaction."

"Your other five business transactions didn't include filing an ethics Complaint," Maizy said evenly.

Five? Math wasn't my strongest subject, but even I could put two and two together. Or five and five. Five business transactions, five arrests. Gilbert Gleason was only a transaction for one night. I could be wrong, but that would make her...

"What made Gilbert different from the others?" Maizy asked.

Miranda's tone dripped disdain. "Very little. Emphasis on the *little.*"

Oh, *eww. Way* too much information.

"Gilbert wasn't in the same financial ballpark as my usual dates," Miranda added.

Oh.

"But I was hired to do a job," she said. "And men are all alike, after all. He's no different from any other."

I didn't know much about men, but I knew that wasn't true. For example, there was an unbridgeable chasm between Curt and Gilbert Gleason.

Wait again. *Hired?* But that would make her...

"How well did you know Nick DiBenedetto?" Maizy asked her. "And don't bother denying that you knew him. We found your name and number in his apartment."

We had? Was that a bluff, or had Maizy gone rogue? I hoped not. Maizy sometimes skirted the edges of legality, but even she drew the line at—

Oh, who was I kidding. Maizy drew no lines, ever, at anything.

Even though she seemed to be drawing one now, from Nicky D straight to Miranda Law, with a stop-off at Gilbert Gleason.

"Nicky D." A little smile touched Miranda's lips. So much for her theory on men's homogeny. "He was just a business deal."

Maizy sat back and crossed her arms. I noticed Eunice's leg wasn't pressed tight to *hers.* Their elbows weren't even touching. It was like Maizy had an impenetrable force field or something. A force field where air circulated freely.

It was possible the heat was making me irritable.

"Tell us about that," Maizy said.

Miranda drained her coffee and set it aside with a resigned sigh. "Nick knew I'd used Gilbert Gleason as my lawyer after a car accident a year ago. He asked me to pretend I had another case then seduce Gilbert and file an ethics Complaint against him. I got the sense he wanted Gilbert gone, but he needed leverage to do it. I didn't know, and I didn't care. Nick paid me. Gilbert did what men do—"

"Not all men," I cut in.

Her smile was pitying. "And the next thing I knew," she went on, "Gilbert wasn't a lawyer anymore."

"And Nicky D was dead," Maizy said. She pushed herself upright to look at me, and I could tell we shared the same thought. Miranda was clearly too cheap to spring for a lousy fan.

Also, that Gilbert Gleason had had a gold-plated motive to kill Nicky D.

CHAPTER THIRTY-ONE

———

"I never trusted that doofus," Maizy said. "Who harasses women down on the road in the middle of the night, anyway?"

Eunice stashed the camera in her bag. It was practically smoking from her nonstop Hank slide show. "Who's Gilbert Gleason?"

Oh, *now* she wanted to participate. I rolled down my window and stuck my head out to dry my sweaty face. My bottom half was just as sweaty after an hour in Miranda's smartly decorated toaster oven, but sticking *that* out the window would have been a little too *Animal House* for me.

"He's a lawyer," I told her. "A *real* one."

"An *ex* one," Maizy corrected me. "Thanks to Miranda Law."

I pulled my head back inside. "Do you trust her?"

"No. But I believe her. It fits. It also gives him motive." She thought for a moment. "Plus he had easy backstage access, and it could easily have been him that I saw."

Great. So despite the bottomless well of motive for Nicky D's bandmates, our killer could be Gilbert Gleason. What next? I was afraid to ask.

"What next?" Eunice asked.

In my defense, she'd had less exposure to Maizy than I'd had.

"Next we extract a confession," Maizy said.

I shook my head. "No. No, no, no. We're not doing that."

"Why not?" Maizy asked. "We have motive and opportunity. And thirty minutes of recording time."

"But Gilbert Gleason drives a van," I said.

"You mean he *also* drives a van," Maizy said. "You said it yourself. The pickup could be in the shop."

"But it would have to have been in and *out* of the shop numerous times." I sounded sort of whiney because I really didn't want to extract a confession, from Gilbert Gleason or anyone else. "What makes you think we can make him confess?" I added.

"The *US Army Intelligence and Interrogation Handbook*," she said. "I read it cover to cover."

Of course she had.

"You certainly know how to prepare," Eunice told her.

"I don't know," I said. "It sounds dangerous."

"Life is dangerous," Maizy said. "But you keep breathing, right? How about this. If we don't get a confession, we'll perform a citizen's arrest and let the police sort it out."

Oh, much better plan.

I shook my head. "We're not doing that, either."

Maizy rolled her eyes. "Why not? He's not so big. The three of us can take him down. And I've got zip ties somewhere..." She rooted around in her backpack. "Here!" She held them up triumphantly.

"Those things are really strong," Eunice said. "I read that they can restrain a three-hundred-pound man." She eyed them thoughtfully. "Can I borrow a couple?"

"You're proactive. I like that." Maizy handed over two. "You might want to practice first. The first arrest is always the toughest."

How would she know? Besides, I had a feeling Eunice had a different use in mind for the zip ties, since she had a date coming up with Hank. She probably planned to zip tie him to a pipe so he couldn't leave.

"Say we arrest him," I said. "Then what? We can't fit him in this car to take him to the police station. We don't even know where the police station is."

"I've got nav," Eunice said helpfully.

"We could strap him to the roof like luggage," Maizy said. "Only we'll have to make sure to tie his head down, or he'll screw up our aerodynamics."

Yeah. Because Eunice's lumpy little Legume was nothing if not aerodynamic.

"I've got a better idea." I didn't, not really, but what I did have was my fallback position, which had never failed me before. "We can get Curt to help us. He'll be thrilled to put this whole thing behind us." And I'd be thrilled to get him off the stage and away from Virtual Waste and Susan Two's moisturized hands.

"Yeah, we could do that," Maizy said doubtfully. "But what if Gilbert goes underground?"

"To him that means crossing the street," I said. Bad enough we had to go back to the Whispering Pines Mobile Park. I wasn't about to go back inside the Norman Bates trailer. Curt could have that pleasure. I'd happily be the wheelman who waited outside the whole time, preferably in a roomy vehicle with air conditioning. Speaking of which. "You ought to get an SUV or something from Honest Aaron," I told her. "You know, for easy transport." And strategic delay.

"Good idea," she said. "A guy strapped to the roof *might* draw attention. Okay. Here's what we do. You." Looking at me. "Brief Uncle Curt on the plan. You." To Eunice. "Do you think you can pretend to be a lawyer again?"

"Of course," Eunice said. "I've been studying Cochran's Law Lexicon. I've memorized all kinds of new words."

"Why do we need a lawyer?" I asked.

"Someone has to bluff us through an arrest if it becomes necessary," Maizy said. "You don't think I actually know how to do this, do you?"

Well, yes, I had. There was no end to the things I assumed Maizy could do. It was a little disappointing to discover I'd been wrong.

"What about you?" I asked her.

"I'll go see Honest Aaron," she said. "I'm going to splurge and pay the disposal fee just in case this goes sideways. After that I'm scheduled for my first self-defense lesson from Bryn. She's going to teach me the spinning elbow."

"Sounds painful," I said.

"For you, maybe," she said. "I'm a natural. Expect me at your place at eleven. Gilbert Gleason's bound to be home at midnight."

"I'll bring snacks," Eunice said.

Oh, good. Back to the Pine Barrens at midnight. I was getting bored with all that sleep, anyway.

CHAPTER THIRTY-TWO

———

"Nicky D set him up," I said. "He's the reason Gilbert Gleason got disbarred, and probably why his wife dumped him. That's why we think Gilbert Gleason is the killer and why Maizy wants to talk to him." Yes, talk. Much better than *extract a confession under threat of zip-ties*. I helped myself to one of Eunice's lemon drop cookies. She'd just arrived at ten thirty, after spending her evening baking, which had been a better use of time than the *Cops* marathon I'd watched, hoping to pick up some tips. I didn't have time for the *US Army Intelligence and Interrogation Handbook*.

Curt nodded. "That would make Miranda Law a—"

"Yes!" I yelled triumphantly. "But she doesn't look it," I added.

"Maybe she's into the barter system," he said.

Eunice stopped thumbing through the cardboard sleeve of Hank photos she'd had printed up at the local drugstore before coming over. "That sounds quite practical. Maybe she needed money for rent or a car payment."

Curt's dimples winked at me. He sat in my recliner, cradling Ashley in his lap. The little fink. When I held her, she suffered the immediate onset of narcolepsy. In his hands she was wide awake, staring up at him with big adoring eyes, tail swishing languidly back and forth. I could hear her purring from five feet away, where I sat cross-legged on the floor, close to the coffee table and the cookies, which I was snarfing at an alarming rate thanks to a whopping case of nerves.

"Your rent is due in a couple of weeks," he said. "Want to barter?"

I almost choked on my lemon drop cookie.

Ashley shot me a look of utter disdain familiar to cat owners the world over. If she walked upright and had opposable thumbs, he wouldn't have to ask *her* twice.

"So my brilliant niece comes up with this plan," Curt said. "And you see nothing wrong with it?"

"I wouldn't say that," I told him. I saw all sorts of things wrong with it. Life was imperfect. But it was easier just to go along. And no, I would *not* jump off a bridge if everyone else did it.

"Did it occur to either one of you to just call the police?" he asked.

It was a good question. One I preferred not to answer. "We called *you*," I said. "Maizy likes to spend time with her favorite uncle."

"Isn't that nice," Eunice said.

"It wasn't always that way," I told her. "They used to argue all the time."

"What on earth for?" she asked. "Maizy's delightful."

"It was just a phase," I said. "Curt outgrew it."

He rolled his eyes. "Did it occur to you that if you're wrong about this guy, he could file all kinds of charges against you? Against *us*?"

"Oh, no," Eunice said. "We have reasonable cause to believe Mr. Gleason committed a felony, i.e., the commission of murder. We have grounds to make a citizen's arrest if we don't get him to confess. In that case the grounds are, well, ipso facto."

I blinked. "Hey, that was really good."

She beamed at me.

"Still," Curt said, "I don't think it's a good idea. In fact, I'm pretty sure it isn't."

"What are you saying?" I asked him. "You're not coming with us?"

"Change of plans," he said. "When she gets here, we're going to call the police and tell them all about Gilbert Gleason. That way there's no chance of this thing going wrong."

"I'm okay with that," Eunice said. "Then I could watch QVC at midnight."

I was okay with it, too. The black silk nightie was folded neatly in my dresser drawer, waiting for a stroke of courage. All

I had to do was get rid of Eunice and Maizy, and then I could launch Campaign Shock and Ho-hum.

I let my attention drift to the ancient *Partridge Family* rerun on the TV. The Partridges were performing at some sort of outdoor fair in front of a wholesome-looking crowd. Not a tube of moisturizer in sight.

Which got me thinking.

"It's a shame you wasted your time with Virtual Waste," I told Curt, "but now you can quit. Want me to get Mike on the phone for you?"

His smile nearly peeled off my shirt. "Way ahead of you. I played my last gig at the Golden Grotto. They found a new drummer."

That was the best news I'd heard since *we're calling the police*. It was turning out to be a pretty good night all the way around.

"I think it's great that you play an instrument," Eunice said. "I'm not musically inclined at all. I have no sense of rhythm. I can't even get the Clapper to work right."

Curt glanced at his watch. "Maizy should be here any minute, right?"

"She said eleven." I glanced at the clock. It was nearly that already. I'd been half hoping that Maizy hadn't been able to contact Honest Aaron, or had lost her supply of zip ties, or had just found something better to do at midnight, like hitting a Herbie Hairston Blue Light Special. I hadn't heard from her since we'd dropped her off at the riverfront, somewhere near Honest Aaron's evil lair. But then I hadn't expected to since she'd said she had a lesson with Bryn. I got that she wanted to add ninja warrior to her skill set, but I was starting to wish Maizy would learn to be a slacker once in a while.

Fifteen minutes later, she still hadn't shown up. Which was so unlike Maizy that I felt a knot beginning to form in the pit of my stomach. I finished off the last lemon drop cookie, which suddenly tasted like cardboard. Curt glanced at his watch once or twice then up at the wall clock, his jaw muscles tightening. Eunice had put aside the photos to flip through an old *Star* magazine, but she kept slipping me surreptitious glances.

"She's late," Curt said.

"She's only a few minutes late," I said. "Maybe she ran out of gas." But I didn't think so. That also wasn't like her. That was like *me*. On her own Maizy had enough skills to survive nuclear winter.

Curt thumbed Maizy's number on his cell phone. I heard ringing on the other end before it went to voice mail. *That* wasn't like her, either.

He dropped the phone into his pocket without leaving a message. "I don't like this. You don't think she went to Gleason's alone, do you?"

I shook my head. "I doubt it. She'd have no reason to do that." Not after Gilbert Gleason's roadside representation of Crazy Town.

"Maybe her lesson started late," Eunice said. "Remember she was going to see her friend Brenda?"

"Bryn," I said. Hadn't her lesson been in the afternoon? Maybe they'd gone out to dinner afterward and lost track of time.

It was eleven fifteen. No one lost track of *that* much time. An ugly loop started playing in my head: Maizy being run off the road on her way home, maybe straight into a lake, maybe knocked unconscious, maybe…

No. I forced myself to stop thinking like that. Maizy could drive better than the average NASCAR driver.

A nasty little voice whispered *It's already happened once.*

No. I couldn't go there. She was probably still with Bryn. She was safe with Bryn.

Curt got up to stand at the window. "Think we should go to that mobile park anyway, just in case?"

I looked at the rigid set of his shoulders and could see he'd rocketed right past concern to apprehension. Which propelled *me* straight to terrified. "We should give her another few minutes," I said. "She might've accidentally left her phone at home." That was weak when we both knew Maizy's cell phone was practically welded to her hand.

Curt stayed at the window, hands on hips, watching for Maizy.

Eunice's worried eyes met mine.

I picked up her photos, trying to keep my hands from shaking. I barely saw each one as I flipped through them. Max's Garage. The vintage Corvette with Hank and his customer at its hood. Hank at the rolling tool chest. Hank wiping his hands on a rag. Hank standing just outside the garage bay talking to the owner of the Corvette, a well-muscled guy in a black T-shirt just a little shorter than Hank but just as brawny. His hair was short and thick. He was standing at a three-quarter angle to the camera so that his face wasn't visible.

Wait.

My breath caught in my throat. I scrambled to my feet and took the photo into the kitchen where the light was brighter.

We'd assumed that Hank's customer was a man, based on the jeans and the work boots and, well, unintentional sexism. But the person in the picture wasn't a man. It was Bryn.

"What is it?" Curt asked over my shoulder.

"I'm not sure," I said. I handed him the photo. "What do you see?"

"Is this a joke?" He glanced at it. "One of Hank's customers, right?"

I shook my head. "Look again."

He did. "It's Bryn from the Pinelands." He looked up, uncomprehending.

"Jamie?" Eunice stood in the doorway. "What's wrong?"

"When you were taking these pictures," I said, "were there any other customers besides the one with the Corvette?"

"Just her," she said. "Why?"

Dread settled onto my chest like an anvil. "We thought we were watching two guys, didn't we? We were *sure* it was two guys."

"I guess so," Eunice said. "But we only saw their legs. They didn't come outside until you and Maizy had gone to get the car." She glanced from Curt to me. "Is that important?"

My legs felt weak. "Maizy saw Nicky D's killer go backstage," I said. "She said he was a guy, in jeans and work boots and a dark hoodie." I pointed with a trembling finger at the photo. "There's only one thing missing, and Bryn would easily be mistaken for a man in that lighting. Even by Maizy."

Bryn had claimed to be busy tossing someone out of the bar between sets when Nicky D had been killed, but no one had mentioned any sort of fight that night, and like Maizy always said, everyone lied to us. It would have been easy for Bryn to slip backstage. No one would question her; they'd probably pay her no attention at all. Why would they? She *belonged* there. She'd even helped them pack up their equipment the next day. And she'd kept herself close to us under the guise of helping when she'd likely just been monitoring how close to the truth we were getting the whole time. Hadn't she mentioned something to Curt about collecting cars? Maybe *cars* included *pickup trucks*. Bryn had to be the driver of the pickup that had chased us around South Jersey! Of course!

I fell back against the counter, trying to remember every interaction we'd had with Bryn. Her unexpected appearance at the Golden Grotto. The night she'd sneaked up on me in the parking lot. The time she'd ridden by on her Harley just in time to save us from Gilbert Gleason. Just on her way home, she'd claimed.

But then she'd turned around and ridden off the way she'd come, instead of continuing on toward home. And we hadn't even noticed.

Because everyone lied to us.

Plus…

"Jamie." Curt's voice was like a razor, slicing through my terror. "Maizy was supposed to see Bryn this afternoon?"

I laid a hand on my chest to make sure my heart was still beating. "More than that," I said in a near whisper. "I think Bryn's sister Brianne dated Nicky D." I stared at him. "Brianne committed suicide when he dumped her."

"Motive," Curt said grimly.

I nodded again. "And she knows Maizy and I are trying to find the killer."

Eunice pressed her fist to her mouth. "Oh, no."

Curt brushed past me to grab the phone.

"Are you calling the police?" I asked.

He didn't answer. "Tommy. Have you seen Bryn tonight?" He listened for a few seconds. "Can you give me her number? It's important." He made that gotta-write-something hand gesture, and I shoved a pen and piece of paper at him. "Thanks," he said when he'd scribbled down the number. "Hey, any idea where she lives? In case I can't get her on the phone?" He forced a hollow chuckle. "No, nothing like that. Strictly business."

Eunice had moved to stand next to me. Her hand on my shoulder was oddly comforting given my state of utter panic.

"Thanks, Tom." Curt hung up and turned, clutching the paper. "Staying or coming with?"

"You're kidding, right?" I pushed him out of the way to get to the door, Eunice on my heels. "Did he tell you where she lives?"

He slammed the door behind us. "She's got a place at the Whispering Pines Mobile Park. He thinks she lives with her boyfriend, but she could be there. Her uncle takes care of the place for her."

Oh, no. Not there. I faltered on the steps and made a grab for the rail.

"What's the matter with you?" Curt snapped.

I turned. "Are you sure he said Whispering Pines?"

"Positive. Keep it moving, will you? We need to find this place so we can find Maizy."

I remembered too well how to find Whispering Pines.

I kept it moving.

CHAPTER THIRTY-THREE

———

I'd tried Maizy's cell continuously until I'd run out of signal, to no avail. Eunice was silent in the back seat, her fingers twisted in her lap, her expression a study in anguish. The expression annoyed me since it spoke of something that might not have happened. Probably hadn't happened. *Couldn't* have happened.

Finally, after a lifetime of driving, during which I tried to convince myself that there *were* such things as coincidences, Curt veered onto the shoulder just outside the Whispering Pines property. No other cars in sight. No breeze. Nothing but the incessant drone of cicadas. At that point, the Jersey Devil could have tapped on the window, and I wouldn't have noticed.

"Hopefully she calls this place home," he said. "See if you can Google the address."

I shook my head in frustration. "There's no signal."

"What?" Curt snatched the phone from me and glared at it before hurling it onto the dashboard. He folded his forearms on the wheel, staring hard into the night. "What's her last name?"

"Bryn?" I tried to remember our introduction, outside the Pinelands, the night I'd picked up Maizy and more trouble than I could have imagined. There was nothing there, not even in the fringes of my memory. "I don't remember. I guess I wasn't paying attention."

"I have an idea," Eunice said. "Why don't we look for that Corvette?"

Yes! The Corvette! Of course, if I had a valuable vintage Corvette, I certainly wouldn't park it at the Whispering Pines. I'd rent a temperature-controlled garage to store it and keep it safe.

Especially if I was a collector. Besides that, there was only room to park one car at each home.

A garage…

I turned to Curt. "The pickup!"

I didn't have to say anything else. Curt shoved the Jeep into gear. "I'll drive down Broadway here. You look to the right. Eunice, look to the left."

"It's hard to miss," I said. It *had* to be.

We crawled through the first intersection. No one spoke.

"How'd she get down here, anyway?" Curt asked, fury infusing his tone.

Another question I didn't want to answer.

"What do you mean?" I asked. I knew full well what he meant. And I knew how she'd gotten there. I'd been an accomplice to it. How would I live with that if anything happened to Maizy?

"I mean, she doesn't have a license." He held up a hand. "Yes, I know that's not important. But she doesn't have a car, either."

Now would be the time to offer platitudes, empty assurances that he was probably right, that Maizy probably hadn't disappeared into the Pine Barrens, that she'd simply been distracted by something or someone much closer to home and wasn't answering her cell phone.

But I couldn't.

"Well…" I bit my lower lip. "That's not exactly true."

"Brody Amherst?" he asked tightly.

I shook my head.

"Herbie Hairston."

I didn't want to be responsible for the maiming of Maizy's maybe-romantic interest or her delinquent–but–underaged purveyor of medieval weapons. As much as Maizy would hate it, it was time to come clean about Honest Aaron.

I'd just opened my mouth when Eunice yelled, "Is that it?" and Curt brought the Jeep to an immediate shuddering stop. We all looked to the left at a giant, hulking pickup truck parked outside of a mobile home.

"Is that it?" Curt asked me.

Why hadn't I paid attention when Maizy had written down the license plate number? The least I could have done was notice the color, or the model, *something* that positively identified it. Of course, I knew why. My inner chicken had distracted me. I'd been worried about Mechanic Yeti making a curtain call. Then Gilbert Gleason had shown up, and the truck had been forgotten.

I hated my inner chicken.

"It could be," I said. "I'm just not sure."

"One way to find out." Curt hooked a sharp left, and we roared down the street in a plume of dust and dirt. He was out of the Jeep almost before it stopped, banging on the door.

"It's after midnight," Eunice said. "Is that wise?"

"Let them call the police," I said. It could only help. I studied the pickup, trying to envision it as I'd seen it so many times, looming larger and larger in my rearview mirror or driving away on the opposite side of the highway after Maizy had dumped the Caddy.

Someone had opened the door to Curt's banging, and the two were in animated conversation. Gradually, the homeowner's gestures stilled as he seemed to comprehend what was going on, until at last they talked quietly before he shook Curt's hand and closed the door.

Curt hurried back to the Jeep and got in. "He doesn't know Bryn, but he said sometimes he sees a woman fitting her description at a home on C Street. We'll knock on every door if we have to."

A coldness settled over me. "C Street?"

"Yeah." He glanced at me. "Why? You know it?"

I knew it. I'd just hoped never to see it again.

CHAPTER THIRTY-FOUR

———

The trailer still looked empty. But I no longer believed it was empty. I cast a glance at the trailer on the other side of the street when we got out of the Jeep. All dark. Hopefully it stayed that way.

"Someone actually lives here?" Eunice whispered.

"Do you see her Harley?" Curt asked.

"It could be on the other side," I said and frowned, looking at the front of the home. So far as I could tell, the only improvements were that someone had shut the windows and removed the ladder. Neither of which made it more welcoming.

"It's completely dark," I said. "What do we do?"

"We get inside," he said. "Any way we can. Right now."

He made a move for the door. I grabbed his arm. "No. Let me."

"I can't let you, Jamie," he snapped. "She's my niece." *And you're a ninety-eight-pound weakling* was the silent addendum.

Let him, my inner chicken clucked. *What could you possibly do against Bryn anyway?*

I had no clue. But it was time I found out.

"I'm going," I told him. "You can follow me if you want. But I'm going first."

"We'll go together," he said.

"What about me?" Eunice asked. "I want to help."

Curt hesitated before pointing. "Go knock on doors, and see if you can find a landline to call the police."

"Don't go—" I began, but Eunice was hustling away toward Gilbert Gleason's door, and I didn't have time to go after her.

I reached for the door handle. Locked but hardly impenetrable. Besides, if I couldn't go through the door, I was prepared to go through the wall. Maizy was in there.

"Hold on a second," Curt whispered. He stepped in front of me and did something Emersonian, and a minute or so later, the door swung open slightly.

I slipped inside.

I was hardly aware of Curt behind me when I squatted, making myself small while my eyes adjusted to the darkness. I was intrepid, but I wasn't stupid. I didn't want to be an easy target.

The inside hadn't gotten any better, either, if the smell was any indication. It was musty with an underlayment of filth. I squinted into the blackness, trying to discern shapes. Especially moving shapes. With weapons. I saw nothing. It sounded empty. More than that, it *felt* empty.

I straightened up and stepped closer to Curt. "There's no one here."

That's when I heard it. The faintest shuffling sound, from the bathroom, as if someone had readjusted her position slightly. Then silence.

We weren't alone.

I squinted in that direction. Was that a dresser in front of the door, blocking it?

Curt laid a finger against his lips. We stood frozen, listening hard. Nothing.

He pointed at his own chest then toward the bathroom. Several agonizing seconds later, he took hold of one end of the dresser and slid it away from the door. Then his hand was on the knob.

He opened it.

CHAPTER THIRTY-FIVE

––––––

"Thank God!" Archie Ritz squeezed through the opening, wild-eyed. "I thought it was *him* coming back to finish me off!"

Him? He had it all wrong.

"That's an easy mistake to make," I said. "But *he* was actually a *she*. She just has a lot of muscles. Put her in boots and a baseball cap, maybe a hoodie to cover up the girls, and you'd never know the difference."

"What girls?" Archie asked.

"You know." I did the time-honored palms-up *hubba-hubba* gesture in the vicinity of my chest. "The bozingas. The chicken cutlets. The *girls*."

"Please stop talking," Curt told me.

Probably a good idea.

Archie made a move to brush past us. Curt grabbed his arm. "Hold on a second. What happened? Who's this guy you're talking about?"

"I don't know who he is. I never saw him before, and I never want to see him again." Archie had swapped his clown clothes for dark jeans, a black shirt, and plain black Nikes. His stack of hair had de-poofed in the heat, but his tiny set of features were fully animated. "This giant broke in and locked me in the bathroom. Sounded like he ransacked the place."

I glanced around. Why would anyone ransack *this* place? And how would you know if he did?

"What was he looking for?" Curt asked.

Archie shuddered. "I don't know. He said I'd better be quiet, or he'd be back to *make* me be quiet. I've never been so frightened in my life." His lower lip quivered, and his eyes started to fill.

That giant had to be Hank. My heart fell for Eunice. At the same time it seemed curious that Archie had never seen Hank before. According to everyone with eyes, Hank followed Susan One to every performance, and he was hard to miss. Then again, by all accounts, Hank stayed outside in the parking lot most of the time, so maybe their paths had never crossed.

But why would Hank ransack Bryn's home? What was I missing? Besides common sense, good judgment, and a well-paying job?

"What are you doing here?" Curt asked him. "We were told this place belongs to a woman named Bryn."

"Bryn is my niece," Archie said. "I keep an eye on the place for her, but I had no idea this neighborhood was so dangerous."

Wait. What? His niece? *He* was Bryn's Uncle Doug? I flashed back to the pictures on his credenza. No wonder I'd felt the distant memory of sisterly compatibility. There'd been the wife, the man who looked like the wife's brother, and the two little girls, one frilly, one tomboyish. Bryn and…what was her sister's name? Brenda? No, Brianne.

Brianne…

"How did you get here?" I asked him. "There's no car outside."

"Oh, dear, he must have stolen it!" Archie clutched his bosom. What a drama queen. "Now I'm trapped here!"

I could practically hear the waterworks gearing up.

"We'll take you home," Curt told him.

Archie's eyes narrowed in my direction. "Aren't you the mother who's going to sue me?"

Curt's head swiveled around to stare at me.

"You must have me confused with someone else," I said lamely.

"I'm sure I don't," he said. "Your daughter was very—" He paused, groping for the right word. "—pregnant."

Curt's eyebrow shot up. I did a no-worries headshake. He met it with a headshake of his own.

"Do you know where Bryn is?" Curt asked him. "It's crucial that we find her."

"I have to get away from here," Archie said. "Before he comes back." He made a move to get past Curt.

Curt held his arm. "Don't worry about him. I need you to focus. We have to find your niece."

"She stays with her boyfriend," Archie said. "I can take you there. Just don't leave me alone again."

"We won't leave you alone," Curt said. "You'll come with us."

"That's very kind of you," Archie said.

Curt and I turned to make our way back outside when Archie said, "Just one thing."

We turned around and froze. Archie was wearing a baseball cap and holding a long, curved, lethal-looking sword. Holding it as if he'd held it before, and often.

A *sword*? Who had a sword, for Pete's sake? And where had it come from, anyway? The seat cushions? The most interesting thing I'd ever found in *my* seat cushions was some spare change and a few Alpha-Bits, and this guy was hauling out fencing supplies.

And why was he pointing it at Curt? And by extension, me?

"Is that what Hank was looking for?" I asked him.

I know one day I'd look back at that question and say, "Duh." I hoped.

"Who's Hank?" Archie asked.

"You know, the big guy who ransacked..." I suddenly forgot what I wanted to say because an epiphany had smacked me in the brain. I realized Archie's hair hadn't de-poofed from the heat. It had flattened under that cap, giving him a severe case of hat head to go along with his slipping-backstage-to-kill-Nicky-D ensemble. No wonder he'd raised no eyebrows at the Pinelands. As the band's agent, he belonged there as much as Bryn did. Maybe more. So long as he'd hid his ridiculous pompadour under a hoodie, he'd have been as unmemorable as me at a fashion show before he'd escaped out the side door.

But that was the least of my worries. The most of them was that at the moment he had the tip of the sword resting at the base of Curt's throat. I did a subtle sidestep until I was hidden behind Curt's back. I was sure he wouldn't mind, although it was entirely possible that sword was long and sharp enough to make shish kebab out of both of us.

Where was Maizy's pregnancy pad when I needed it?

"Thank you for releasing me from my little prison," Archie said, "but now I'm afraid I must ask you to take my place."

"You don't want to do that," Curt told him. Only he didn't say it in that empty threat kind of way you hear from people on television, right before they make an ill-fated grab for the weapon. Curt wasn't dumb enough to make a grab for a sword. Judging from his utter stillness and his deep, even breaths, he planned to go Jedi warrior on that sword and melt it with the searing heat of his stare.

He could leave the shaking and the hyperventilating to me. I'd gotten a head start.

"I think I do," Archie said, almost pleasantly. "I suggest you comply. I'm a kendoka, you see."

I peeked around Curt's shoulder. "What's that?"

Archie pivoted slightly, whipped his arm around, and suddenly Bryn's floor length drapes became valances.

Oh.

I swallowed hard. "Hank didn't lock you in the bathroom, did he?"

Yeah, I know. Again, "Duh." But Archie hadn't locked *himself* in there.

Irritation flickered across his tiny features. "Who is this Hank you keep talking about?"

"If you don't know, I'm not going to tell you," I shot back.

Archie and Curt did a simultaneous eye roll. It figured. The first time Curt moved anything besides his diaphragm, he was rolling his eyes at *me*.

When their irritating male bonding moment had ended, Archie jiggled the sword at Curt's throat again. "If you'll be so kind as to step lively, I really should be on my way."

"On your way?" Curt repeated. "It's a long, lonely walk to anywhere in the dark."

"But I have a car," Archie said. "Hand over your keys. Now, please."

Curt didn't move. "Don't have them."

He had them. Curt never forgot his keys. Would it be weird if I stuck my hand into the front pocket of his jeans and handed them over myself to avoid a skewering?

"Of course you do," Archie said. "Give them to me."

"I left them in the Jeep," Curt said. "Seemed like a safe neighborhood."

Of course, since I was standing behind Curt, I couldn't actually *see* the front pocket of his jeans. I'd have to feel my way. And with my acute sense of direction, I might end up in unexpected places, doing unexpected things best done in the dark and without a witness. And that would definitely be weird. Right?

Archie's mini-face puckered and creased, and when it smoothed out again, his eyes were glassy with wetness. "I don't want to have to hurt you. Really, I don't. But I'm afraid this is nonnegotiable. I can't have you following me."

"We just want to talk to Bryn," Curt said. "That's all. We have no grudge with you."

I frowned up at the back of his head. Maybe *he* didn't, but *I* sure did. I had one whopper of a grudge with Archibald Dougal Ritz, going way back to his skepticism over my fictitious exotic dancing career all the way up to and including that condescending eye roll.

Archie looked at Curt through teary eyes. Did he have any other kind? "You seem like a nice person," he said. His gaze shifted momentarily to me. "You, I'm not sure about."

"Me? I'm a sweetheart," I assured him. "I foster small children and feed stray animals and belong to the Sierra Club. You couldn't find a nicer person than me, honestly." I dug out a crumpled tissue and waved it around Curt's arm like a tiny white flag. "Here, have a Kleenex."

Archie speared it with the tip of the sword and flicked it away. Unnecessary showmanship, if you asked me, since I'd already gotten the point with his seamstressing demonstration.

"Why'd you kill Nicky D?" Curt asked him with dead calm.

Good approach. Keep him talking until an opportunity for escape or attack appeared. Given the length and lethality of Archie's sword, my money was on escape. Of course, I was broke.

"That *boy*." Archie practically spat the word. "I had no choice. Someone had to do it. How many young women's lives could he be permitted to ruin?"

I went still. Brianne.

"Yes," Archie said, although I hadn't realized I'd actually spoken. "Brianne. I adored my niece. Such a beautiful, innocent child…before she met *him*. She was pregnant when she committed suicide." His lip began to tremble. His eyes began to well. "That darling sensitive girl was *rebuffed* by Nicholas, and it drove her straight to her grave. He didn't even care. He simply refused to take responsibility for his actions."

"I'm sorry," I said. Surprisingly, I realized that I was. Which was a strange realization, given that Archie's sword was still threatening a tonsillectomy on Curt.

He ran a finger under one eye. "I couldn't tolerate it. So I took the job as their agent, knowing what I had to do, and I bided my time, waiting for my chance. And my chance came. Thankfully, someone left the side door open, and I walked right in. I knew if I was recognized, it wouldn't matter. I belonged there, you see."

"And you hit him with the amplifier," I said.

"A stroke of luck," Archie said. "I had planned to use my dagger, my *tanto*, to educate him. The amplifier made it look like an accident. Either way, I taught him that actions have consequences."

"But she could have gone after him for child support," I said. "You know that. You're a lawyer."

"Child support." He snorted. "A pebble in a roiling sea. Assuming he would have even paid it. No." He pulled back the sword to skim his finger reverentially along the blade. "I would have preferred to teach him a more elegant lesson, but one must seize opportunities as they appear. He was alone backstage. It was a fait accompli."

I wasn't sure what that meant, but it sounded deranged.

"And you." He'd focused on me again, those stupid bushy eyebrows lowering like storm clouds. Honestly, didn't the guy own a pair of tweezers? "You and your delinquent little friend had to keep asking questions and involving yourselves in a situation that I'd already neatly resolved."

Neatly resolved?

"You murdered a man!" I blurted out. "And then you just walked out of the bar and went home as if it was nothing! And then you threatened my friend!"

Curt's face grew even darker, if that was possible. "He did what?"

I ignored him. I was on a roll. "And for your information, she's *not* a delinquent. She's incredibly smart and brave and independent and—"

"Foolish," Archie said mildly. "Sadly, she's also a fairly good driver, and so I was unable to capitalize on her inexplicable affection for well-worn vehicles. Although I gave it a few tries."

"You drove the pickup truck," I said. "You wrote the notes."

"Correct." He smiled like a proud teacher after his student had grasped a difficult mathematical concept.

"Where is she?" Curt asked him.

"I have no idea," Archie said. "I haven't seen the child. Perhaps she's at the hospital delivering her sofa cushion."

Okay, I'd had that coming. But that's *all* I had coming from Archibald Dougal Ritz. I had no intention of standing there and letting this crackpot make a colander out of me. I could make a run for it, but there was no way I would abandon Curt, even if the rich irony was that there was also no way I could help him. Plus he had the keys to the Jeep in his pocket.

Archie glanced at his watch, and his mouth formed a tiny *O* of surprise. "It's getting quite late. I really must insist that you step into the bathroom right now."

"Fine." Curt looked down at me. "You first."

Oh, wasn't *that* gallant. Push the skinny stupid girl into the path of the crackpot's sword. And here I was trying to be all noble, refusing to run out on him. That eye roll should've told me something. I should have been nothing but a vapor trail at this point.

Curt took my hand and dragged me across his chest until I was in front of him. I barely noticed the chiseled hardness under his shirt. It was purely an accident that my free hand skimmed across it on the way. Archie raised the sword like a lift gate while I stomped past him, muttering, every muscle in my body clamoring to go in the other direction, toward the door and beyond, straight to a realtor to find a new apartment. I heard Curt moving behind me, but I no longer cared. I was *so* over Curt. What had lusting after him ever done for me? I could have slid out of bed in that silk nightgown and wound up with a concussion. Or a bad chest cold. Or some nasty razor nicks, all for nothing.

"It's obscenely hot," Curt said suddenly. "Mind if I take off my shirt before we go in there?"

Time for me to roll *my* eyes. "You've got a lot of nerve," I snapped. "Don't think for one minute that staring at your naked chest will make me any happier about this."

He stared at me for a few beats before tipping his head toward Archie. "I was talking to him."

Well, that was weird.

Archie made a hurry-up gesture, and Curt went all Chippendales without the oil, peeling his T-shirt over his head on a wave of rippling muscle. I assumed. I refused to watch. I crossed my arms and tapped my toe and stared at the ceiling. Okay, I sneaked one quick peek, but that was only because the flexing of his abs caught my peripheral vision.

"Feel better now?" Archie herded us toward the bathroom with the sword. "If you please."

I shot him the dirtiest look I could muster and stepped into the bathroom doorway. Curt followed about two feet behind, with Archie prodding him the whole way. Curt's eyes met mine, and he gave a tiny movement of his head that indicated I should step back from the doorway.

Well, he wasn't the boss of me. If he wanted more room to spread his muscles, he could darned well get himself locked up someplace else. This bathroom was taken.

Then it happened.

Archie lowered the sword and turned slightly to pull the dresser closer to the door to block us inside.

Immediately Curt was on him, slinging his T-shirt over Archie's head and holding it tightly with both hands while Archie thrashed and bucked in a blind struggle to free himself. The sword glinted as it swung back and forth with the movement, and then I lost sight of it because both came crashing back against the wall and into the bathroom doorway, straight into me. I stumbled backward, lost my balance, and fell backwards onto my right hand. Which was suddenly at the bottom of the toilet bowl.

Eww!!!

Also, wasn't that just typical of a male, to leave the seat up?

I scrambled to my feet, grabbed a towel from the rack, and wrapped it around my hand. No time now to peel off the top layer of skin; I had to find some way to help Curt. Now that I knew he'd had a plan all along, and it had never involved being ogled by me.

Except he didn't seem to need my help. When I burst out of the bathroom, he still had the shirt over Archie's head and was steering him, kicking and struggling, toward the door. I wasn't sure that was such a good idea. In the open with room to operate, Archie's sword could do a lot more damage.

My gaze fell on a table lamp. It wasn't a bazooka, but it was better than nothing. I snatched it up. "Curt, here!"

He glanced back for a millisecond, and that's all it took for Archie to break free and bolt for the door, all hope of imprisoning us forgotten as he darted outside into the night.

Curt followed him out. I followed Curt, clutching the lamp in my now dry, if forever contaminated, right hand.

As I'd feared, Archie brandished the sword with fury in his eyes, and I knew it would no longer satisfy him to lock us in the bathroom and go away. He now wanted to teach *us* a lesson.

Suddenly high beams blazed into life from the corner of Broadway and C Street, piercing the night like Archie's sharpened sword.

There was barely time to register the giant pickup truck before it leapt forward. I wanted to dive back into the trailer, but my feet wouldn't move. Curt and Archie stood directly in the path of the pickup with no time to react and no place to take shelter. Everything froze except for the snarling engine, and then the awful ear-splitting air horn rent the darkness.

It braked hard four feet away, flinging cinders and dirt. The driver's door opened, and a pair of work boots and jeans came into view, followed by a hot pink T-shirt.

"Uncle Doug, don't!"

Bryn.

"Turn around," Archie said. "You shouldn't have to see this."

She approached slowly, moving so lightly she practically floated. "It's too late, Uncle Doug. The police are right behind us."

I squinted past her into the darkness. Not close enough. Hold it. Us?

Maizy slipped out of the passenger seat and rushed over to me. I wrapped an arm around her shoulders, so weak with relief I practically needed her for support. "We were so worried about you," I whispered. "We thought Bryn had—"

"It's *his* truck," Maizy whispered. "It's not Bryn's."

I nodded. "I know."

"We only took it to go to the police," she said. "None of the neighbors would let us in, and there's no cell service and—"

I nodded again. "I know. What happened?"

"She was giving me a lesson when he called her from his office," she said. "He asked her to stop in at her trailer at ten. He said he'd been letting a friend use it, and there was some kind of problem."

Gilbert Gleason, I thought.

"She doesn't even live here anymore," Maizy went on, "so she didn't know anything about that, but she came anyway, and she brought me with her. Jamie, it was so weird. He was sitting there looking at all these pictures of her sister. It's like he just broke or something."

I thought maybe that had happened a year or two ago.

Eunice crept up behind me. "I tried, but I couldn't find anyone with a landline. I woke up half the block. That man across the street is very upset. He said he'd told the FBI something was going on when he saw Mr. Ritz practicing with that sword, and they only sent two dim-bulb agents out to talk to him."

I was willing to let that slide now that Maizy was safe.

Maizy frowned. "How'd Ritz get out of the bathroom, anyway?"

I squeezed her shoulders. "Let's not talk about that right now."

"You shouldn't have locked me in there!" Archie was saying. "I only did what I had to do."

"Brianne wouldn't want this," Bryn said. "She wouldn't have wanted to see you go to jail."

"It was worth it," Archie said. His voice trembled. I wasn't close enough for a good look at his eyes, but I'd bet they were welling with tears. "Brianne was a *child*. He took advantage of a child!"

"You got your revenge," Bryn said calmly. She was nearly within arm's length of him now, moving without hesitation or fear. "That has to be enough."

"But these people," Archie said, flicking his sword toward Maizy and me. "They'll turn me in."

"*I'll* turn you in," Bryn said. "I won't let you hurt anyone else."

Archie's face changed when he looked at her, growing harder and colder and meaner. "You can't do anything to stop—"

Bryn pounced in a whip-fast blur of legs and arms, sending the sword flying. When the onslaught was over, Archie was lying on the ground crying. Naturally.

"Bryn is *fierce*," Maizy whispered.

A police car screeched around the corner and down the street, its lights flashing dizzyingly.

"You bet she is," I said.

"You people are disturbing the peace!" Gilbert Gleason yelled from across the street. "I'll sue you all!"

CHAPTER THIRTY-SIX

———

I stood in front of the mirror, running a hand across the black silk. Maybe I'd finally managed to gain a few pounds, because the nightie seemed to be flowing smoothly rather than puddling across my chest, lying along my hips in a very flattering way. A small smile touched my lips as I twisted to assess the rear view.

The smile fell away. Not much to see there. Maybe after the next bag of Kisses.

Ashley sat primly in the doorway, watching every move I'd made since I'd stepped from the shower. I was pretty sure her interest centered around the proximity to her dinner hour more than my reincarnation as a vixen, but it was still interest.

I'd managed to iron most of the frizz from my hair and left it loose around my face. I'd even broken out the heavy hitters: clear lip gloss, a touch of mascara, and a spritz of some perfume I'd never heard of that Maizy had bought from what she'd called Herbie Hairston's Summertime Beauty Special. He'd probably ransacked a drugstore cosmetics department, but I was willing to let it pass. Although I wasn't too sure about the name: Obsession-Compulsion.

I reached down and peeled off my socks. The tile floor felt cool and refreshing beneath my feet. No goose bumps at all. I dropped them into the hamper along with the other clothes I'd collected from chair backs and doorknobs throughout the apartment.

The bathrobe hung on a hook on the door. I left it there, stepping into the living room barefoot. I'd never noticed before how soft and thick the carpet was. The sofa bed was folded up and laundry-free. I found the remote and switched the TV to one of those stations that plays continuous soft jazz without videos or commercials.

Ashley wove in between and around my legs, meowing plaintively for some food. I detoured into the kitchen to pour her a fresh bowl of Meow Mix and change her water. I added a few treats to the platter as a reward for her attentiveness.

That done, I checked the oven. Not up to temperature yet. I'd set the table with my finest Corelle and the cut glass, fake crystal stemware that had been a Christmas gift years ago. A single candle took center stage on the table. Dessert was in the fridge: a cherry cheesecake from Leonetti's. Six slices of frozen pizza on the cookie tray awaited baking.

I padded into the living room again, shutting off lights as I went. Finally, I lit two vanilla-scented candles, both with three wicks for maximum olfactory effect in case Ashley and I were working at cross-purposes at some point throughout the night.

Everything was ready.

On cue, a knock on the door.

Ashley's ears pricked up, but the night wasn't for Ashley. It wasn't even for Curt. It was for me. I'd finally triumphed over my inner chicken. I'd conquered my fear. I'd stared death in the face and—

Yeah, okay. So I'd gone back into the Norman Bates trailer. But in fairness, it *was* a really disgusting trailer.

I hesitated, smoothed the black silk that already looked like liquid mercury, and took a few deep breaths.

Then I opened the door.

ABOUT THE AUTHOR

From her first discovery of Nancy Drew, *USA Today* bestselling author Kelly Rey has had a lifelong love for mystery and tales of things that go bump in the night, especially those with a twist of humor. Through many years of working in the court reporting and closed captioning fields, writing has remained a constant. If she's not in front of a keyboard, she can be found reading, working out, or avoiding housework. She's a member of Sisters in Crime and lives in the Northeast with her husband and a menagerie of very spoiled pets.

To learn more about Author, visit her online at
www.kellyreyauthor.com

Enjoyed this book? Check out these other reads available in
print now from Gemma Halliday Publishing:

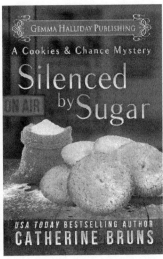

www.GemmaHallidayPublishing.com

Made in the USA
Middletown, DE
25 February 2018